Ann Barker was born and brought up in Bedfordshire, but currently lives in Norfolk.

For more information about Ann Barker and her books, go to www.annbarker.com

LADY OF LINCOLN

For Emily Whittaker living in Lincoln, the closest thing to romance is her lukewarm relationship with Dr Boyle. But a new friendship with Nathalie Fanshawe brings interest to her life. Then Canon Trimmer and his family move into the cathedral close. When Mrs Trimmer's brother, Sir Gareth Blades visits them, he seems a romantic figure, and apparently attracted to Emily. But she finds a mysterious side to Sir Gareth with the arrival of Annis Hughes, not to mention his connection with Mrs Fanshawe ... Is Sir Gareth really a gallant gentleman or would Emily be better off settling for Dr Boyle after all?

ANN BARKER

LADY OF LINCOLN

Complete and Unabridged

ULVERSCROFT
Leicester

First published in Great Britain in 2007 by
Robert Hale Limited
London

First Large Print Edition
published 2008
by arrangement with
Robert Hale Limited
London

British Library CIP Data

Barker, Ann
Lady of Lincoln.—Large print ed.—
Ulverscroft large print series: historical romance
1. Lincoln (England)—Social life and customs—
Fiction
2. Love stories 3. Large type books
I. Title
823.9'2 [F]

ISBN 978–1–84782–284–0

Published by
F. A. Thorpe (Publishing)
Anstey, Leicestershire

Set by Words & Graphics Ltd.
Anstey, Leicestershire
Printed and bound in Great Britain by
T. J. International Ltd., Padstow, Cornwall

This book is printed on acid-free paper

For Jane, a good friend, and the best teacher I ever had.

My grateful thanks to the Society for Lincolnshire History and Archaeology for their invaluable help, and to the volunteers of Lincoln Cathedral, all of whom coped patiently with my many questions. I would also like to thank the Dean and Chapter for their care of the cathedral, and the staff of the White Hart who looked after me so well during my stay.

Ann Barker

1

'Miss Whittaker, I am fortunate indeed to find you alone, for I have something of a very particular and private nature to say to you.'

Emily Whittaker looked at the gentleman who was standing in front of her and barely repressed a sigh. Arthur Boyle's failure to find her alone previously had had nothing whatsoever to do with chance, she reflected guiltily, for short of deliberate rudeness, she had done everything that she possibly could in order to avoid him. She had carefully refrained from walking past his house, even though that was her quickest route to and from the market. She had deliberately absented herself when she knew that he was due to pay a professional visit to her grandfather. She had even missed the whole of a series of lectures upon the wild flowers of Lincolnshire, which had been given in the assembly rooms, just round the corner in Bailgate. This was a topic that interested her, and she would normally have gone out of her way to attend, but because she knew that the good doctor would also go simply in order to see her, she had kept away on purpose.

Naturally, she could not miss services in Lincoln Cathedral. Not only did she live literally a stone's throw away in Priorygate, but also her grandfather and her father, with whom she resided, were both canons (although Grandpapa's state of health no longer permitted him to be present). After worship was over, however, she was always careful not to encourage any private conversation with the doctor.

Now, despite all her careful tactics, the moment that she had been putting off had arrived. Dr Boyle had visited her grandfather on a different day from usual, and since he had managed to catch her just as she had finished conferring with Mrs Ashby, the housekeeper, she had no obvious reason to escape. Judging by the earnestly determined expression on his face, he had decided to propose and had no intention of leaving until his errand was accomplished.

There would be plenty of people among her acquaintance who would be ready to tell her that she would be well advised to accept him. She knew it herself. At the advanced age of thirty, she would be very unlikely to get another offer. She had little private fortune, and her mirror told her that her looks were not exceptional. She was not tall, and her hair was of an unremarkable shade of brown. Her hazel eyes, her best feature, were expressive, and her face was a neat oval. In short, there was nothing objectionable in her appearance, but there was nothing about it that would cause gentlemen to beat a path to her door. The house in Lincoln Cathedral precinct in which she had been born and where she now lived with her father and grandfather did not belong to her family, but to the cathedral. She needed to provide for her future. The most obvious way of securing this provision would be to accept Dr Boyle as a suitor for her hand.

Unfortunately, the doctor could not in any way be considered to be a figure of romance. His nose was rather long and pointed, and his eyes were on the small side, so that when he narrowed them in concentration, he bore more than a passing resemblance to a weasel. He was well respected, Emily had to concede. She had never heard anyone speak ill of him. She would almost have preferred it if someone had. He was thin in build, with a slight stoop to his shoulders, and his hair, although still covering his scalp well enough, looked as if it might soon give up the struggle. Worst of all, his hands were cold and damp, and Emily could not imagine his even doing such a decorous thing as taking hold of both of hers, without feeling a shudder run right through her.

None of these thoughts showed on her face, however, as the discretion cultivated all her life from being a clergyman's daughter came to her aid. 'By all means, Dr Boyle,' she replied in her low, cultured voice. 'Will you not be seated?'

She sat down herself, and gestured towards another chair which was set at a decorous distance. The doctor sat down, but after only perching there for a maximum of three seconds, sprang up and began to pace about the room. Emily looked beyond him and through the window towards the cathedral which for the whole of her life had seemed to gaze benevolently down upon her.

'I . . . er, that is to say . . . hrmph!'

'You are agitated, Dr Boyle,' said Emily. 'Would not a breath of fresh air be beneficial?'

The doctor stared at her uncomprehendingly and, for a moment or two, Emily wondered whether perhaps she had spoken in a foreign language. 'No indeed,' he began; then halting abruptly he went on, 'And yet, of course, perhaps it might . . . um . . .' He took a deep breath. 'Miss Whittaker, would you

4

care to stroll about the close a little? The day is fine and warm.'

Sensing the possibility of at least escaping the confinement of the room in which they sat with its heavy dark furniture and drab hangings, Emily replied 'Very well, Doctor. Pray excuse me while I fetch my bonnet.'

No sooner had she made the suggestion than immediately she began to regret it. It had seemed like a good one at the time, she reflected as she went up the stairs. The drawing-room had begun to feel stifling in the doctor's presence. Now, however, she recalled all the different pairs of eyes that would be drawn to the interesting spectacle of Dr Boyle escorting Canon Whittaker's daughter around the Minster Yard. The drawing-room might have been stifling, but it was at least private. She was now faced with the prospect of receiving the doctor's proposal in front of an unseen but fascinated audience, and bearing in mind his agitated state, she could even imagine him throwing himself down upon his knees on the cobbles in front of the great west door! She was very tempted to tell Arthur Boyle that she would rather stay indoors, but the last thing that she wanted was for him to think her indecisive. He might then suppose that when she refused him, she did not know her own mind!

Once in her room, she found the dove-grey bonnet that toned with her lavender gown and shawl. It was a sensible, modest item of headgear, at least three years behind the times, and admirably suited to a clergyman's daughter of mature years. Her fingers paused briefly in tying the ribbons. Just a few days before, she had seen a frivolous confection on display in the window of Mrs Phillips's milliner's shop. It had been in an impractical shade of white, trimmed with artificial rosebuds, and Emily had coveted it intensely. It had come into her mind as the ten commandments had been read on Sunday, and she had listened to the last commandment, 'Thou shalt not covet', with a stab of guilt. But, she had heard a little voice saying inside her head, I do not want anyone else's ox or ass, I want that bonnet. After all, it is for sale and it is so very pretty.

She pulled herself together and tied the grey ribbons of her bonnet firmly under her chin. However subject she herself might be to temptation, she could never be accused of leading anyone else into thinking wrong thoughts. No right-minded person whom she encountered that day would covet *her* bonnet, or indeed, any other part of her apparel, she decided ironically.

Sternly repressing these thoughts, she left

her room and, conscious that she had kept the doctor waiting, she hurried down the stairs, pulling on her gloves, only to find that her father was standing at the bottom, looking up at her with a gentle expression of reproach in his eyes.

'Emily, Emily, my dear,' he murmured, his tone sorrowful. 'Such indecorous haste!'

'I beg your pardon, Papa,' she replied automatically. She had long since learned that the more she protested, the longer the incident would be remembered.

'I am sure your gallant swain will wait a little while longer for you,' her father went on, with rather ponderous playfulness.

'Dr Boyle and I are simply going to take the air,' she replied, hoping that the doctor had not heard her father's words.

'Well, you may invite the doctor in for tea when you return,' smiled her father.

'Thank you, Papa, but the doctor has patients to see, I think,' Emily answered. She had no idea whether this was true or not, but she had no wish to entertain to tea a man whose proposal she had just refused. She also slightly resented the fact that her father seemed to think it necessary to give her, a woman of thirty, permission to invite someone to tea.

Mercifully, the drawing-room door was

closed, and Boyle had not heard any of the conversation between Emily and her father. Just before they left, however, Canon Whittaker said, 'I cannot tell you how much comfort it gives me, Dr Boyle, to know that my dear Emily is in such safe hands.'

The doctor straightened his shoulders. 'I shall do my best to ensure that your trust is not misplaced,' he said nobly.

Emily could not allow this piece of nonsense to pass without comment. 'Really, we are taking a turn about the cathedral, not venturing into a den of marauding pirates,' she exclaimed.

'Emily, my dear, such forcefulness,' her father replied reproachfully.

'There can be dangers anywhere, even in the safest seeming place,' the doctor replied.

Emily stepped out of the door, looking about her as the two men parted on the step. Dangers indeed! She muttered to herself. Falling masonry, a cloud of dust, a swarm of wasps, perhaps? Or what of something more dramatic? A runaway carriage? A rabid dog? A licentious libertine on the prowl? Chance would be a fine thing!

The doctor joined her on the path, and politely opened the gate for her, then together they turned left to walk around the close. Boyle held out his arm politely for her to take it, but pretending not to notice, Emily turned away, pointed out a rather attractive tree in blossom in one of the gardens, then walked at a decorous distance with her hands clasped loosely behind her back. She had no wish to demonstrate to her neighbours any particular closeness between herself and the doctor.

Dr Boyle had been living in Lincoln for some six months now. His father had been the resident physician before him, but following the older man's death the previous year, the son, who had been practising in a nearby country area, had come to take over his father's business.

Emily could not imagine why his fancy should have lighted upon her. A realist, at least as far as her own appearance was concerned, she knew that she was no more a figure of romance than was he. She could only conclude that he saw her as being a useful helpmeet for a busy doctor. Unfortunately, she could not think of herself in the same way.

They had not walked very far, when the doctor cleared his throat again. 'Miss Whittaker, I wonder whether I might be so bold as to address you on a very private and . . . hrmph . . . intimate matter?'

It could not be avoided. With a flash of insight, Emily understood that the reason that she had wanted to put off his proposal was because she did not yet want to close the door completely on that particular avenue. It would, at least, represent an escape from a dull life, in which sometimes the only thing that lifted her spirits was the cathedral itself. If married life with the doctor proved to be as dull as spinster life with two ageing clergymen, she told herself that at least she would still have that place of refuge.

Then suddenly, the whole matter of the doctor's proposal and her reply became irrelevant, when the door of one of the houses that gave on to the close flew open, and an enchantingly pretty, heavily pregnant young lady with tears filling her eyes came running out, a handkerchief fluttering in one hand.

2

'Mrs Fanshawe, whatever can be amiss?' Emily exclaimed, recognizing the young woman immediately. 'Is the baby coming? Surely it cannot be right for you to agitate yourself in such a way!'

'No indeed,' agreed the doctor, immediately becoming practical and decisive when confronted with a professional matter. 'You must come and sit down at once, Mrs Fanshawe.'

The young lady's eyes darted from one to the other, her expression one of great anxiety. She looked as if even now, she might still take flight. 'Oh, but I was just going — ' Abruptly she halted, and her shoulders drooped. 'But it is not as if I *can* go,' she finished, then burst into tears.

'Miss Whittaker, we must take her inside at once,' the doctor said. 'Mrs Fanshawe, can you walk?' The lady did not speak, but nodded into her handkerchief. 'Then pray, lean upon my arm, ma'am,' he went on. 'Miss Whittaker will go on ahead to make sure that your bed is prepared for you.'

'I don't want to go to bed,' was the muffled response.

'Perhaps not, but I would like to examine you, if I may, to make sure that all is well with the baby.'

Once Mrs Fanshawe was lying down on her bed, Emily began to make her farewells, but the younger woman protested. 'Pray do not leave, Miss Whittaker. I would like to speak with you when the doctor has gone.'

Emily was shown into an adjoining pretty sitting-room, but she did not have long to wait. The doctor soon came in to see her, and he was smiling. 'There's nothing amiss,' he told her. 'Ladies in her delicate condition are sometimes subject to strange fancies and humours, and I fear that Mrs Fanshawe has allowed her spirits to become overset by some of them.'

'Did she tell you what was concerning her in particular, Doctor?' Emily asked. She could not dismiss from her mind that picture of the hunted expression on the younger woman's face.

'She did not confide in me,' the doctor replied. 'I am hoping that she might say something to you. Naturally if that matter is confidential then you must keep it to yourself. But I must urge you that whatever you do, you must attempt to give her thoughts a more cheerful direction. A lifting of the spirits will do her more good than anything.'

When Emily entered Mrs Fanshawe's room, she was sitting up on the bed with a cup of tea in her hand.

'That's better,' Emily said, smiling encouragingly. 'You will soon feel more the thing.' Seeing that there was a tray on a little table by the window on which someone had placed a teapot, milk, sugar and another cup, Emily poured herself some tea and sat down next to the bed. They were in a charming room, very pretty and feminine with wallpaper with a design of pink flowers and leaves, curtains at the window and at the corners of the bed that matched the exact shade of the flowers, and a thick carpet with a toning design. Everything in the room seemed light and delicate, and appeared to have been designed with its occupant in mind.

As if to echo Emily's thoughts, Mrs Fanshawe said, 'Ernest had this room decorated especially for me.'

'That was kind of him,' Emily observed, thinking briefly of her own room, clean, tidy, sensible and, in all honesty, rather dull.

'Oh he is very kind,' Mrs Fanshawe agreed eagerly. 'I do believe that no husband on earth could be more kind and generous and truly Christian! Which is why it is so ungrateful of me to feel unhappy at this time.'

'But happiness has nothing to do with gratitude,' Emily observed. 'One can be conscious of all kind of benefits that fall to one's lot and yet still not be happy.'

Mrs Fanshawe leaned forward, to the imminent danger of her cup of tea, and grasped hold of Emily's hand. 'You *do* understand,' she exclaimed. 'I thought that you might. You have always looked to me to be truly sympathetic.'

'That is good of you to say so,' Emily replied, taking hold of Mrs Fanshawe's cup and setting it to rights. 'Dr Boyle tells me that ladies in your condition often have strange and unaccountable humours. Might your present unhappiness be something to do with that?'

'Yes, I dare say that it might,' the other lady agreed. 'But just because the reasons for my unhappiness can be explained away does not mean that I can just stop feeling unhappy. Anyway, there is something else.'

Emily simply nodded sympathetically. She had for some time been interested in the very pretty wife of the Reverend Ernest Fanshawe. Mr Fanshawe had not been in Lincoln for long, and he was one of the most junior clergymen attached to the cathedral. He had arrived with his young wife just a few months

14

ago, and since Mrs Fanshawe was expecting their first child, and seemed to be inclined to be delicate, no one had seen a great deal of her. Mr Fanshawe, tall, blond and far more handsome than any clergyman had a right to be, might well have caused a flutter or two in the cathedral close had he not been so clearly devoted to his lovely wife. Indeed, this very devotion had given rise to some criticism. Emily had overheard the end of a conversation between Mr Fanshawe and the dean, in which the latter had been heard to say rather severely, 'The cathedral comes first, my dear sir; always first. Your wife must wait her turn.'

Emily's interest, however, did not mean that she had any intention of prying. Over ten years of sympathetic listening as a clergyman's daughter had taught her that when people were in a confiding mood, then sooner or later they spilt everything out.

Sure enough, moments later, Mrs Fanshawe said, 'You do not ask me what it is.'

'It is not my place to ask any questions about your private affairs, Mrs Fanshawe,' Emily replied.

'Pray call me Nathalie,' begged the other. 'And may I call you Emily? I still feel so strange here and I have few friends.'

'Of course you may.'

'The reason for my unhappiness is no

secret,' Nathalie said, after a few moments. 'The fact of the matter is that Ernest has been promising to take me away to the sea, to build me up for my confinement.'

'A very wise idea,' Emily interpolated.

'Yes, and Dr Boyle is of the same opinion,' Nathalie answered eagerly. 'So Ernest decided that the best thing would be to take me to Mablethorpe. It is only a little place on the coast, but he knows of a very respectable woman who would have been very glad to put us up, but now it is all come to nothing!'

With that, Mrs Fanshawe showed a remarkable inclination to burst into tears again, so Emily said quickly, 'What is the problem? Does the woman have another booking? Surely another place can be found.'

'No, no, it is nothing like that,' Nathalie assured her. 'It is just that Ernest has been told that he will not be permitted to go. He is needed for something in the cathedral. Oh Emily, you cannot imagine how I had been looking forward to that little visit. I know that you have lived here all your life, but I am a stranger here and just recently I have started to feel so hemmed in and trapped that I fear that I will lose my mind.'

'Oh, surely not,' Emily protested.

'Well perhaps I am exaggerating a little, but

I am conscious of a lowness of spirits and I had been so looking forward to getting away.'

'Are there no relatives to whom you could go?' Emily asked her.

'No, nobody at all,' Nathalie replied in a subdued voice.

At that moment, the door opened and the exceedingly handsome young clergyman about whom they had been speaking came hurrying into the room. 'Nathalie, my darling!' he exclaimed. 'I have just chanced upon Dr Boyle in Bailgate and he told me that you were unwell.' He sat on the edge of the bed and took his wife's hand in his. 'You must take care, dearest,' he added fondly.

'Oh, I shall, I promise you, and Dr Boyle and Miss Whittaker have been so kind.'

The clergyman stood up, came over to where Emily had risen to her feet, and took her hand, kissing it in quite the grand manner. 'God bless you for that,' he said fervently.

'It was nothing, really,' she told him, a little flustered, for gallant gestures such as his seldom came her way these days. 'And now I must leave you. Nathalie, I do hope that you will be feeling better soon. May I call tomorrow and see how you do?'

'Oh, yes please,' Nathalie answered. 'I should like it of all things. Thank you so much for your kindness to me.'

Emily went out, closing the door gently behind her. She left the Fanshawes' house and looked round a little anxiously to see whether Dr Boyle had lingered. Then she recalled that Mr Fanshawe had said that he had met the doctor in Bailgate. She was conscious of a feeling of relief. She had steeled herself to receive a proposal of marriage from him. The moment had been put off and she could only be thankful. It felt like a reprieve.

Upon returning to her own home, she found that her father had gone to visit the dean about some matter, and she was glad to have a little time in which to decide how to tell him the story of the afternoon's adventures. She was well aware that there were some in the close who were all too willing to condemn Mrs Fanshawe as being a little flighty. The image of the clergyman's wife flinging herself out of her own front door and into the street would do nothing to improve that image; Emily would find it hard to pursue a friendship with the younger woman without her father looking reproachful and making gentle remarks about the wrong company.

Emily could never decide whether it would have been better if her brother had lived. He had been some ten years older than herself, had attended Eton, and had by all accounts been a promising scholar, diligent in his work and quick of apprehension. It had always been intended that he should go into the church, but before he could begin his degree at Cambridge, he had drowned in an accident whilst on holiday with a friend. Because of the gap between their ages, Emily had not known him very well, and although she had grieved his loss sincerely, it had been more the grief that one would feel for a distant relative than for a brother.

She had often felt a degree of curiosity about the accident which had taken his life, for it sometimes seemed to her to be quite the most interesting and romantic thing about him, but her father would never speak of the matter. He did occasionally refer to his lost son as 'dearest Patrick', the name seldom being used without either that or some other sentimental adjective. On such occasions, he would bemoan the fact that he did not have a son who could also take his place among the staff at Lincoln Cathedral. At these times, Emily became aware that she was a very poor second. She privately owned that the idea of yet another man in clerical black hovering about the place and regarding her with gentle and kindly disapproval was almost enough to drive her to screaming point.

Even if Patrick had lived, therefore, he might very well have been just as disapproving of her friendship with Nathalie as her father would undoubtedly be. That was a pity; it was probably the most interesting thing that had happened to her in a very long time.

3

'Did you have an agreeable walk with Boyle, my dear?' Emily's father asked her at dinner. Their meal was simple but well cooked, for Canon Whittaker, whilst not being mean in his provision for the family, was very much averse to extravagant display.

'It was agreeable, but quite brief,' Emily replied, thankful that she had had time to think about what she might say about the day's events. 'Quite unexpectedly, Dr Boyle was called in to attend Mrs Fanshawe, so we were unable to complete it.'

'That was unfortunate,' her father answered. In appearance, Canon Whittaker was very like his dead son. He had the same sharp features and slim figure, and his hair, like his son's, had also been fair, until the years had turned it to a rather drab shade of grey.

'No doubt there will be other opportunities,' said Emily calmly. 'Are you preaching on Sunday, Papa? What is your text for the day?' In this deft way, she managed to turn the subject, and Dr Boyle was not mentioned at all during the rest of the meal.

After Canon Whittaker had finished, he

made his excuses and went to his study, leaving Emily on her own. She went upstairs to see her grandfather, but finding that he was asleep, she collected her sewing for the poor from the linen cupboard and went downstairs to occupy herself until the tea tray should be brought in.

Her father came in a little later and smiled approvingly at her occupation. 'It is very pleasing to see you engaged so unexceptionally, my dear,' he said. Fleetingly, she thought of all the other occasions when he had come in and seen her similarly occupied. Pleasing it might be; unusual, by no means. If he had found her with her feet up, reading a scurrilous novel now . . .

'Shall I read you one of the sermons from this volume?' her father asked, interrupting her musings.

Emily saw that in his hand he had a book from which she had heard him read on countless occasions. 'Yes please, Papa,' she answered. 'Would you be so good as to read the one which concerns diligence?'

'By all means,' her father answered, beaming. He would have been less pleased had he realized that she had only chosen it because she knew it off by heart, and would be perfectly capable of answering any questions upon it, even if she allowed her

mind to wander so much t⌐ ⌐
hear a single word he said.
Canon Whittaker was readin⌐
gence, obedience and sobriety, a
bending her neat head over a pl⌐
finishing it off with plain stitche⌐   ⌐⌐
was picturing that frivolous little ⌐onnet in
the milliner's window.

*   *   *

'I think I shall call upon Mrs Fanshawe today,
Papa,' Emily said, as they sat at breakfast the
following morning.

'Mrs Fanshawe?' her father repeated,
looking as if he did not entirely approve of
such a course of action.

'Yes, Papa. She is expecting a baby, you
know.'

Her father looked as if he would have liked
to reprove her for being indelicate, but all he
said was, 'Yes, indeed.'

'She is becoming rather anxious and
nervous,' Emily went on, then added craftily,
'The doctor thought that I might be able to
raise her spirits.'

The canon's face lightened. 'Of course,' he
agreed. 'You might lift her thoughts to a
higher plane. She is a delicate young thing,
and might easily not survive the coming

ut if you can turn her from worldly rs and prepare her mind for Heaven, u will have done some good.'

Emily was surprised at how annoyed she felt at the tenor of this speech, and was glad that the servant came in with the newspaper at that point, thus distracting her father with the news of Nelson's latest exploits.

She did not make the mistake of thinking that her visit to Mrs Fanshawe would be welcomed early in the day, and busied herself with household tasks until eleven o'clock. Even so, she discovered on arrival at the young clergyman's residence that his pretty wife was still abed, but would welcome a visit from her new friend in her chamber.

Emily entered Mrs Fanshawe's room with a kind of envious longing, for the contrast between this feminine environment and her own rather plain accommodation seemed even more stark now that she had had the chance to view her room in the light of this very different one.

As she went in, Nathalie laid aside the book that she was reading with rather a guilty expression. 'It is an . . . an improving book,' she said hastily.

'Really? What is it?' Emily asked her, prompted by a spirit of pure mischief.

Mrs Fanshawe bit her lip. 'It is a novel, but

pray do not tell anyone,' implored the younger woman. 'It would be sure to get back to the dean or the bishop or some such person, and then Ernest would be in trouble and all on my account.'

'I should not dream of telling anyone,' Emily replied. Then after a moment she added curiously, 'Is it very entertaining?'

'Oh, extremely so,' Nathalie replied, regaining her complexion as soon as she realized that her secret was safe. 'Would you like to borrow it when I have finished it?'

'I doubt whether I would ever get away with reading it,' Emily replied regretfully.

'But you are quite ol — that is to say, you are of age,' Nathalie said, correcting herself hastily. 'Surely no one can tell you what you may or may not read?'

'You wouldn't think so, would you?' Emily answered ruefully. 'Well, perhaps they cannot do that, but sometimes, you know, the thought of disapproval can simply stop one from even trying.'

'That sounds very sad,' Nathalie commented. 'Have you always lived in Lincoln, Emily?'

'Yes, always. So you will have to tell me about London, for I have never been.'

'What, never?' Nathalie exclaimed, aghast.

'No, never. What is it like? Is it very busy and noisy?'

Mrs Fanshawe rang for tea, and for some time, whilst they were waiting for it, and then after it had arrived, they were happily engaged in exchanging stories of London life on the one hand and existence in the provinces on the other.

'Of course, we have a theatre now,' said Emily eventually. 'You must persuade your husband to take you when you are well.'

For the first time since Emily had entered the room, the anxious look reappeared on Nathalie's face. 'If I ever do get well,' she murmured.

'Of course you will,' Emily answered encouragingly, very conscious of what the doctor had said concerning the need to raise the young woman's spirits.

'If only I could get away,' she said wistfully. 'But the dean will not hear of Ernest leaving at present, and I cannot go alone.'

They sat there in silence for a time and, as they did so, a thought came into Emily's mind that seemed to be so daring that she could hardly imagine giving voice to it.

Just as she was about to speak, she looked at Nathalie and saw that the younger woman had been taken by the very same idea. 'Oh, Emily, would *you* come with me?' she asked.

Because Emily had had the same notion, she did not immediately say no, but answered slowly, 'I wonder how it could be done?'

'I am sure that Ernest would be very happy to send me to Mablethorpe in your care,' Nathalie declared.

'Yes, but what of my Papa?' Emily asked. 'I must persuade him to give his consent.'

'Oh Emily, please try,' Nathalie begged. 'It would do me all the good in the world.'

Soon after this, Emily made her excuses and walked slowly down the stairs. She could see that Nathalie thought her a pathetic thing for needing, at the age of thirty, to get her father's permission to go somewhere. She was not surprised. She thought it a little pathetic herself. She had a vague feeling that there had been a time when she might have stamped about in order to get her way. But then Patrick had died, all the household had been plunged into grief, with herself caught up in it although not fully understanding it, and she had begun to suppress any of her own feelings and desires so as to not upset anybody. This had become a habit, she freely acknowledged and she had never found a really powerful reason to change it. Now, for some strange reason, she found herself very much wanting to go to Mablethorpe. It was such a little thing; yet even Nathalie Fanshawe, with all the feminine wiles which even a blind man might detect that she possessed, had not been able to sway the issues in her direction. How then could she, dowdy spinster that she was, expect to achieve such an object?

She got to the gate, paused briefly, then instead of walking back to her own house, she turned and entered the cathedral. There was something about its lofty expansiveness that seemed to enable her mind to think more clearly. She wandered up the nave, pleased not to encounter anyone, and went into St Hugh's choir, where her gaze lighted upon the dean's seat. If the dean were to decide that Mrs Fanshawe should go away for her health and for the sake of her husband's peace of mind, then it would happen she mused. She turned her head and glanced up at the Lincoln imp, who seemed to be grinning down at her from his position at the top of one of the pillars. Suddenly she smiled as an idea came to her. She might not have any feminine wiles, but she could be cunning!

She left the cathedral more decisively than she had come. She walked in the direction of the dean's house, where she was fortunate to find his wife at home. That august lady was pleased to receive Emily very graciously, and for a time they indulged in polite chit chat. Emily was just wondering how to bring up the subject of Mrs Fanshawe, when her hostess saved her the trouble. 'The dean is very concerned about Mr Fanshawe,' she remarked. 'He is wondering whether the young man has his mind on his work.'

'I can understand the dean's anxiety,' Emily agreed.

'As can I,' agreed the other lady. 'But you know, I can see the matter from the other side too. How well I remember being a young mother! But you, as a single woman, would of course know nothing about such things, Miss Whittaker, and it is entirely right and proper that you should be ignorant about them.'

Emily glanced down, not wanting the dean's wife to see the irritation in her eyes. She might never have been a mother herself, but she had visited many homes where a baby was expected, or had just been born. 'As you say, I am comparatively uninformed about those delicate matters,' Emily responded diplomatically, 'but I have seen much of cathedral life, and I can understand how hard it must be for the dean to spare Mr Fanshawe.'

'Yes of course,' agreed the dean's wife grudgingly. She had lived in Lincoln for far less time than had Emily. A fashionably dressed lady, she was accustomed to a much more varied society than that which was to be found in Lincoln.

'It must be very worrying for the dean to see so conscientious a young man with worries that threaten to distract him.'

'Naturally it is,' the dean's wife agreed again. 'My husband knows the Fanshawe family which is why he has taken such a keen interest in his ministry.'

'If only it were possible for some other person to take Mrs Fanshawe away for a short time — say, to the seaside,' Emily observed.

'Some other person?'

'It would have to be a reliable person — a lady, of course — who had no official duties to carry out here, and no children of her own to care for, but who was old enough and sensible enough to be of help to Mrs Fanshawe. Then her husband could concentrate upon his work with his mind relieved of care.'

'Indeed,' responded the dean's wife thoughtfully. 'But where might such a person be found?'

'We must think very hard,' answered Emily. 'I will tell you if anyone comes to mind. Well, you must excuse me now, ma'am, I really ought to return home. Not that Papa needs me very much, of course. I do declare, our Mrs Ashby is so efficient that I could simply disappear for weeks on end and no one in the house would feel the loss of me at all.'

That very evening, the dean came round to the Whittakers' house to ask that, for the sake of Mr Fanshawe's peace of mind in particular, and for the good of the cathedral as a whole, Miss Whittaker should be permitted to take Mrs Fanshawe to the seaside for her health.

4

Emily had not been to the sea for some years, and she found that as they drew near to the coast, and as she observed Nathalie becoming more excited, she became conscious of a feeling of excitement welling up inside herself as well.

No younger or older sisters with babies had ever demanded her attention; no school friends had ever invited her to visit; no godmother had ever summoned her. Consequently, she could not remember the last time that she had spent a night away from home.

As she had correctly surmised, her father had immediately agreed to the dean's suggestion that she should go away with Mrs Fanshawe. A part of her had felt resentment that he should so readily accept an idea from such a source, when the same plan, if coming from herself, would undoubtedly have been rejected out of hand. Yet another part of her, however, had rejoiced that she had found a devious means to achieve her end. 'I am a designing woman,' she had said gleefully to herself one night in bed before she had left Lincoln.

The lodgings that Mr Fanshawe had procured for his wife were within easy reach of the sea. The ladies walked to the shore nearly every day, but if the weather was inclement, they could still see the vast expanse of water with its changing moods from their upstairs sitting-room window.

Freed from anxiety about her health, and under the care of a local doctor who dealt sensitively with all her fears, Nathalie's spirits improved. She had brought with her some material to make tiny garments for the new baby and Emily gladly put her dull sewing for the poor on one side and instead made a tiny dress with exquisite stitches.

'This is such a change,' she murmured one day, as she was busy working on a piece of smocking. 'I get so fed up with sewing in brown or grey.'

'Forgive my saying so, dear Emily, but do you not get fed up with wearing it as well?' Nathalie asked curiously.

Emily stared at her for a moment, then said, 'I did not mean sewing for myself, I meant sewing for the poor.'

'Oh, I beg your pardon,' murmured Nathalie, blushing. 'I thought that as you wear . . . that is . . . you must not think that you do not always look very . . . very . . . ' Her voice tailed off. Eventually, she added,

'Of course you are at liberty to wear whatever colours you choose, ma'am, but has anyone ever asked the poor if they would like to wear any other colours?'

'I don't think anyone has ever thought to do so,' Emily answered. Then on impulse, she said quickly, 'Nathalie, do I really look as if I have been dressed out of the poor box?'

'Oh no!' Nathalie exclaimed hastily, her tone unmistakably sincere. But later, Emily wondered whether somehow she had got herself into a position where she had as little choice about what she wore as the poor did. She resolved to consult Nathalie about the suitability of the bonnet in the milliner's window.

When they got tired of sewing one day, Emily offered to read to her young friend, and somewhat guiltily, Mrs Fanshawe handed her a book entitled *The Fateful Bells*. 'It is so thrilling, and I would so like to discover whether Veronica, the heroine, manages to escape from the haunted monastery with the little blind girl.'

'Oh my,' breathed Emily.

'Of course, it is just horrid stuff,' Nathalie said hastily, 'and if you should have a . . . a book of sermons or homilies, I should be just as happy with that.'

'Well, I should not,' said Emily frankly. 'I

can hear Papa read me one of those any day of the week. Where did you leave off? Will you tell me briefly what has gone before?'

This Nathalie did very willingly, and after that, the ladies whiled away many an hour enjoying the improbable exploits of the characters to be found within the pages of the books that Nathalie had brought with her.

'What does Mr Fanshawe say about your reading novels?' Emily asked curiously one day.

Nathalie looked at her cautiously. 'Promise you will never tell?' she asked.

'Of course,' Emily replied.

'Well he does not care for *The Fateful Bells* very much because he thinks that the clergyman in it is very silly and improbable, but he liked the one that we read together before that — I've forgotten what it was called, now.'

'He reads novels with you?' said Emily in a surprised tone.

'Oh yes,' Nathalie answered. 'He says that if we were only to read what was proper in some people's eyes, we wouldn't read half of what is in the Bible, and that it is how people conduct themselves in real life that matters.'

'How very sensible,' murmured Emily, much struck. 'I think he ought to become a bishop.'

'He certainly should,' Nathalie agreed. 'He is the best of men, and when I think what he . . . how he . . . ' She coloured, then went on hastily, 'Do you think that it is sunny enough for our stroll, now?'

Emily looked curiously at her companion, but did not make any remark. If the young clergyman had indeed behaved in some gallant way, she was sure that Nathalie would tell her about it eventually when she was ready.

'I wonder how it is that some people come to write novels,' Emily said thoughtfully, as she and Natalie sat in their little sitting-room one afternoon. It was about a week after Emily's arrival in Mablethorpe. They had just finished *The Fateful Bells* and both had cried a little over the ending in which the little blind girl, who had also turned out to be consumptive, had died with blessings on her lips for her rescuer's union with the handsome viscount.

'I don't know,' Nathalie replied. 'I'm very sure that I couldn't.'

'Well somebody must do so,' Emily declared incontrovertibly, 'and they must have a great deal of imagination. After all, no one could possibly experience all the mishaps which the characters suffered in *The Fateful Bells*.'

'I should hope they would not,' Nathalie agreed fervently. 'To be chained to a rock as the tide was coming in on one page, and then to be immured in a dungeon just one chapter later must surely be beyond anyone's experience.'

'Exactly,' Emily answered. 'Nobody could have such things happen to them; which is why I should think almost anyone could write a novel, given a reasonable standard of literacy and the will to do it.'

'Anyone?' Nathalie echoed.

'Why yes; in fact, even I could do so. After all, I do have some experience that may be relevant.'

'*Really?*' exclaimed Nathalie, her eyes opening very wide.

'I don't mean that I have ever been kidnapped, or seen a ghost, or been threatened with murder, like some of the characters in *The Fateful Bells*,' Emily answered her hastily. 'But I *have* attended death-beds and visited people in prison.'

'*And* you live close to the cathedral,' Nathalie put in with enthusiasm. 'That could appear in some splendid scenes; especially at night.'

'Yes, yes, it could,' Emily agreed slowly.

Nathalie gave a gasp. 'I know!' she cried. 'You could have a corrupt clergyman!'

'Goodness!' Emily breathed. 'It had never occurred to me that I could have such a thing. Of course,' she went on after a short pause, 'I have no experience of romance.'

'None at all?' queried Nathalie in pitying tones. 'But surely, Dr Boyle . . . ?'

'Oh no,' Emily responded hastily. 'There has been nothing of that nature between us. But I have my observations of how other people behave.'

'And I could help you with the more . . . *sentimental* passages,' Nathalie suggested.

'Yes of course; if I ever did such a thing,' Emily agreed. 'But I never shall.'

'Oh, why not?' Nathalie demanded, her imagination now fairly caught by the idea. 'It would be such fun! I know, you could put all the people that you know into the book under different identities!'

'But how would I face anyone when it came into print?' Emily asked her.

'You could publish under an assumed name,' Nathalie suggested. 'Or just call yourself 'a gentleman' or 'a lady'.'

'But where would be the fun in that?' Emily asked her. 'If I had a book published I would want to boast about it to everyone.'

After Mrs Fanshawe had gone upstairs to rest, Emily went for her usual walk along the beach. On this occasion, she had something new to occupy her mind, however, for she began idly to turn over in her mind the various characters that she would put in any novel that she might write.

Her heroine would definitely not be young and beautiful, she decided. Why should such people have all the fun? Instead, she would be an older lady, possibly a companion to someone young and beautiful, who would, for a change, be a minor character in her story. This older lady would be sensible, respectable, and pleasant looking if not precisely pretty. She would give her heroine a sensible name, too; something like Susan, or Margaret, not one of the fanciful names that novelists seemed prone to use.

She would be a thirty-year-old spinster, the daughter of a clergyman, in comfortable circumstances, and living a life that was comfortable and happy in a way, but rather dull. She smiled wryly as she thought again about this description. It could be herself.

The story would begin on a dark and stormy night. Her heroine would be returning home from laying someone out, and would be obliged to walk past the Minster, which loured threateningly through the mist.

She frowned. No, that wasn't right at all. To others, the cathedral might appear to lour, but for her it was an old friend whose demeanour was welcoming, never threatening. But that would not fit with the dark and stormy night. It would just have to lour and that was all. Then, as her heroine hurried through the gloom, she would suddenly encounter a tall, dark man, powerful and muscular, with strong features and swathed in a long cloak, who would exclaim at her clumsiness, and seize her in a vice-like grip.

A sudden crash of a breaking wave brought Emily back to the present with a start. Good heavens, where upon earth had he come from, she wondered? The hero of *The Fateful Bells* had been fair-haired and slender. The leading male character in *The Haunted Forest* which they were to read next, and at which she had already glanced, looked to be much the same, and, if truth were told, promised to be rather dull. It was the villain who was always dark and muscular, who seized hold of the heroine and swore at her.

If the heroine was unlike other heroines, of course, the hero could be unlike other heroes too. Whoever this character might be, hero or villain, he would certainly give sparkle to the whole narrative. And there the similarity to her own life ended, she sighed, as she turned back towards their lodgings. There was nothing in her life that sparkled. The nearest thing in her life to a hero was Dr Boyle, and whoever would want to read about a hero named Boyle who looked like a weasel?

★ ★ ★

Whilst they were in Mablethorpe, both ladies were diligent as regards their correspondence, and Emily wrote to her father every week. Nathalie wrote to her husband rather more frequently and seemed to receive a missive from him almost every day. In addition, he wrote to Emily, enquiring as to his wife's health, and Emily made sure that she sent him cheerful replies. She could only hope that with all this letter writing to occupy him, he was spending as much time on his sermons as he should.

He often asked about the skill of the local doctor, and Emily was able to say truthfully that she had formed a very good opinion of Dr Saddler. Certainly Nathalie had every confidence in him. 'I like him so much better than Dr Boyle, who I always think looks like a weasel,' she remarked one day when they were enjoying a cup of tea after the doctor had gone.

'Oh do you think so?' Emily said, trying to sound surprised, but guiltily aware that she had always thought the same.

Nathalie looked mortified. 'Oh, I do beg

your pardon,' she whispered. 'I had forgotten that you had an understanding, and I do assure you, Miss Whittaker, that I meant a particularly handsome weasel.'

'Is there such a thing?' Emily asked quizzically. 'No, my dear, I do not have an understanding with him. Although I have wondered . . . '

'Oh no, surely not,' Nathalie exclaimed.

'Well, it is not as if I am falling over offers of marriage,' Emily said candidly. 'And at least I would have a home and a role and perhaps children . . . '

'Yes, but he isn't exactly exciting, is he?' said Nathalie frankly.

'Excitement isn't everything,' Emily pointed out.

'No. No, you are right, and I am the last person who should need to be told that,' Nathalie agreed in a subdued tone.

'Did . . . was your life in London very exciting, before you met Mr Fanshawe?' Emily asked tentatively.

'I — ' Nathalie halted abruptly, her hand to her mouth. 'Forgive me,' she blurted out, before hurrying from the room.

Emily sat, her tea cup in her hand, not knowing what to do. Clearly Nathalie was distressed, but would she welcome the presence of the woman whose conversation had been the means of distressing her? And how could her words have possibly been construed as any kind of criticism?

While she was still pondering, Nathalie came back into the room, her handkerchief in her hand. 'I beg your pardon,' she said softly.

'No, it is I who should beg yours,' Emily insisted, getting up in order to help Nathalie to her chair. 'I was intolerably intrusive.'

'No, you were not,' Nathalie answered. 'The fact of the matter is . . . well, I cannot tell you the whole story for it is not all mine to tell. But suffice it to say that life in London was rather more exciting than I could bear, and when matters became too overwhelming for me, it was Ernest who rescued me from the consequences of my folly. His chivalry, his goodness are greater than I deserve, and I shall never cease to love him for all that he has done for me.' She looked at Emily with an expression that was half pleading, half defiant.

'Well, for my part, I am very glad to hear that you love your husband so sincerely,' Emily replied. 'Is there any news yet of when the dean will release him?'

'Not yet,' Nathalie replied, putting away her handkerchief. 'But I have hopes that I may hear good news any day now.'

The next day brought more than good

news: it brought Mr Fanshawe himself. The ladies were sitting at their small dining-table enjoying a light luncheon, when the door opened, and the young clergyman came in, his handsome face beaming with delight. Nathalie sprang up from the table and cast herself into his arms, quite regardless of Emily's presence, and Mr Fanshawe pressed a firm kiss upon his wife's pretty lips.

'Nathalie, my dearest, how lovely and blooming you are,' he declared, his voice vibrating with sincerity. 'The sea air has done you good, I see.' He turned to Emily. 'Miss Whittaker, your servant.'

Emily returned his greeting with a curtsy. 'Welcome, Mr Fanshawe,' she replied. 'Yes, the air has done us both a lot of good, which is why I shall go now and enjoy a little more of it.' So saying, she went out and left the young couple to their privacy.

As she walked down to the sea she was conscious of a stab of envy. No gentleman had ever taken her in his arms in that way. No gentleman had ever kissed her upon her lips. Doubtless Dr Boyle would be glad to oblige, but the very idea filled her with disgust. She would have to face the fact that romance had by now passed her by. No doubt she would have to be content either with imagining how the muscular gentleman in the novel that she would never write would perform such a salute, or with being glad at the happiness experienced by such as Mr and Mrs Fanshawe. If she was especially lucky, perhaps they would invite her to be a godmother. This thought should have comforted her; sadly, it only succeeded in making her feel rather desolate.

They made a companionable party for dinner that night, but Emily was very conscious of being not exactly an intruder, but a third person where a couple would have been quite sufficient.

The following morning, when Emily left in the carriage in which Mr Fanshawe had arrived, she went away with very mixed feelings. On the one hand, she had thoroughly enjoyed her visit to the sea, and the chance to share confidences with a female friend, an opportunity which had rarely come in her way; but on the other, she knew that Nathalie now only wanted her husband and she did not want to get in the way. Furthermore, she knew if she was honest with herself, that their friendship would never be one of true mutuality. For Nathalie, she would always be someone to depend upon.

Going back to Lincoln did have its bright side, after all. She had her various duties and interests which she had missed. There was the little group of children that she met every week for reading practice, and the ladies with whom she sang sacred songs, not to mention the time that she spent each day reading to her grandfather and her prison visiting . . . my goodness, she thought to herself, is that really what my life amounts to? Suppose someone like the hero whom she had pictured so recently were to appear on the scene? In which of these settings would he ever feel at home?

The carriage brought her back to Lincoln during the middle of the afternoon, setting her down outside her house in Priorygate.

'It's good to have you home, miss,' said Mary, as she opened the door.

'Thank you, Mary. It's good to be here,' Emily replied, not entirely sure that she was speaking the truth. 'Has anything exciting happened whilst I have been away?'

'New family's just moving into Canon Mitchell's old house,' the maid answered. 'I saw Pickford's men carrying things in only today.'

Emily went straight up to her room to take off her outdoor things, but later, she asked her father who the new arrivals might be.

'It is Canon Trimmer and his wife,' her father told her. 'He has come here from Salisbury. His wife is the sister of a baronet, I understand. Emily, my dear, I am very pleased that you are home. The house has been strangely silent without you. I am sure that your grandfather will have missed you too.'

Emily thanked her father and went upstairs to supervise her unpacking. In truth, she was a little taken aback at the warmth of his welcome. Somehow, she had not supposed that he would miss her very much.

That evening, she went to sit with her grandfather, a duty which she had performed every day, until she had left for Mablethorpe. The elderly clergyman had had some kind of seizure some weeks before and since then had lain in bed neither speaking nor moving. Only the fact that it was possible from time to time to coax him to swallow some thin gruel gave his family any hope that he might eventually recover; but it was a very small hope indeed.

Dr Whittaker was a distinguished scholar, with a number of books published under his name. He had not always lived with his son and granddaughter. Before his wife's death five years ago, he had occupied a post at York Minster. After that sad occasion, however, all the heart had seemed to go out of him, and he had come to live in Lincoln, preaching occasionally and performing light duties in the cathedral.

His grief had made him withdraw, and so it was that apart from dining with them, conducting himself with quiet politeness at such times, he spent very little time with his family. Even after five years, Emily could not really say that she knew him well.

But if by chance he could hear, even though he gave no sign of it, he would surely have learned more about his granddaughter over the past few weeks than he had ever learned previously.

Before she had left for the seaside, she had visited him, telling him that she would be away, and promising to inform him about all that she had been doing. It was strange but now that he lay immobile in the bed, he seemed to have become the safe confidante that she had never had; the one to whom she could tell the secrets that she could never, ever bring to her father. Now, on her return, she entrusted him with just such a secret.

'Would you like to know what I have been doing?' she whispered to him, drawing a little closer. 'I have been reading novels! Yes, I know it is very shocking, but you will never tell Papa, will you? And really, I cannot see that they are at all harmful. Mrs Fanshawe and I talk about all kinds of things, and she seems to feel just as she ought on important matters. Anyway, I was wondering whether you would like me to read you something from a novel? I promise that it will have a very good moral tone, but I think that you must be as bored with Papa's book of sermons as I am, and it will give you something else to think about.

'Anyway, Grandpapa, we have new neighbours, so I shall go and see them soon, and of course I shall tell you all about them.'

5

In fact, she went to see the new neighbours and welcome them to Lincoln on the following day. Remembering Nathalie's morning habits, and not wanting to discommode strangers, she left it until quite late in the morning before going. She found that her arrival coincided with that of another, for a gentleman was getting down from a splendid black horse at the very gate of the house that she was intending to visit.

'Forgive me, madam,' he began, taking off his hat, 'but I wonder if I might ask whether you know if this is the residence of Canon and Mrs Trimmer?'

Emily, looking up at the gentleman, saw a strongly featured, good-looking man about ten years older than herself. She knew nothing of fashions, but even in her ignorance, she could tell that he was dressed expensively and with style. He was of medium height only, but of a powerful build, with dark hair flecked with grey.

All at once, she was suddenly transported to another world in which they were standing, not in the warm sunlight, but in the midst of a wild storm, with the wind howling around the cathedral, and the gentleman before her, instead of making a polite enquiry, swore at her for her clumsiness.

'Ma'am?' he questioned, his brow wrinkling a little. She continued to stare at him. He tilted his head, looking at her quizzically. His eyes were of a dark charcoal grey, and there was a deep cleft in his chin. Slowly, he began to smile, an expression that indicated good humour and conjured up a rather surprising dimple in one cheek.

'Oh!' Emily exclaimed belatedly, blushing. For no reason that she could fathom, her heart had begun to beat rather quickly, and she felt breathless all of a sudden. 'I beg your pardon! I was . . . was thinking of something else.'

'Something else?' echoed the stranger.

'Something that I had read in a novel,' she said hastily, anxious to avoid any more embarrassing silences. Then, fearing that he might gain a false impression about her, she added, 'Not that I read novels, of course.'

One of the gentleman's eyebrows went up. 'So in fact, you were thinking of something that you had not read in a novel. How intriguing.'

To Emily's great relief, at that moment an

elegant-looking lady in a fashionable, high-waisted sapphire-blue gown hurried out of the house and down the path towards them. 'Gareth, my dear, how wonderful to see you!' she cried, embracing the gentleman. 'But you should not bring your horse round here to the front of the house; it must go to the stables.'

'That, my dear Aurelia, was my intention, but I had no idea of where to go. I was about to ask this young lady, when you came out and cast yourself upon my bosom.'

'This young lady?' murmured the one whom he had addressed as Aurelia.

'Forgive me,' said Emily, blushing and curtsying, for it was some time since anyone other than an octogenarian had referred to her as a young lady. 'I am Emily Whittaker, and I live in the close. My father is one of the canons of the cathedral. I had come to bid you welcome, but I see that you have a visitor so I will leave you now, and call again another time.'

'Oh, pray do not,' replied the lady to whom she was speaking. She looked to be about Emily's own age, or possibly a little older. 'I am very much obliged to you for wishing to welcome me. I am Aurelia Trimmer, and my husband Alan has come to serve in the cathedral. As for this gentleman, he is not really a visitor as such, but my own dear

52

brother, so pray allow me to present him to you. Miss Whittaker, this is Sir Gareth Blades.'

'Miss Whittaker, I am delighted to meet you,' said Sir Gareth in his rather deep voice. 'Have you lived in Lincoln for long?'

'All my life,' she admitted. 'I was born in the house in which I now reside.'

'Good heavens,' murmured Mrs Trimmer.

'That isn't so strange,' Sir Gareth replied reasonably. 'I could say the same thing myself, and so could you have done, before you married.'

'Pray come inside, Miss Whittaker. My husband will be delighted to meet you.'

Emily hesitated, partly because she did not want to intrude upon a family occasion, and partly because she had suddenly found herself feeling more dowdy than usual. Strangely enough, it was not the charming gown worn by Mrs Trimmer, but the elegance of that lady's brother that gave her this feeling.

Seeing her hesitation, Sir Gareth said, 'Please do join us, ma'am. If you refuse, my sister will be sure to say that you did not like the look of me.'

Emily glanced up at his face, and quickly looked away, blushing. 'Well, perhaps just for a little while,' she agreed.

'Just as well you agreed, ma'am,' he murmured in an undertone, as they followed his sister into the house, 'Or I would have had to reveal your guilty secret'

Emily wrinkled her brow. 'Sir?'

'A canon's daughter and novel reading? Oh fie, Miss Whittaker!' he retorted archly.

They entered the house just as two boys, aged about ten and eight came clattering down the stairs. 'Uncle Gareth! Uncle Gareth!' the older one exclaimed. 'There is an attic, and I think it might be haunted!'

'Gareth, do be careful! Mind your shoulder!' Mrs Trimmer turned to Emily. 'My brother suffered an injury a short time ago, and I don't want him to have a set-back.'

Sir Gareth stepped forward laughing. 'Nonsense, Aurelia!' he declared. 'I'm as fit as a fiddle.' He bent, picked up and swung each boy round in turn. 'Good grief, James!' he exclaimed as he put down the younger one. 'You have grown so much, I can scarce lift you!'

'Feel my muscles,' the boy demanded, stretching out his arm.

'Very impressive,' his uncle answered solemnly, as he did as instructed. 'But what is this about the attic being haunted?'

'I really ought to go,' Emily said to her hostess. 'I am intruding.'

'By no means,' declared Mrs Trimmer. 'Come through into the drawing-room.' Emily followed her in, and found that already the new occupant had put her own stamp upon the room with chairs covered with straw-coloured satin, and curtains which toned with them, and which were in marked contrast to the drab brown ones that had formerly hung in the windows.

Noticing her visitor looking round, Mrs Trimmer said, 'Did you know this house before?'

'Not well, but I have visited it on occasions.'

The boys, who had entered the room behind them, heard her words, and the older one came forward saying, 'Do *you* know if the attic is haunted, ma'am?'

'Oliver! I am surprised!' exclaimed their mother in shocked tones. 'You have not even been introduced.'

The lad coloured. 'I beg your pardon, ma'am,' he said, bowing.

'That is quite all right,' Emily replied. 'It is sometimes hard to remember everything, isn't it?'

'Yes ma'am. I am Oliver Trimmer and this is my brother James. Please, ma'am, *is* the attic haunted?'

Emily looked at the face of the younger

boy, who was looking a little anxious, and then at Mrs Trimmer, who shook her head discreetly. She was also conscious of the figure of Sir Gareth entering the room, presumably after having given instructions as to the care of his horse. 'My name is Emily Whittaker,' she told the boys with a smile. 'In answer to your question, I have never heard that it was haunted. Canon Mitchell, who lived in this house before you did, was here for many years, and I am sure that he would have said something, had he seen any ghosts.'

'Did he die here?' Oliver asked with relish. 'Because if he did, his ghost might haunt the house.'

'No, he did not die here,' Emily answered. 'He spent his last days with his daughter who lived in another part of the town.'

'But he still might haunt it,' Oliver persisted.

'Well, if you ever do see a kindly old man with a smiling face, then I expect it will be him,' Emily responded matter-of-factly. 'He might have a bag of sweets with him, too,' she went on. 'He was always giving me sweets when I was a child.'

She saw that James looked relieved, as did his mother and she was content. Oliver was not satisfied, however, and he said, 'But surely *something* around here must be haunted! What about the cathedral?'

'Well I suppose it might be,' Emily agreed. 'After all, it is very old. You would have to ask the dean about that. All I can tell you is that I have been in there many times after dark and have never seen anything to frighten me.' She thought for a moment, then added nonchalantly, 'Not even when I have been up in the roof or on the tower, actually.'

'You have been right up there?' James asked, his eyes very round.

'Yes, certainly, many times,' Emily replied.

Oliver opened his mouth to speak but their mother held up her hand. 'Boys, I really cannot believe that you have unpacked all your books and set them out properly on the shelves in the schoolroom. Please go and finish your task.'

Whilst Emily had been talking with the boys, their mother had sent for refreshments, and after they had gone, having bade a polite farewell, Sir Gareth poured two glasses of ratafia and took one to each of the two ladies before pouring a glass of wine for himself.

'Pray enlighten me, Miss Whittaker,' he said to her after she had taken her glass from him. 'Was Canon Mitchell really a kindly old dispenser of sweets?' He was looking at her, a quizzical expression on his face.

'No, I'm afraid he was a miserable old

curmudgeon,' she admitted. 'When I was younger, I used to walk nearly all the way around the cathedral in order to avoid bumping into him.'

Sir Gareth burst out laughing. It was a full, rich sound, and Emily glanced at him, then at Mrs Trimmer in surprise. She could not remember anyone laughing out loud in her own house. It would have been considered quite improper. 'You'll be telling me next that he really did die here,' he said, as soon as he was able.

She looked at him indignantly. 'Certainly not,' she answered with dignity. 'If that were the case, then I must have lied to your nephews and I would never do such a thing.'

'I am sure you would not,' Mrs Trimmer agreed, looking reproachfully at her brother. Then she rather spoiled the effect by adding, 'Children always find out if one has done so, and then it is very hard to convince them of the truth of anything that one says afterwards.'

There was a brief silence, then after a moment's thought, Emily added, 'His wife did, though.'

Sir Gareth, who was on the point of sipping his wine, spluttered and choked. 'My God, Miss Whittaker, you'll be the death of me,' he declared, as soon as he was able. 'How did it happen?'

'She fell down the stairs,' Emily answered shortly, half regretting that she had said anything at all.

'Better and better,' murmured the baronet. 'Did she fall, or was she pushed?'

'Gareth!' exclaimed his sister in shocked tones.

'I have sometimes wondered,' said Emily quietly, 'whether Canon Mitchell's unfriendly disposition sprang partly from grief at the loss of his wife, whom he found at the foot of the stairs after he had returned from worship in the cathedral.'

There was a lengthy silence, after which the baronet walked over to Emily's chair and stood in front of her. 'You do right to reprove me,' he said ruefully. 'That was a crass thing to have said. You must lay the blame for my frivolity on my delight in the fact that I am reunited with my sister after quite a long absence. Am I forgiven?' He was holding out his hand to her. It was a strong, square hand, devoid of rings, and as she looked at it, it seemed as if she could do no other than put her own out so that he could take it. His grip was warm and firm.

'We all say things that we do not mean from time to time, sir,' she replied frankly.

'How many of us would want them to be held against us?'

'You are very generous, ma'am,' he told her, bowing over her hand before releasing it. Then, after a short silence, he said, 'You show some skill with boys, Miss Whittaker. Do you have nephews of your own?'

'No, I do not,' she replied. 'I had only one brother and he died childless some years ago. But I do teach a Bible study class each week.'

Whilst Mrs Trimmer asked Emily about the number of children and the content of the lessons that she took, Sir Gareth wandered over to the window and stood looking out at the cathedral. 'It's a fine building,' he said, when the ladies fell silent.

'It is indeed,' Emily agreed. 'Everyone believes their own cathedral to be the best, but I am of the opinion that Lincoln must be one of the finest to be found anywhere, and I love it dearly. It is like a second home to me.' She coloured because she feared that she had sounded too effusive, put down her glass and stood up. 'Thank you for your hospitality,' she said. 'I must return home now, but I hope that you will call soon.' She smiled at her hostess, then looked at Sir Gareth whose eyes were twinkling, and she suddenly wondered whether he supposed that she was trying to flirt with him in some way. She gave a little gasp of horror, stammered a final farewell and hurried from the room.

'Oh Gareth!' Mrs Trimmer declared, looking roguishly at her brother. 'I fear you have slain her with your fine eyes.'

'Slain her? What nonsense!' he declared, pouring himself another glass of wine.

'I dare say you are the only personable gentleman she has seen for a long time,' his sister went on, as if he had not spoken. 'You heard her say that she has lived here all her life. She probably seldom sees any male of the species who is not an elderly clergyman.'

'I expect she is simply shy,' answered Sir Gareth.

Mrs Trimmer nodded. 'Perhaps. Mind you, she didn't let you get away with that stupid remark about Canon Mitchell. Really, Gareth, how could you be so insensitive?'

'Call it thoughtless, rather.'

'She certainly knew how to talk to the boys, didn't she?'

'Perhaps she has been a governess,' he answered. 'And she did say that she taught a Bible class, remember.' At that point, The Reverend Alan Trimmer came through the door that led into his study, and the recent visitor was forgotten, at least for the time being.

6

Sir Gareth Blades greeted his brother-in-law with great pleasure. 'Alan, my dear fellow,' he declared, flicking the touch of grey at the other man's temples. 'You're getting very distinguished. When do I greet you as my lord bishop?'

Alan Trimmer laughed. 'Never, I hope,' he answered. 'I fear I don't have the legs for gaiters.' He was a man of about forty with finely drawn features and light-brown hair. He was a little taller than his brother-in-law, but much slimmer. 'In fact,' he went on thoughtfully, looking down at the other man's muscular calves, 'I'm not sure whether you don't have a much better figure for them than I.'

The baronet held up one hand in a defensive gesture. 'Heaven forbid!' he declared fervently. 'I suspect that even the church at its most lax would not consider good legs for a bishop's gaiters to be sufficient reason for entering the ranks of the clergy.'

Trimmer grinned wryly. 'You'd be surprised,' he answered. 'What brings you here, anyway?'

'Purely a desire to visit my dear sister and her charming family,' Gareth replied, raising his glass to the lady in question.

'Gammon,' his sister replied frankly, even while she bestowed a fond smile upon him. 'I very much suspect you've been with friends in the area and have outstayed your welcome.'

'Not at all,' her brother replied. 'Quite the reverse, in fact. Houghton begged me to stay a little longer, but, out of loyalty to you . . .' He glanced at Aurelia, broke off, then added in another tone, 'Oh very well, then, if you must have it. Christina Langland turned up with all four of her daughters in tow, and they wouldn't leave me alone. If I had stayed, I would have ended up either being very rude to them, or finding myself in parson's mousetrap, so I pleaded family reasons and made good my escape.'

'I knew it!' his sister declared. 'Forty years old and you are still evading your responsibilities.'

'By no means,' Sir Gareth replied, getting out a box of snuff and offering his brother-in-law a pinch before taking some himself. 'I've no more objection to my responsibilities than any other man; it's my pursuers I want to evade.'

'Stop splitting hairs, Gareth,' said his sister

firmly. 'You know that it is high time you married.'

'Possibly. But I haven't yet found a woman that I want to put in Mama's place, and until I do, I'll remain a bachelor.' His sister looked unconvinced, so he added coaxingly, 'My dear Aurelia, I have before me in you and Alan an example of perfect wedded bliss. Surely you don't wish me to settle for anything less?'

'You don't want the title to die out with you, though,' put in Alan Trimmer.

'I'd rather it didn't, but I'm not going to get worked up about it. Worldly vanity, my dear brother,' he added piously, casting his eyes to heaven.

'Play actor,' laughed the other, cuffing him on his arm.

'Besides, who's to say that I couldn't arrange for the title to go to one of your boys?' Gareth suggested.

'*I* say that you *shouldn't*,' said Aurelia firmly. 'The title should go to *your* son, not mine.'

'Well, don't try to marry me off whilst I'm here,' said the baronet firmly. 'Not to that plainly dressed spinster, nor to anyone else of your acquaintance!'

They were all quiet for a few moments, then Sir Gareth changed the subject by saying: 'There was another matter that I wanted to bring to your attention. It has come to my ears that our disreputable cousin Bernard is no more.'

'Good heavens!' exclaimed Aurelia, dropping her embroidery in her surprise. 'Do you mean he has actually . . . passed away?'

'Yes, if such a peaceful sounding expression could be used to describe his manner of death. He was killed in a drunken brawl in Paris.'

'Paris!' Alan Trimmer echoed. 'Last time you heard of him he was in London surely.'

'He made London decidedly too hot for himself,' the baronet answered. 'He was forced to flee abroad. The authorities sent his effects back to me. There were precious few of them, in all truth; but among them was a cravat pin.' He reached into his pocket as he spoke. 'I've a feeling that this was made from a brooch belonging to Grandmama which was promised to you, Aurelia, and which he purloined. I thought you might like to have it back.'

Aurelia put out her hand reluctantly, and accepted the ornament that he placed in it. 'It *should* have been mine,' she agreed, 'but I feel strangely reluctant to take possession of it now.'

'Then keep it for one of the boys,' her

brother suggested. 'I should have thought that something with a grisly history would suit Oliver down to the ground. In fact, only convince him that Bernard was wearing it at the moment of his demise and it will no doubt become his favourite piece.'

Aurelia gave a short laugh. 'You're absolutely right of course,' she agreed, putting the pin away amongst her sewing things.

At that moment, the boys came in announcing that they had completed their task, and the subject was changed.

★　★　★

'But surely my dear Aurelia, you do not intend to ignore your brother's expressed wishes?' Alan Trimmer asked his wife that evening when he went to her bedchamber in order to say good night.

'Certainly not,' she replied with dignity. She was sitting up in her bed, a light shawl about her shoulders, for the evening was warm, and a rather fetching night cap upon her head. 'It is simply that I do not believe that Gareth knows his own mind in this matter.'

'Not know his own mind? A man of his age? I hope you will not allow him to hear you express that opinion!' He wandered over to the bedroom window, lifted the curtain to glance out, then let it drop again. 'Aurelia, my dear, it never ceases to amaze me how wherever we go, you manage so quickly to contrive to make the place seem like home.'

'Thank you, my love,' replied his wife, much gratified, 'Which is exactly why I desire dear Gareth to find a wife who will make him comfortable. And how is he to find one, pray, if his nearest and dearest do not make shift to help him?'

'From what I have heard, my dear, plenty of ladies have already been making strenuous efforts on his behalf,' said the clergyman, sitting on the bed again, taking hold of his wife's hand and turning her wedding ring idly with his long fingers. 'I see no reason why you should add to their ranks.'

'There is every reason, Alan. All of those ladies have some other aim in view apart from Gareth's happiness. Christina Langland's girls are as plain as a set of schoolroom chairs, and she is desperate to marry them off; why, the oldest one must be quite twenty-four! If I do not miss my guess, Millicent Copthorne was there as well, and everyone knows that that family has nothing to offer but debts! As for Annis Hughes, she has been chasing him for ever. If he did marry her, I doubt very much if he could ever be sure that any child she produced really was his.'

'Aurelia!' her husband declared in shocked tones.

'Well, it's true,' she replied firmly. 'Would you desire a sister-in-law like that?'

'I confess I would not,' he admitted, 'but as for the other ladies, I have only heard you say that one is poor and others are not pretty. Would you condemn them for such reasons?'

'Not condemn them, no; but I refuse to permit any woman to marry my brother simply to get herself out of her own difficulties. No, say what you will, Alan, I am much more likely to find him a suitable bride. After all, my motives are by far the purest.'

'But how are you to achieve that, dearest?' Trimmer asked his wife. He got up to blow out the candles on the mantelpiece and on the dressing-table. 'After all, you have no acquaintance here at all — unless you count the lady who was visiting earlier on today.' His task accomplished, he wandered back to sit on the bed again.

Mrs Trimmer, who had been leaning back against her pillows in a relaxed manner, suddenly sat bolt upright. 'Alan! What a splendid idea!'

Her husband frowned. 'My dear Aurelia,

do not think me a fault finder, but did you not say that the oldest Miss Langland, at twenty-four, was too old for your brother? My suspicion is that Miss Whittaker may easily be older than that.'

'No no, I do not mean that she would make a match for him,' his wife said hastily, 'but she said herself that she has lived here all her life. She will be bound to know all the young ladies who live around here and which ones are eligible and which are not. She will be the perfect person to consult.'

'My dear, are you sure that that is wise?' he ventured, his brow creasing a little.

'I see no reason why not. Oh, I will be discreet, of course, but anyone could tell from looking at the lady that she is transparently honest.'

'That is not what I was thinking,' he replied.

'Explain?'

'I overheard you telling your brother that he had captivated her with his fine eyes, or some such thing. If she has become enamoured of him, then surely it would be cruel in the extreme to ask her help in finding a wife for him.'

'Oh fiddle,' declared his sensible wife. 'People do not fall in love in that kind of instantaneous way. She was flustered at meeting a strange man, that is all.'

'I'm sure it is just as you say, my love,' replied Mr Trimmer with a smile. 'I was just wondering . . . ' His voice tailed off as he stopped fiddling with his wife's ring, and ran his fingers up the inside of her arm to her elbow.

'Yes, Alan?' she replied innocently.

'I know you have had a good deal to do today,' he continued, looking down at the coverlet.

'That's true,' she agreed.

'I was wondering if you were very tired, or . . . ?'

'No, Alan,' she answered, pulling back the coverlet in invitation. 'I'm not tired at all.'

★   ★   ★

The members of Canon Whittaker's household had never kept very late hours, and after Emily had retired for the night, especially in the summer months when she would go to her room before it was properly dark, she would find it impossible to sleep before she had read a few pages of a book.

Before meeting Nathalie, her reading matter had often been Shakespeare. She would sometimes close her eyes and try to imagine what the different characters might

70

look like and how they might sound as they spoke their lines.

Now, she had slightly different subject matter to absorb her, for she had borrowed from Nathalie a copy of Mrs Radcliffe's novel, *The Mysteries of Udolpho*, published just a few years ago. Yet although she picked it up once her bedroom door was closed, she sat with it unopened on her knee, her thoughts going instead to the ideas that she had had for a book when she had been in Mablethorpe. As she recalled the pictures that had come into her mind, the hero seemed to take on new life, and she now realized that he bore the features of Sir Gareth Blades. Blades! Now there was a fine name for a character in a book.

She remembered the conversation that they had had concerning Canon Mitchell. Of course it had been very shocking for Sir Gareth to suggest that the clergyman might have pushed his wife down the stairs. What a splendid incident it would make in a novel, however! Perhaps the principal characters might discover that an elderly clergyman had murdered his wife. Perhaps the heroine might discover the body and fling herself into the hero's arms out of shock!

Blushing at the very thought, Emily opened the novel on her lap and began to read.

71

Minutes later, she burst out laughing, for on reaching the third page, it became clear that the heroine was called Emily! Perhaps, then, she was destined to be a heroine after all.

7

Mrs Trimmer did not waste any time in furthering her acquaintance with Emily Whittaker, and the following day, she made her way to Canon Whittaker's house. Emily was already about her household duties when her new neighbour arrived, but she gladly left the sorting of the linen cupboard to Mrs Ashby, and came downstairs to greet her guest and offer her refreshment.

'Thank you, I should be very glad of something,' Mrs Trimmer admitted. 'The boys can be quite exhausting first thing in the morning, but Alan and Gareth have taken them to walk about the town a little. They talked of going to a place called Brayford. Is it very far?'

Remembering what her husband had said, she watched Emily keenly when her brother's name was mentioned, but Emily did not even look conscious let alone blush at the mention of the baronet. Instead she said with a smile, 'It's not very far, and they will have a fine view of the cathedral, but they will have a very steep climb back up.'

'Oh, splendid,' Mrs Trimmer replied. 'That

will have the double advantage of occupying them and tiring them out.'

'The boys, or the gentlemen?' Emily said humorously. Then she blushed at her own temerity, for she hardly knew Mrs Trimmer and, as far as she could remember, had never before addressed a visitor in such a flippant way.

Her new neighbour laughed. 'I meant the boys, but you are quite right, of course. Gentlemen can also be a nuisance under one's feet. I dare say you sometimes find it to be the case?'

Emily gave a little gasp. She had never before presumed to think of her papa or her grandpapa in this kind of way. She could hardly take offence, for it was she who had first spoken presumptuously, and she found herself saying slowly, 'I do not think that they mean to be so.'

'No, I am sure they do not,' Mrs Trimmer agreed. After a moment or two's thought, she went on, 'Speaking of the boys, I have not yet decided what to do about their education.'

'Will you send them away to school?' Emily asked curiously.

'I had always thought that I would do so eventually, but I am now in two minds,' the other woman admitted. 'What kind of education is provided at the grammar school?

Do you know anything about it? They are too young yet, of course, but I think that Alan intends to remain here in Lincoln, so I need to look ahead.'

'I believe that it was very good at one time,' Emily answered, 'but I understand that people are not as satisfied with it as they were. One should not speak ill of the dead, I know, but the master who died a year ago held other livings and didn't really give enough time to it. Perhaps this new century will bring an improvement. I am in no position to provide a personal recommendation, or a personal criticism. I had a governess, you see, and my brother Patrick went to Eton.'

'Like Gareth,' put in Mrs Trimmer. 'I wonder whether they knew each other? Did your father not think highly of the local school?'

'I don't think that it was because Papa had a low opinion of the local school,' Emily replied. 'I think that he wanted my brother to gain a wider view of life than that provided within the city.'

'He did not think that the same thing was necessary for you, evidently.'

'No. No, he didn't,' Emily agreed after a short silence.

'Well, I shall visit the school and see what I

think,' concluded Mrs Trimmer. 'In the meantime, of course, they will need a governess.'

'Do you teach them yourself at the moment?' Emily asked her.

Mrs Trimmer sighed. 'Unfortunately at present I have no choice in the matter,' she answered. 'They did have a governess until we moved. She was called Miss Bright and she was an excellent person and both the boys liked her, but she got married just before we came to Lincoln. I am fending for myself at the moment, and Alan is very capable of taking them for some lessons, but it can only be a temporary arrangement. Can you think of anyone who might be prepared to teach them?'

Emily thought for a moment. 'There is no one whose name springs to mind,' she admitted. 'But I will let you know if I think of anyone.'

After a brief silence, Aurelia said, 'That was one subject that I wanted to consult you about. Now I have another, and since we are upon visiting and consulting terms, pray call me Aurelia; may I call you Emily?'

'Yes of course,' Emily replied, trying to think of another lady, apart from Nathalie, with whom she was on Christian-name terms.

'There is a matter about which I need to

glean information and you, as a lifetime resident of the Close, will probably be able to help me better than anyone.'

'Of course I will, if I can,' Emily answered, happy to be of service.

'I am really hoping to find out from you if there are any eligible young ladies living in the Close, and if there are, what their dispositions may be like.'

'Young ladies?' Emily echoed, puzzled.

Aurelia leaned forward and dropped her voice a little. 'I am thinking of Gareth,' she said.

'Gareth?'

'My brother Gareth,' Aurelia explained, the tiniest hint of impatience in her voice. 'He is forty years old now, and it is high time that he married. He has a title and property, and there are no more brothers or even male cousins in our family now, so the line will die out if he does not set up his nursery.'

'I see,' said Emily. She was remembering what a very attractive man Sir Gareth was. It seemed strange to her that his sister should feel it necessary to find a wife for him.

Almost as if she could read Emily's thoughts, Aurelia spoke again. 'He does not seem to be able to find a woman to suit him, the foolish man. In fact, he has run away from a houseful of eligible females; that is why he comes to be here.'

'Perhaps he does not wish to be married,' Emily suggested.

'Nonsense! Of course he wishes it,' replied the baronet's sister. 'He has said himself that he would like to be as happy as Alan and I. The only difficulty lies in finding the right woman.'

At that moment, Mr Whittaker came in, and Emily presented him to their new neighbour. She was a little afraid that Mrs Trimmer's decisive manner might give her father the impression that the clergyman's wife was over-bold, but she need not have worried. That lady had a wide experience of social and ecclesiastical gatherings, and she was able to strike just the right note.

'I was just saying how grateful I was to your daughter for coming to see me yesterday, Canon,' she was saying. 'Her act in welcoming the stranger showed true Christian charity.'

'I am delighted to hear you say so,' answered Mr Whittaker, smiling gently. 'I very seldom have to blush for anything in Emily's behaviour.'

'Papa, I am thirty, not thirteen,' Emily protested.

'Emily!' said her father in a tone of gentle reproof. He turned to Mrs Trimmer with an apologetic smile. 'Still headstrong, I am afraid ma'am.'

Mrs Trimmer smiled back, but briefly. 'You have a fine cathedral here,' she remarked. 'I am very much looking forward to getting to know it.'

'If you ever wanted me to take you round the cathedral, I should be glad to do so,' Emily offered diffidently.

'I expect the dean will want to take Mr Trimmer around the cathedral himself,' her father said. 'I doubt whether our little efforts will be needed, my dear.'

'I am sure that the dean and my husband will have a fascinating visit together, but I do not think that they would want myself or the boys in the way,' murmured Mrs Trimmer. 'We should be very glad of your daughter's services.'

'Well, that is very good of you to find Emily something useful to do,' answered the canon. 'But for now, I must leave you, if you will excuse me. It is time for me to visit my father. Emily, I trust you will not be negligent in that respect.'

'No, Papa,' Emily agreed.

Her father went out and closed the door. After he had gone, Mrs Trimmer looked at Emily's tightly clasped hands, then glanced around at the room, spotted the fire irons and set them up in a clear part of the floor. Then she took a cushion off the rather old-fashioned sofa, handed it to Emily and, indicating the fire irons, said, 'Go on, throw it. You'll feel better, I promise you.'

After staring at her visitor for a moment or two, Emily took hold of the cushion, pressed her lips firmly together, and threw it at the fire irons, which fell with a tremendous clatter.

When the maid came in moments later to see what on earth the noise had been about, Mrs Trimmer was standing the irons up in the grate and saying, 'Oh my goodness, how clumsy of me. I must have caught them as I turned.' Emily was standing at the window with her back to the room. Once the maid had ascertained that there was nothing for her to do, she withdrew. As she did so, Aurelia heard a strange choking sound, and for a dreadful moment wondered whether Emily was crying. Then the other woman turned round and it was clear that she was laughing, rather in the manner of a person who does not know how.

'Have you never wanted to do that before?' Aurelia asked curiously, when Emily had calmed down and they had ordered a fresh pot of tea.

'I think I have, often,' Emily admitted, 'but

I have only just realized that that is what I had wanted to do.'

'What do you usually do?'

'I go to the cathedral,' Emily replied simply. 'I can be myself there. That is where I have always gone if ever I have felt troubled about anything.' She looked straight at the other woman and said, 'The Lincoln imp always makes me smile.' With that she turned upon her visitor a smile of great sweetness that made her look considerably younger than her thirty years.

The second pot of tea had just arrived when there was a knock at the front door, and soon the sound of voices in the hall told them that Mr Trimmer and Sir Gareth had arrived. Had Mrs Trimmer been looking at her hostess at that moment, then some of her earliest suspicions would have been confirmed, but she was suddenly afflicted with a sneezing fit, and by the time she looked at Emily again, that lady was standing up in order to greet the visitors.

In between the arrival of the gentlemen and their entrance, Emily had told herself severely that her strange reaction to Sir Gareth Blades the previous day had simply been some kind of nervous condition, probably brought on by too much novel reading. There was nothing special about him. He was perhaps a little more stylish than most of the men she had met, but that was all.

Then the door opened and, as she caught sight of him, her heart and breathing played the same stupid trick upon her as they had done before. Both gentlemen were dressed in top boots and tan breeches, but Sir Gareth was in a dark-blue coat which seemed to impart some of that colour to his eyes, and his smile was just as devastating as she had remembered.

'Miss Whittaker, good morning,' he said in his deep voice, as he bowed politely. 'Finding that Aurelia had come to see you, we made so bold as to do the same.'

'You are very welcome,' Emily managed to say without stammering. 'Would you like some tea, or . . . ' She paused, not sure what else there might be in the house that would be suitable for two gentlemen who had just been for a long walk.

'Tea would be delightful,' Sir Gareth answered, smiling at the maid who disap-peared in order to fetch two more cups. 'But you must allow me to introduce my brother-in-law to you, for I do not think that you met him when you came yesterday.'

Emily greeted the new clergyman, and was soon put at her ease by his calm manner. 'Did you have an agreeable walk?' she asked them.

'Your sister mentioned that you might perhaps go to Brayford.'

'The walk *there* was agreeable,' Mr Trimmer qualified, 'but I think that it will be some time before my muscles recover from that climb back up the hill.'

'For shame, Alan!' Sir Gareth exclaimed mockingly. 'What you really need to do is tackle the same walk every day for a week, then you'll soon be in shape.'

Mr Trimmer looked less than enthusiastic. 'It's my belief that you are in conspiracy with the boys,' he retorted, 'for they certainly declared themselves ready to take the same walk tomorrow; by the way, we left them at home as we came past.'

'And what did you reply, sir?' Emily asked him.

The clergyman looked a little guilty. 'I told them that I had a sermon to write,' he admitted.

'Oh Alan, what a shocking untruth!' exclaimed his wife. 'You will have no credibility with them at all if they find out.'

'I believe I lost most of my credit with them as I staggered behind them on the way up Steep Hill,' he replied. 'And I am rapidly losing what remains every time Oliver asks me a question about Lincoln to which I don't know the answer.'

'Well what can you expect?' his wife asked in reasonable tones. 'Children never believe that their parents know anything, do they?' she added, turning to Emily.

To her great annoyance, Emily found herself stammering and blushing again, for she could not remember challenging her father upon any matter. 'I . . . I cannot say,' she murmured.

'Fie, Aurelia,' Sir Gareth declared. 'Anyone can see by looking at Miss Whittaker that she was an obedient child.'

'Unlike myself, I suppose you will say,' his sister retorted.

'If the cap fits, my dear, I would be the last man to prevent you from wearing it,' he replied with a smile.

There was general laughter in which Emily joined, and she reflected that she had not laughed as much as this in her own home for many a long year.

The tea had just arrived when Mr Whittaker came back in and, of course, Emily was then obliged to introduce him to the two gentlemen. Mr Trimmer greeted his fellow clergyman with courtesy and a deference that was pleasing to an older man.

Sir Gareth murmured polite gratification at the introduction then said, 'Since I met your daughter yesterday, sir, I have been trying to remember where I have met someone by your name before. Today, I have been looking at the portrait above your fireplace, and I wonder whether perhaps it is of Patrick Whittaker?'

They all looked at the picture. It was of a fair-haired young gentleman, captured almost at that very moment when youth turns to manhood. He was rather too sharp-featured for handsomeness, with a shock of fair hair and hazel eyes, very like Emily's own. His expression was serious and he was dressed severely in black with a high, plain neck-cloth.

The elderly clergyman suddenly became still. 'You knew my son Patrick?' he asked quietly.

'I certainly did,' answered Sir Gareth. 'This is a fine likeness, as I recall. He was with me at school, and we were to have gone to Cambridge together. His death was a sad loss, sir.'

Mr Whittaker shook his head. 'A sad loss indeed,' he agreed. 'My sainted Patrick! He was to have gone into the church, you know,' he explained. 'Alas, we shall never know the blessings of three generations all serving the cathedral, shall we, my dear Emily?'

'No Papa,' Emily replied dutifully.

'But you must call again and we will have a

long talk about Patrick,' the canon went on.

'Thank you, you are very good,' Sir Gareth answered, but when her father turned to speak to Mrs Trimmer, Emily thought that she caught the baronet looking up at the portrait and smiling wryly. She could not help it; she simply had to look at him whilst he was unaware of her regard.

His dark hair, which he wore a little longer than was dictated by the current fashion, was swept back from his face, throwing the line of his jaw into relief. That chin of his was firm, very masculine with a hint of shadow that indicated a strong growth of beard, and the way that he lifted it seemed to say that he could be stubborn at times.

Her gaze travelled down to his shoulders, which so substantially filled that well-cut coat. She recalled James demanding that he feel his muscles. What would the baronet's own muscles feel like?

Suddenly colouring at such an indelicate thought, she looked up, and saw that he was regarding her quizzically, and all at once she knew that he must have observed her staring at him. Then, to her great astonishment, and so imperceptibly that she could not be sure afterwards that it had really happened, he winked at her!

Looking away hurriedly, she discovered

that Mrs Trimmer was inviting her and her father to dinner. 'It would be a splendid opportunity for you to tell us more about the town and the cathedral,' she was saying. 'We do so want to learn all that we can.'

'That is very kind of you, but I fear that Emily may not be able to come,' said the canon politely. 'She usually sits with her grandfather in the evenings. Furthermore, she has been away visiting friends recently, and has been neglecting her duty, and she is not one to shirk, are you, my dear?'

'No, Papa,' Emily replied, feeling almost sick with disappointment.

'I am quite sure that she is not,' agreed Mrs Trimmer, 'but on such an occasion, her duty would be calling her in two directions, would it not? Duty of kindness to the stranger is important too.'

'Why yes, indeed,' the canon agreed thoughtfully.

'Perhaps, then, Miss Whittaker might sit with her grandfather earlier in the day; then if it would ease your mind, dear sir, I could send my old nurse round to sit with him whilst you are away from the house.'

'That would be very kind, Mrs Trimmer. Emily, we are very grateful, are we not?'

'Yes indeed, Papa,' Emily agreed, wishing that she could make her own thanks without looking as if she needed to be prompted to do so.

She glanced at Mrs Trimmer and, seeing her smiling, suddenly remembered the fire irons and could not help smiling back. It occurred to her that in this new friendship with Mrs Trimmer, she might find the mutuality that her relationship with Nathalie would always lack.

'Then shall we say next Tuesday?' asked Aurelia. 'Emily, I shall rely upon you to help me with finding dependable tradesmen to supply the things that I need.'

'Of course,' Emily replied, before her father could assure their visitor that his daughter would do all that was proper. 'Shall I call round tomorrow, perhaps?'

'Please do.'

With that, polite farewells were made, and the visitors were gone, and although they had only been there quite briefly, it seemed to Emily that the house felt quite empty after their departure.

8

'I have heard from Mrs Fanshawe today,' Emily told her grandfather that evening as she sat at his bedside. 'She is keeping very well, she tells me, and she is so happy that Mr Fanshawe is with her.' She sighed and put the letter down on her lap for a moment. 'Was that how you felt with Grandmama?' she asked him. 'I suppose it must have been.' She stroked the white, papery hand that lay on top of the coverlet. 'I don't mean to pry,' she said apologetically. 'It's just that I — ' She stopped suddenly, then picked up the letter again.

'The sea air is doing her good, she says. Mr Fanshawe is making her walk by the sea every day, and she is sleeping much better at night, but that may be because — ' Again she broke off. This time, she was silent for quite a long time. Then at last, she said softly, 'Grandpapa, I met a gentleman this week. His name . . . no, perhaps I won't tell you his name just yet, but . . . ' Again she paused. 'Grandpapa, do you think it is too late for me? I mean, to have what Mr and Mrs Fanshawe have; what you and Grandmama had? This gentleman

would never look at me, I feel sure, but — '
She stopped, hearing footsteps outside and, as the door opened softly and her father looked in, he heard his daughter reciting the words of the Lord's Prayer.

★ ★ ★

The following day, as she had promised, Emily walked around the cathedral to the house where the Trimmers resided. She had only just reached the gate at the bottom of the path when the two boys came hurrying out.

'Miss Whittaker, Miss Whittaker!' they both exclaimed, so excitedly that it was difficult to distinguish one voice from another. 'Have you come to take us up the tower? May we go now?'

Seeing that she could easily find herself dragged through the cathedral doors by main force before she had even had a chance to speak to Mrs Trimmer, Emily said 'I need to speak to your mama. Then perhaps we may talk about it later.'

'We'll take you in,' said the older boy, who, Emily remembered, was called Oliver.

'Thank you,' Emily replied. Clearly she was not going to be allowed to escape without at least making some kind of future arrangement for climbing the tower.

Mrs Trimmer was with her housekeeper, but she stood up as soon as Emily came in with the boys. 'Thank you, Mrs Gibson,' she said. 'You see, Miss Whittaker has come to see me just as she promised. I shall soon be able to give you all the information you need about procuring necessities for the house.'

Mrs Gibson curtsied and withdrew at the same time as the boys groaned. 'Oh no, not shopping,' they declared, in despairing tones.

'Shame on you, boys,' declared the deep voice of Sir Gareth from the doorway. 'It's the duty of every gentleman to learn to enjoy shopping; otherwise, who would be able to escort the ladies and appreciate the purchases that they made?'

Emily, looking at his smiling face, could well imagine the kind of shopping to which he referred. It would be a frivolous expedition, no doubt, conducted in Bond Street, or one of the other London thoroughfares, of which she had read but which she had never seen. 'I don't suppose we engage in the same kind of shopping,' she surmised.

He smiled and inclined his head. To her great surprise on his face was an expression that might have been pity. 'Then you will have to instruct me,' he told her. 'If you and my sister want to engage in making any kind of purchases, then I will consider myself committed to accompany you. And,' he went on, before anyone could interrupt him, 'I will promise to carry any purchase made, whether it be eggs, turnips, or a dead hen, still with its head and feathers.'

Emily had to smile at that, but Mrs Trimmer assured her brother that they would not be making any such purchases. 'A dead hen indeed,' she exclaimed. 'The very idea! I am simply calling on Emily's expertise to show me which shops can be relied upon, that is all.'

'But this is excellent!' the gentleman exclaimed. 'I may take all the credit for being gallant enough to offer to carry your purchases, without the inconvenience of actually having to do so.'

'Now you are being absurd,' retorted his sister. 'Do you really mean to accompany us?'

'Certainly,' he responded at once. 'And in addition, may I make a suggestion? After we have discovered all that the shops can offer, perhaps if Miss Whittaker is not too fatigued, she might be willing to escort us up the tower of the cathedral.'

'Us?' queried Mrs Trimmer.

'Oliver, James and myself,' he explained. 'You know they will not be content until they have been right up there, and I would be glad to see the view, I must admit.'

'Perhaps Emily does not want to climb the tower today,' Mrs Trimmer ventured.

'Oh no, I should be quite happy to go,' Emily assured her. 'It is a favourite view of mine.' The boys, who had wisely kept quiet whilst this matter was being discussed, let out a cheer.

'Why do you not play in the garden until we return?' said their mother. 'Nurse will keep an eye upon you.' This they agreed to do, whilst protesting vigorously that they would have no need of Nurse's attentions.

In no time, the three adults were walking out of the cathedral precinct and through the Exchequer gate into Castle Square. There they paused for a few minutes to look around, and Sir Gareth asked Emily to tell them about the castle.

'It was built by the Normans, but this part of Lincoln was a stronghold even in Roman times,' she informed him. 'It is where the assizes are held, and the sheriff's court, and it also houses the county gaol. I don't like going there much,' she confessed.

'Then you must behave yourself better, and thus avoid being committed so frequently,' Sir Gareth replied in tones of mock severity.

She stared at him uncomprehendingly,

then made the same sound, half choke, half chuckle, that Mrs Trimmer remembered from the previous day. Sir Gareth, hearing it, drew the same conclusion as his sister: this lady did not often get the chance to laugh.

'I visit some of the inmates,' she told him unnecessarily. 'Some of Papa's congregation at St Mark's get themselves into debt, you see.'

'I see.' It occurred to Sir Gareth that this spinster lady who led a very narrow and uneventful life in some people's eyes, must find herself going into situations that were far beyond the experience of those who would make such judgements about her. 'Do you pay their debts for them?'

She shook her head. 'If we did that for one we would have to do it for all; then we should be in debt ourselves. No, I generally take them some home comforts, and news from their loved ones. Then on the other hand, I try to keep an eye on the families and help them to organize their affairs, so that the debt can soon be paid.'

'Very commendable,' the baronet murmured.

Suspecting a slight, she flushed and said, 'It is not as exciting as going on the strut in Bond Street no doubt.'

He looked back at her narrowing his eyes.

'On the contrary, I would have said that it was much more exciting,' he answered her smoothly. 'Besides, we do not all spend our time walking up and down and looking in shop windows, you know.'

Realizing that she had made unfair assumptions about him, Emily turned away, murmuring, 'I beg your pardon', in mortified tones, and thus did not see the twinkle in his eye as he inclined his head in gracious acknowledgement of her apology.

Mrs Trimmer, feeling that the conversation needed a lighter touch, said, 'No, some of you spend half your time in Jackson's boxing saloon.'

The baronet laughed. 'I do try to look in there whenever I can,' he admitted. 'No doubt, though, Miss Whittaker will think that just as frivolous as looking in shop windows.'

'Not at all,' Emily answered in a flustered tone, wishing that she did not sound like a middle-aged spinster. Then, not wanting to seem abrupt, she went on, 'Do you really fight in there, or are you just pretending?'

'I have always wanted to ask that, but I have never had the courage to do so,' Mrs Trimmer interjected.

'Yes and no, Miss Whittaker,' the baronet replied with a twinkle. 'No, the fighting is not real, insofar as it is not done in anger;

although I must admit that on one occasion, I saw two fellows there who clearly had a grudge against one another and things got a little savage. But the activity is just as strenuous as in a real fight and the moves are the same.'

By this time, they were walking along Bailgate and Emily began to point out the various shops to them.

'Do you go marketing yourself, Miss Whittaker?' Sir Gareth asked.

'Certainly I do,' she replied. 'It is one of the things that I enjoy the most.' Again he cast a pitying glance in her direction. Did she never have the chance to do anything simply for her own enjoyment?

It was quite a novelty for Emily to have companions with whom she could visit the shops. When she had been growing up, there had been very few other girls of her own age about. Then, with Patrick's death, it was as if the outside world had become closed to her. Her mother had lost the will to live, and had gradually dwindled into an invalid, eventually needing nursing and constant care. She had finally died when Emily was twenty-three. After the family's period of mourning was over, there had been no lady who had seemed to feel it to be her responsibility to bring Emily out, so she had stayed chiefly at home, going out to make necessary purchases for the house, or to take her Bible classes, or attend worship in the cathedral, but seldom being invited to social functions, apart from the occasional dinner with other clergy families.

This opportunity to show another lady the shops was a pleasure that seldom came her way, therefore, and she made up her mind to enjoy it, even though the sky had clouded over, and the day that had begun so promisingly now seemed set to deteriorate.

Mrs Trimmer seemed interested in all the shops, not just the ones that were noted for their good food, and Emily made up her mind to show her new friend the bonnet in the milliner's shop window that had caught her eye. To Emily's surprise, Sir Gareth also came over to the window, and to her embarrassment, raised his quizzing glass in order to get a better look at the head gear in question.

'Yes, it is charming,' Mrs Trimmer agreed. 'Quite charming.'

'I agree,' Sir Gareth answered. 'Charming, but definitely not for you, Miss Whittaker.'

He had not intended to insult her. In London, he was a gentleman whose impeccable taste had frequently been called upon by friends of both sexes. He had a fine eye for colour, and his own dress was always well chosen and appropriate for his dark colouring. Female acquaintances consulted him with regard to their choice of wall coverings, carpets, curtains and other furnishings. They invited him to their gardens, and asked his opinion about their flowerbeds. When they could, they persuaded him to go with them to the dressmaker or milliner so that he could enable them to be as well dressed as he was.

This expertise was sometimes something of a burden to him, for if he was not firm, he could find himself dispensing advice twenty-four hours a day. However, for certain favoured friends, he was prepared to offer his help, and so when he saw Miss Whittaker, a pleasant woman with whom his sister was disposed to be friendly, possibly intending to purchase a bonnet which would not flatter her in any way, he could not help speaking out.

To Emily, however, his remarks simply told her what she had already suspected: she was too old even to think of wearing something so pretty. She looked up at his face and, as he glanced down at her, he saw from her expression that he had hurt her. Before he could work out how he could have done it, they were addressed by two ladies who had approached them from behind.

'Miss Whittaker, what a delightful day,' said the older lady, whose name was Mrs Cummings. She was accompanied by her daughter Jennifer, and she greeted the canon's daughter far more effusively than usual. As she did so, her glance flickered speculatively towards Mrs Trimmer and, more particularly, her brother. 'Are you going shopping?'

Feeling disappointed, although she could not think why, Emily introduced her new acquaintances to the two ladies.

'Are you shopping as well, Sir Gareth?' Mrs Cummings asked.

'Not as such, ma'am,' the baronet replied politely. 'I'm simply here to guard these ladies from all the perils that Lincoln might provide.'

'How gallant!' Miss Cummings exclaimed admiringly, and cast down her lashes.

'And how are you enjoying Lincoln, Mrs Trimmer?' the young lady's mother asked. 'Miss Whittaker and I know it well, do we not?' By such means, Mrs Cummings managed to engage both Emily and Aurelia in conversation, leaving Sir Gareth free to entertain Jennifer, a circumstance which, from the girl's expression, seemed to please her enormously.

In this way, they walked to the end of the street. Emily responded to Mrs Cummings's pronouncements about the various shops and tried to suppress the resentment that she was feeling at her suspicion that that lady appeared to be taking over her new friend. At the same time, she was very conscious of the conversation going on behind her, Jennifer's tinkling laughter being punctuated by the richer sound of Sir Gareth's deep voice.

At last, they reached Mrs Cummings's carriage, and Sir Gareth politely handed the ladies in. 'It has been so agreeable to meet you, Mrs Trimmer,' said Mrs Cummings, smiling graciously. 'So pleasing to have some interesting female company nearby, for a change. You must call and see us very soon, and of course bring your husband and your brother. We have some delightful gardens which you will enjoy exploring.'

'Thank you, you are very kind,' Aurelia replied, smiling. 'My sons will enjoy doing so as well.'

Mrs Cummings opened her eyes very wide. 'Oh, you have sons!' she exclaimed. 'Well, I am sure they will . . . will . . . ' Her voice tailed off.

Mrs Trimmer's eyes took on a decidedly martial sparkle, but before she could say anything Sir Gareth said with a twinkle, 'It will, however, be difficult to call upon you when we do not know your direction.'

'Oh, Miss Whittaker knows where we live,' said Mrs Cummings carelessly.

'Then she must bring us next time she visits you,' Sir Gareth responded, bowing.

As the carriage was leaving with a clattering of wheels along the cobbles, Mrs Trimmer stared after it in indignation. 'Oh, you have sons!' she said, mimicking Mrs Cummings's plummy tones with a fair degree of accuracy. 'Detestable woman! Why, anyone would think that they were Barbary apes, from the way that she was speaking!'

Sir Gareth pursed his lips. 'Well, now that you come to mention it,' he murmured.

'Oh, you!' exclaimed Mrs Trimmer, laughing and hitting her brother in the midriff with her reticule. She turned to Emily apologetically. 'I am sorry for speaking in such a way, for I gather that Mrs Cummings is an old acquaintance of yours, but really, I cannot allow anyone to speak disparagingly about Oliver and James.'

'I suppose that is why you have inflicted damage upon me which may be lasting and, who knows, even fatal,' the baronet remarked, rubbing his midriff.

'Nonsense,' answered Mrs Trimmer calmly. 'You are not hurt at all. In any case, you know that I am referring to strangers and bare acquaintances, not to those who, like yourself, know and love the boys already.' She looked at Emily. 'I do beg your pardon,' she said. 'We are monopolizing the conversation with family concerns, which must be dull to you.'

'Not at all,' Emily replied, feeling a little envious of their closeness. 'It is simply that I am not used to the kind of informal relationships that you enjoy. And please do not worry about speaking about Mrs Cummings. I . . . I have sometimes found her a little trying, myself.'

'Miss Cummings seems to be a sweet child, however,' Sir Gareth remarked casually.

The three companions passed the last of the shops and continued walking, keeping the cathedral to their right. 'How old is this place?' Sir Gareth asked Emily after they had walked in silence for a short time. 'Part of the west front looks Norman, but the rest of the building is not, surely?'

Emily proceeded to tell him about the construction of the cathedral, a subject that interested her very much. As they walked, however, the deterioration in the weather continued, so that by the time they reached Emily's house, drops of rain had begun to fall. Bidding a brief farewell, Mrs Trimmer, no doubt concerned for her charming straw bonnet, hurried off in the direction of her own home at what looked suspiciously like a run. Sir Gareth, however, apparently oblivious to the rain, escorted Emily right up to her front door.

'Would you like to come in?' she asked him, not wanting him to get wet, but then feeling dreadfully bold, for she knew, as the baronet did not, that her father would certainly not be within at this time.

'Thank you, no,' he answered, stepping close to the porch so as to shelter a little. 'My sister will be expecting me to follow her.'

'I . . . thank you for bringing me home,' Emily stammered. She was now faced with a dilemma. The front door was rather heavy, and somewhat prone to shut of its own volition; so as long as Sir Gareth stood here almost in the doorway, she was obliged to hold the door open whilst she was speaking with him. Consequently, they were standing rather close to one another, and this had the effect of making her feel confused. If only he were not so very attractive!

So flustered was she that she actually missed most of what he was saying, only catching his last few words: ' . . . quite magnificent.'

This word seemed to be so much in tune

with her thoughts concerning his appearance that she found herself simply repeating it whilst looking up at him. He grinned down at her. 'I was referring to the view from the cathedral tower in good weather, Miss Whittaker,' he explained, his dimples more pronounced than ever.

'Oh!' exclaimed Emily, feeling as if she was all one blush from her head to her feet. 'Of . . . course! That . . . that is what you meant. I knew it all the time . . . ' Her voice tailed away.

'Of course you did,' he answered her soothingly. 'After all you could not possibly have been lost in the pages of some unsuitable novel, could you?' She stared at him, quite unable to think of an answer. After a moment or two he spoke again. 'As an excursion is clearly impossible today, may we presume upon your good nature on another occasion?'

'Yes, yes of course,' Emily replied, by now quite desperate to close the door on him before she embarrassed herself any further. 'Please, do hurry home before it really begins to rain hard.'

Sir Gareth smiled and tilted his hat. 'I am not made of icing sugar, Miss Whittaker,' he said with a twinkle. 'Anyone would think that you wanted to get rid of me.' Then, after bidding her good day, he hurried after his sister.

9

Emily did not see Sir Gareth again until the following Sunday, when she attended the morning service in the cathedral. She sat in her usual place, and kept her head down when he entered, escorting Mrs Trimmer and the two boys. But even with her gaze averted, she noticed that he was looking very elegant in a coat of charcoal grey cloth that matched his eyes, and her heart churned inside her in the most disconcerting way.

It was very annoying that this should happen, she reflected, for ever since that meeting with the Cummingses in Bailgate, she had been telling herself very firmly that she should stop thinking about the baronet immediately. He did not belong to her world; he was clearly destined for someone like Jennifer Cummings. She would be very well advised to put him out of her mind. So she had kept out of his way, avoided all the Trimmers, and even responded to Aurelia's kind enquiry with a message that she had a headache and needed a day or two's quiet.

Then she had applied herself energetically to her duties, both at home and with the

Bible class, forcing herself to think about other things. But now, she only had to see a shaft of sunlight picking out the silver flecks in his hair and she was as captivated as she had ever been.

She recalled a conversation that she had heard years ago between two girls who lived in the Minster Yard. They were both married now and living far away, but at that time one of them had become infatuated with one of the younger clergymen who had come to serve in the cathedral. When it had been revealed that he had become engaged to be married, she had cried her eyes out. 'It's no good,' she had wailed. 'I know that he is not for me; but it does not seem to make any difference. When I see him, my heart beats twice as fast as it should, and I feel myself blushing. When he is not there I look for him, and I have to stop myself from walking past his house all the time, just so that I will catch a glimpse of him.'

At the time, Emily had thought that the girl was rather foolish. Now, she could recognize many of the same symptoms in herself. No wonder novel reading is frowned upon, she concluded. I will beat this infatuation. I'm thirty years old, after all; not a silly schoolgirl!

With all the determination that she possessed, she concentrated on the Dean's sermon so fiercely that afterwards, that good man read carefully through his notes to try to find out what he might have said concerning the lost coin that had made Miss Whittaker look so annoyed.

After the service when everyone left by the west door, Emily hung back a little, not wanting to risk being made to feel small again by Mrs Cummings. As she was lingering inside, she heard a voice speak her name, and turning, she saw Dr Boyle standing next to her.

'Miss Whittaker, what a pleasure to see you again,' he declared.

Observing him now, having had a chance to admire Sir Gareth's looks, she thought that he looked more like a weasel than ever; but he was a friend of comparatively long standing, so she smiled back at him and said, 'It is a pleasure to be home, Dr Boyle.'

'I trust you left Mrs Fanshawe in good health?' he asked her, as they walked to the door together.

'She seemed very well the last time I saw her,' Emily informed him. 'I have also had a letter from her which gives the same news. I think that the presence of her husband has done her as much good as the sea air.'

'Ah yes,' the doctor agreed, bending gallantly over her hand in the doorway. 'True affection must always make a difference.'

Looking up, she saw Sir Gareth, his sister and Mrs and Miss Cummings standing a few feet away. Sir Gareth was listening attentively to something that Jennifer was saying, but his eyes flickered towards the door, and Emily knew that he had seen them. She noticed, with a pang, that Jennifer was wearing what she had thought of as 'her' bonnet, and that she looked ravishing in it.

The fact that the doctor was with her lent her courage, and laying her hand on his arm in a way that she had not done before, she said to him, 'Come, sir, I think you have not met the latest arrivals in the Close.'

Mrs Trimmer was very pleased to meet the doctor and asked him to leave his direction at her house. 'I am sure that if you attend my friend's family, you must be more than competent,' she said, smiling.

'You are too good, ma'am,' the doctor replied, gratified.

Mrs Trimmer began to ask the doctor about a treatment for influenza which she had heard of elsewhere, and whilst Mrs and Miss Cummings were speaking with the dean and his wife, Sir Gareth came over to Emily's side.

'Tell me, are there really three hundred and

twenty-seven steps up to the top of the tower?'

'Yes really,' she answered with a smile. 'Do not tell me that you are losing enthusiasm, sir.'

'Certainly not,' he replied with mock indignation. 'More screwing my courage to the sticking place, really.'

'Please do not limit your interest to climbing up the tower,' she begged him. 'There is much more to be seen in the cathedral.' Then it occurred to her that he might think that she was fishing for the chance to show him round, and she coloured. 'That is to say . . . of course, you know that that is the case for you are now in it,' she said hastily. 'At least, you were until a few minutes ago.' Then she wanted to slap herself for sounding like a silly middle-aged spinster.

'So I was,' he agreed. 'I do seem to have an unfortunate ability to embarrass you,' he went on, confounding her.

'No, no, not at all,' she responded, still sounding flustered.

'To distress you, then,' he said.

'To distress me?' she echoed blankly.

'Mm. When we were shopping the other day, I managed to upset you in some way, and I have been trying to decide how I might have done it.'

'No, no, there was nothing; nothing,' she told him, trying to speak calmly. 'It was not anything that you had done . . . ' Her voice tailed away, and involuntarily, her gaze lit upon the bonnet that adorned Miss Cummings's golden head. The beauty turned and smiled winningly.

The baronet smiled back, looked at Emily again and said 'Ah,' a note of understanding in his voice.

'I beg your pardon?' she said startled.

He looked at her without speaking for a moment, then said, 'I'm very sorry if you were hankering after that bonnet, but the truth of the matter is that it's not your colour.'

Again she said, 'I beg your pardon,' this time in a voice that was frankly puzzled.

'I said, it's not your colour. Take it from a man who knows. Cream, perhaps, or gold, or straw colour, but not white. It would not flatter your complexion at all, believe me.'

At that moment, Aurelia approached them, saying, 'Do not forget, Emily, you and your father are to dine with us on Tuesday.'

Forget? When it was the first dinner invitation that she had received and been able to accept in months? 'I shall not forget, Aurelia,' Emily replied quietly.

'Are we upon first-name terms, now?' Sir

Gareth asked, grinning at her.

She looked up at him, coloured, said 'Excuse me,' and hurried off home.

★ ★ ★

'Gareth, how could you so put her out of countenance?' his sister asked him later.

'I'd be able to tell you a good deal better if I had any idea to whom you were referring,' he answered her lazily. They had enjoyed a good meal, the boys were upstairs, and Mr Trimmer was in his study. Sir Gareth, choosing not to sit in the dining-room in solitary state, had brought his glass of port through into the drawing-room.

'I am speaking of Emily Whittaker, of course,' his sister replied, her eyes on her sewing.

'I still don't understand what you mean,' he told her, after he had taken another sip of wine.

'You know perfectly well,' his sister retorted, putting down her work. 'She has said herself that she is quite unused to the kind of banter that comes so naturally to you. You embarrassed her very much, and for what reason? You knew perfectly well that she and I were on first-name terms already.'

'I'd forgotten,' he answered blandly. 'Anyway, if she's embarrassed because of a little gentle teasing, then she needs a good deal more banter, not less.'

'She needs you to leave her alone,' Aurelia said severely. 'You will only arouse expectations that you have no intention of fulfilling. If you must flirt, flirt with such as Jennifer Cummings, who know how to play the game.'

'And I suppose that I won't arouse expectations in her breast — or, which is more important, in the rather more ample breast of her mother?'

'And if you did, she's a charming child . . . ' Her voice tailed off.

'Aurelia, I did warn you, didn't I?' he said, his voice suddenly serious. 'Don't play games with my future. When I decide to marry, I, and only I, will choose my wife. Miss Cummings is just as you have described her — a charming child. But I have no desire to look as though I am marrying someone who might well be my daughter.'

'Well, in the meantime, just take care that you don't hurt those you're tangling with. Emily Whittaker and the doctor clearly have an understanding. I should hate it if any thoughtless love games of yours spoiled her best chance of a good match.'

He stared at her incredulously. 'A good

match? With Dr Pimple? You must be joking!'

'I am not,' she retorted. 'I had it from the dean's wife. Local people are living in expectation of an engagement announcement, apparently.'

The baronet shook his head. 'No, no,' he said decisively. 'She's a pretty woman, and would be prettier if she dressed becomingly. She could do so much better for herself.'

Alan Trimmer came in at this point, having looked up the reference that he had wanted to find. Whilst he and his wife indulged in a little domestic conversation, Sir Gareth looked down into his wine and thought about Emily Whittaker.

Why was it that he kept feeling an impulse to tease her? Looking back on their brief acquaintance, he had done so on almost every occasion when they had met. It was certainly not because he wanted to embarrass her as his sister had suggested. After considering the matter, it occurred to him that the reason had something to do with wanting to encourage that slightly rusty, unaccustomed laugh of hers. Her life had been too serious.

Of course, there were times when seriousness was called for. As a landlord with a substantial estate to administer, he had many matters to deal with, some being of the utmost gravity, but he believed that life was to be enjoyed as well. It seemed to him that the canon's daughter had missed much of the enjoyment that life could bring. He would like to correct that; if the consequence was that the light of amusement came more into those lovely hazel eyes, then he would be very well satisfied.

'Would you not agree, Gareth?' The baronet looked up blankly. He had no idea what his sister might have said. 'Good heavens, you were miles away,' Aurelia exclaimed. 'What were you thinking about?'

'Oh, nothing much. I was just thinking that it was a pity Miss Whittaker has no one to laugh with,' he told her.

Aurelia made no comment, but simply repeated the remark she had made before and which he had not heard. But at the back of her mind, the beginning of an idea began to form.

* * *

'I am going out to dinner tonight, Grandpapa,' Emily told her grandfather on Tuesday afternoon. 'Mr and Mrs Trimmer have invited us, and Mrs Trimmer's nurse is to sit with you while I am out.' She paused. 'Grandpapa, would you think me very wicked if I said that I wished I had something pretty to wear? All

114

my clothes are so dull and unfashionable, and I want to look my best. Do you think that I should wear the brown silk? Yes, so do I. I will come and show you how I look before we leave.'

Emily had three evening gowns, a black one, a grey one and the brown silk. The latter was not any more fashionable than the other two — they were all several years old — and cut lower in the waist than the current style dictated but the colour was more becoming to her creamy complexion, and the fabric was of an excellent quality.

In the past, she had usually worn the gown with a white shawl. Since Sunday morning, however, she had been thinking about the white bonnet that she had longed for, and Sir Gareth's comment that it was not her colour. Her father was not mean with the housekeeping, and she had a little put by that she had been saving for a special occasion. On impulse, therefore, she had gone to the mercer's in Bailgate on Monday and bought a length of yellow silk, and some matching fringe. Since then, she had worked diligently until she had managed to produce a shawl whose colour enriched the brown of her gown rather than deadened it.

That evening when she got ready, it was with some excitement that she added the finishing touches to her outfit. Feeling very daring, she had bought a length of yellow ribbon at the same time as the fabric for her shawl, and now she used it to arrange her hair into a slightly looser style than usual.

When she was ready, she went to her grandfather's room. She had decided not to go downstairs until it was time for her and her father to leave. She did not want to risk being sent upstairs to dress her hair in a more severe style.

'Well, Grandpapa, what do you think?' she asked him, as she twirled around in front of the bed. 'Do I look smart enough? Grandpapa, I am so excited. I hope it is not wrong but I can't help it.' She hurried over to sit next to him, loving the way in which the silk rustled as she moved. 'Grandpapa, do you remember my saying that there was a gentleman? Well, he is to be there tonight. Do you think he will like me?' The little clock on the mantelshelf chimed, and Emily stood up, then leaned over to kiss her grandfather's withered cheek. 'I'll come and tell you all about it tomorrow. Goodbye, dear Grandpapa.'

She left the room, not noticing that on the coverlet, the thin white hand twitched faintly.

* * *

To Emily's relief, her father made no comment either about her hair or her new shawl, but simply offered her his arm so that they could walk the short distance around the north side of the cathedral from their own home in Priorygate to the Trimmers' house in Minster Yard.

They talked very little as they went, her father merely commenting briefly on the balminess of the evening. Emily was glad of this, for she was feeling unaccountably nervous about the forthcoming occasion. She was glad that her father had not said anything about what she was wearing. Her confidence in her improved appearance was diminishing with every step. By the time they reached the front door of the Trimmers' house, the yellow of her shawl, which had seemed earlier to give a welcome touch of colour, had become to her mind unforgivably garish and bold, whilst her new hairstyle seemed rather blowsy.

None of those who greeted them seemed at all struck by what now seemed to Emily to be the blatant vulgarity of her appearance. On the contrary, Sir Gareth, who was dressed very stylishly in cream knee breeches with a black coat and blue waistcoat, with dazzling white linen, greeted them both politely, saying, 'You look charming this evening, Miss Whittaker. Do you not agree, sir?'

He had turned politely to Emily's father, who looked at his daughter in some surprise. 'Yes indeed,' he agreed, in a tone of rather puzzled dawning awareness. It was the first time that Emily could remember his making any kind of complimentary remark about her attire. But then, she reflected, he could hardly do otherwise when Sir Gareth had applied to him for corroboration.

Mr Trimmer also came forward to greet them, and Mrs Trimmer, wearing a high-waisted gown in a fresh shade of green decorated with tiny yellow flowers around the hem and the edges of the sleeves, managed to look both fashionable and modest.

It seemed as if they would be a very small party indeed, until the door opened to admit Mrs Cummings with her daughter Jennifer, to be followed very shortly afterwards by Dr Boyle.

Mrs Cummings was resplendent in a rich shade of plum, and Jennifer looked absolutely ravishing in snowy white muslin. Emily noticed that, unsurprisingly, Sir Gareth's eyes were drawn immediately to the younger woman. She could not blame him. Jennifer's slender figure was shown to great advantage in the flimsy fabric, and her young face glowed with health. Suddenly, Emily felt dull and old.

'Your patients have no need of you tonight, then,' the baronet remarked to the doctor, after they had exchanged greetings.

'No, they all seem to be remarkably well at present,' the doctor replied. 'I have left a message with my housekeeper, so that if an emergency occurs, I can be found easily.'

'Then let us trust no one will fall ill suddenly and deprive us of your company,' Sir Gareth responded politely. 'But do not let me keep you from the other guests.' The doctor bowed, and turned to approach Emily, who looked up and smiled. She looked happy, but not as happy as she had immediately after her arrival, the baronet decided, before turning to speak to Mrs Cummings and her daughter, who were hovering nearby.

'I wonder, were you in London for the season, Sir Gareth?' the older lady asked him.

'I was,' he replied, with a slight bow.

'Was it very exciting?' Miss Cummings asked him, her eyes shining. 'How I long to go to London!'

'I am very sure you do,' he responded, smiling politely. 'Are there plans for you to attend in the future?'

'I am to take her next year,' Mrs Cummings answered, in a tone which suggested that the baronet ought to be gratified by this information. 'We were to have gone this spring, but my friend Lady Gresham, who is Jennifer's godmother, and is to act as our hostess, suffered a bereavement in March, so it was quite inappropriate for us to stay with her.'

'Ah yes, I recall, the dowager Lady Gresham passed away,' Sir Gareth replied. 'And so you have had to wait, Miss Cummings. I hope you did not find it too trying?'

'She was naturally a little disappointed, Sir Gareth,' Mrs Cummings put in, before Jennifer could say anything. 'But she did not make a fuss about it. She has the best nature of any girl I have met, although I do say so myself.'

'I am pleased to hear it,' replied the baronet politely. 'Are you an only child, Miss Cummings?'

Again, Jennifer's mother answered for her. 'Yes indeed, she is my only child, and my great solace, for since Mr Cummings passed away, there has only been Jennifer and myself.'

'You will have to tell me what you find to do in Lincoln for entertainment, Miss Cummings,' said Sir Gareth, resolving that this gambit would be his last attempt to get Jennifer to answer for herself.

Fortunately, at this moment Mrs Cummings had found her attention claimed by

Mrs Trimmer. 'Well, I shall try,' Jennifer replied, 'but there isn't a great deal to do, really. London must be far more exciting.'

Sir Gareth smiled wryly. 'Ah, but for me, you see, Lincoln has all the advantage of novelty. For you, London is a new place, but since next season will be my twentieth, you must excuse me if I do not get very excited about it.'

Miss Cummings's eyes opened very wide. 'Your *twentieth?*' she exclaimed. 'Why, you must be — ' She stopped abruptly, blushing profusely.

'Very old,' he completed for her with a twinkle. 'Yes, I am,' he agreed. 'But pray don't tell anyone.'

Jennifer laughed out loud, drawing a look from her mama that was half approval, because she and the baronet were getting along so well, and half reproof, because such conduct was a little unladylike.

Dr Boyle, who had been enquiring of Emily about her grandfather's health, turned to look at the young lady in question. 'How very lovely she looks tonight,' he remarked in tones of heartfelt admiration. 'She looks exactly like a fairy. Does she not, Miss Whittaker?'

'Exactly,' agreed Emily in a colourless tone. The doctor had shown no sign of noticing her

121

new shawl and the different manner in which she had dressed her hair. If marriage to him meant continually hearing his praises of other ladies while garnering none for herself, it would be a bleak business indeed.

Sir Gareth turned away from his conversation with Miss Cummings and, as he did so, he noticed Emily Whittaker. A little while ago, she had looked happy and animated. Now, it seemed as if all the light had gone out of her face. He wondered why, and all at once felt an urge to kick whoever was responsible for the change in her expression. He hoped that it might be Dr Boyle.

It was very soon after this that dinner was announced. Mrs Trimmer took her brother's arm, whilst her husband escorted Mrs Cummings, leaving Emily to follow with the doctor, with Canon Whittaker escorting Jennifer in the rear. At table, Sir Gareth was placed on his sister's right, and Emily, to her surprise, found herself on Mrs Trimmer's left, with Dr Boyle sitting on the other side of her. Sir Gareth had Jennifer sitting next to him on his other side, a fact that pleased that young lady's mother greatly, whilst Mr Trimmer had Mrs Cummings on one side and Canon Whittaker on the other. Because the company was small in number, Mrs Trimmer announced that talking across the table was allowed, and they proved to be quite a cheerful party. Whilst Emily's father chatted with Jennifer in a kindly, indulgent style, Emily found herself engaged in cheerful banter with Mrs Trimmer and her brother.

'He is the most infuriating man,' Mrs Trimmer was saying to Emily. 'In fact, he always has been. Do you know, I quite depended upon him to introduce me to all his friends when I first came out, but do you think that he did?'

'I would guess that he did not, from what you have just said,' Emily ventured, looking at brother and sister with something like envy. Again, she regretted that she had never had the opportunity to take part in this kind of lively exchange.

'You are quite correct. He did not. He came to my ball, danced his duty dances with me, disappeared into the card room, and then retired to his club. Would you believe it?'

'Miss Whittaker, this is most unfair. You are only hearing half the story,' Sir Gareth protested in his deep tones. 'Imagine, if you will, a group of young women, all of them in their first season, all following me around, egged on by Aurelia, if you please. 'Oh, my brother will take you here, my brother will take you there',' he cried, in a falsetto voice. Then he continued in his normal tone, 'If I wanted to escape, the only place that I *could* go where I could be sure that they would not pursue me was my club!'

'My heart bleeds for you, Gareth,' retorted his sister, unimpressed. 'So handsome, so wealthy, so sought after.'

'No, Sister dear,' he corrected her. 'I'm not handsome. Take it from one who looks in the mirror every day.'

'Nonsense,' Aurelia declared. 'Of course you are handsome. Is he not, Emily?'

Emily stared at them both, horrified, blushing furiously. All at once she recalled the moment when they had stood on the threshold of her house and she had said 'magnificent' whilst looking straight up at him. She had considered Sir Gareth to be the most attractive man that she had ever seen, from the moment that she had first set eyes on him. It was one thing to think it, however, quite another to speak it. 'I . . . I . . . '

'Perhaps Miss Whittaker has higher standards than yours, Aurelia,' Sir Gareth suggested.

At that moment, Emily's attention was claimed by Dr Boyle, and when she next spoke with Mrs Trimmer, she found that Sir Gareth's attention had been claimed by Jennifer Cummings.

'Do forgive me, my dear,' Mrs Trimmer

said in an undertone. 'I did not mean to embarrass you.'

'I was a little embarrassed,' Emily confessed, 'but it is only that I am not used to this kind of jesting.'

'I think that you would have been had your brother lived,' the other lady replied.

'Yes, perhaps,' Emily agreed. 'But he died when I was only eight, and he had been away at school for much of the time. I did not really know him.' She sighed: 'I just wish that someone could tell me what he was really like.'

'I can.' While Emily had been speaking, Sir Gareth's conversation with Jennifer had ceased and that young lady had had her attention claimed again by Canon Whittaker.

Emily turned her head to look at him. 'Can you really?' she asked.

'Certainly. Don't you recall that I said that we were at school together?'

'Oh yes, yes,' Emily agreed hastily. 'But schools are large places. I imagine that one could be in the same school as a person and never really know him.'

'Yes, that is true, but I *did* know Patrick very well indeed,' Sir Gareth told her.

'What was he like?' Emily asked him.

Sir Gareth looked across at the eager face, and suddenly thought how very appealing she looked. 'I cannot tell you here,' he said. 'Would you do me the honour of escorting me around the cathedral tomorrow? I could tell you about him then.'

'Yes, of course,' Emily answered, trying not to sound too excited.

'One thing I *will* tell you now,' he remarked, 'is that he was alive.' She looked a little puzzled and he added impatiently, 'What I mean is that he wasn't a plaster saint' — here he directed a swift glance in her father's direction — 'but that he was really alive.'

As Emily and her father were walking home, her father said to her, 'I had a most illuminating discussion with Sir Gareth about Patrick tonight.'

'Did you, Papa?' Emily asked him, recalling what the baronet had said.

'Yes, I did,' her father replied. 'He was a fine scholar, apparently. 'Everything came to him so easily'. Those were his very words. And he used his skills to help those less gifted. How proud we would have been, would we not, Emily?'

'Yes indeed, Papa,' Emily replied, thinking that this was the longest conversation that she and her father had had about Patrick since his death.

After her father had gone to bed, Emily

slipped back downstairs and went into the drawing-room where the portrait of her brother hung over the fireplace. It looked just the same as it had always done.

He was really alive, Sir Gareth had said. What had he meant?

10

Before they had left the Trimmers' the previous evening, Sir Gareth had suggested in an undertone that they should meet in the cathedral the following morning at ten o'clock, and Emily had nodded her assent. The secrecy had seemed a good idea. Had her father been aware of their meeting, he would almost certainly have decided to join them so that he could find out more about Patrick. Had Mrs Cummings heard about the expedition, she might have tried to get her daughter included. As it was, they would be able to talk uninterrupted.

As Emily prepared to slip out of the house after her father had retired to his study, it suddenly occurred that she was bent upon an assignation. I am meeting a man in secret, she thought, and all at once felt like some kind of *femme fatale*. Then she caught sight of herself in her prim bonnet and gown and instantly revised her opinion. No one seeing her would ever make such a judgement.

Normally, if she was simply visiting the cathedral for her own personal reasons, she would enter by the small entrance known as the Richard door. On this occasion, however, because the building was unfamiliar to Sir Gareth, and because he would be approaching it from the other end, she decided to enter by the west door.

Once inside, she found as always that her eyes were drawn upwards by the soaring pillars, and from there to the windows, which, on this bright sunny day, filtered the light through on to the stone, painting it with blue and red.

'Glorious,' said a deep voice behind her, making her jump, and she turned, a startled expression on her face. 'I beg your pardon; I didn't mean to alarm you,' said Sir Gareth, smiling.

Her heart gave a little lurch at the sight of him, but this she sternly repressed. However attractive she might find him — and she had to admit that she did — he was destined for someone more like Miss Cummings. His sister had made that clear. She, Emily, could not possibly be the heroine of any romance in which this man featured as the hero.

'Not alarmed; surprised, merely,' she replied, her calm tone at variance with her inner turmoil.

He inclined his head. 'I am looking forward to hearing about the cathedral from one who knows and loves it,' he said.

Her expression softened. 'I will be happy to tell you all that I can,' she replied. 'In my turn, however, I am hoping to hear about my brother from one who was his friend.'

'And I, too, will be happy to tell you all that I can,' answered Sir Gareth. 'Let us stroll about the cathedral and as we go, you can tell me about the things that we see and I can tell you about the things that I remember.'

'All right,' Emily replied. 'Shall we walk up the south side first?'

'By all means,' he answered. 'I have a very strong desire to stand in one of the places where the sunlight falls through the windows.'

'I have always liked doing that,' Emily admitted, as they moved towards the pillar on the south side that was presently bathed in coloured light. 'When I was small, I used to think that it was magic, but when I told Papa, he was angry with me, for even mentioning such a word as magic in connection with a place like this.'

'That rather depends what you mean by magic,' the baronet remarked, as he stood in the light, looking up and wrinkling his brow as he observed the path of the sun through the window. 'If you're thinking of witches and warlocks and such, then I would say he was right. If, on the other hand, you are thinking of something special and beautiful and just a little mysterious, then I would have thought that this was the very place to find it.'

'I'm sure that that must have been what I meant at the time,' Emily exclaimed, looking up at him. 'How clever of you!'

He looked down and saw the glow on her face that resulted partly from the effect of the sunlight, and partly from the joy of being understood. Her hazel eyes sparkled, and the neat brown hair that peeped from beneath her unfashionable bonnet seemed touched with flashes of gold. All of a sudden, he found himself wondering why the deuce the canon's pretty daughter was still unmarried.

For her part, Emily found her eyes locked with his; her gaze dropped to his mouth and the shocking nature of her thoughts caused her to gasp, turn away and say, 'This way, sir! I really must . . . must show you the . . . the bishop's eye!'

She hurried off, leaving the baronet to follow after her. In fact, she got so far ahead of him that she had turned into the south transept long before he had reached it, and stood there breathing rather fast for a moment or two, her hand on her heart.

What on earth had she been thinking of? Bad enough that her thoughts should have been so wicked; for as she had looked up at the baronet's well-shaped, generous mouth, she had wondered for a moment or two what it might be like to have his lips pressed to hers. How much more magical that place would have been had he done such a thing! She had swiftly repressed that shocking thought. But what had she done after that but treat Mrs Trimmer's brother to a piece of childish rudeness by running off in another direction? Now, thanks to her inability to keep her unruly imagination in order, he was probably lost in the cathedral.

She hurried back around the corner at exactly the same moment as Sir Gareth had reached it, and she bumped into him, causing him to catch hold of her by her elbows, as he laughed down at her. 'My my, you do seem to be in a hurry today,' he exclaimed, as he released her. 'I do hope I'm not detaining you from anything.'

'No, no, not at all,' Emily replied, flustered because she had almost ended up in his arms.

'So what is this bishop's eye that you were going to show me?' he asked her, looking round. 'I take it that it is an architectural feature of the cathedral, and not one of the two that are to be found in the bishop's head?'

She laughed at that. 'The bishop's eye is the round window immediately above us,' she told him. 'Although, to be truthful, the dean's eye is seen better from here.' She pointed to the round window set high up at the end of the opposite transept.

'That is very fine,' he remarked. 'Which do you prefer?'

Her face took on a thoughtful look which, he decided, was strangely becoming. 'I know that I am in a minority, but I prefer the bishop's eye,' she told him. 'It is true that the window does not have any pictures, but the tracery is so very beautiful.'

They both considered the windows in silence for a time, then the baronet said, 'Your brother was never afraid of holding a position adhered to by the minority.'

'Oh yes, you were going to tell me about him,' Emily said eagerly.

'Yes, I was, wasn't I?' he agreed. 'Shall we go and sit down somewhere?'

She led him into a side chapel known as the works chantry, that opened out from the south transept, and sat down beneath a brass plaque on one of the stone seats by the wall.

'Patrick and I were the same age,' the baronet said, when they were both settled.

'Oh. So you are — ' Emily stopped abruptly.

'I'm forty; yes,' Sir Gareth agreed with a smile. 'Had you been wondering, Miss Whittaker?'

'No, certainly not,' she replied defensively, and, it must be confessed, not entirely truthfully. 'Do go on.'

'We met at Eton, and soon became friends. We always stuck together, looking after each other; defending each other if anyone tried to act the bully. In fact, it very soon became known that to attack one of us was to attack both. We even acquired a shared nickname — Thunder and Lightning.'

'Which was which?' Emily asked curiously.

'Oh, I was Thunder; bigger, darker. Patrick was lightning; bright, quick, with flashes of brilliance.'

'I didn't realize that you knew him so well,' Emily responded. 'Although you did tell Papa some things that pleased him very much last night.'

He smiled ruefully. 'Everything I told him was true, but I held a few things back. Patrick certainly was a fine scholar, and he did use his gifts to help those less fortunate.'

'How did he do that?' Emily asked curiously.

'Well, he let me copy his work occasionally.'

Emily stifled a giggle. 'No, Papa would not have approved of that,' she agreed.

'I thought not. Though to tell the truth, he was looked up to by the other boys. He was very kind to the younger ones. Not all of the older boys were. Some of them liked the power that they had through age and superior strength, and used it to intimidate others. He never did.'

'Papa would have liked that.'

'Yes, but as for the rest, I didn't want to tell him a lot of lies, and nothing that he said to me the other night gave me the impression that he would relish the recounting of schoolboy pranks.'

'He might not,' Emily agreed, 'but I would. What did you do, Sir Gareth? The two of you, together, I mean.'

The baronet laughed. He told her many stories of the camaraderie that had existed between himself and the canon's son, making her laugh as well. Then, eventually, in carefully unemotional tones, he told her about that fateful day when, with some other friends, they had gone down to the river to go boating. A child had fallen into the river and Patrick had been the one to jump in and try to save her.

'They both got into difficulties,' Sir Gareth said, in a calm tone that masked the distress that he still felt at this particular memory. 'I jumped in after them, but it was no good. I dived and dived . . . ' He paused and collected himself. 'Even now, I find it difficult to believe that he has gone; all that

135

brightness, that life, that promise.' Again he paused. 'Now that you have heard how close we were, you must wonder why I did not come to the funeral, or even make contact with you. The truth of the matter is that having tried to save them, I then succumbed to a fever which laid me low for some time, and after that, well, I suppose I was just not brave enough. I think I wanted to blot what had happened from my mind.'

He was sitting looking down at his hands which were clasped between his knees. To his great surprise, he saw one of Miss Whittaker's hands reach out and grasp his. 'You were only a boy yourself,' she said. 'It's not surprising that you could not bring yourself to come, but you have come now, and I am glad that you have told me about Patrick. You are right. He was alive; really alive. I have tended to think of him as being like a figure in one of these stained-glass windows. Now, I feel as if I knew him. Thank you.'

He turned slightly to face her, took hold of the hand that she had placed over his, and raised it to his lips.

A sound of footsteps on the stone flags broke the spell, and they both got to their feet. 'That stone seat is dam — decidedly cold,' the baronet remarked, recollecting his surroundings just in time.

'But very convenient,' Emily responded. 'Have you never heard the saying, 'let the weakest go to the wall'? That's so that they would have somewhere to sit down.'

'Is that what it means?' Sir Gareth exclaimed. 'I never knew.'

Further up the south side of the cathedral they came to a tomb underneath an archway, which Emily pointed out to her companion. 'This is the tomb of Katherine Swynford,' she said. 'She was — '

'The mistress, then wife, of John of Gaunt,' Sir Gareth put in. 'You see, I didn't rely on Patrick for all my answers. The tomb is very plain: surprisingly so.'

'There should have been brasses on there but they were taken at the time of Oliver Cromwell,' Emily told him.

They strolled on into the Angel choir where stood another, more ornate tomb, with shields of arms at the base. 'This is very fine,' remarked Sir Gareth, crouching down to take a closer look at some of the markings. Emily, observing him, suddenly realized that she was looking, not at the tomb, which she knew well anyway, but at how the breeches he was wearing did nothing to hide the powerful muscles in his thighs.

Horrified by the increasingly depraved nature of her imaginings, she exclaimed, 'The imp! I . . . must tell you about the imp. Have you had him pointed out to you? Lots of people cannot find him for ages and ages . . . '

The baronet rose easily to his feet, dusting off his hands, and caught hold of her by the elbow. 'What is it?' he asked her, wrinkling his brow. 'You seem to be very jittery today, and I'm blessed if I can think what I might have done to make you so.'

'It's . . . it's just hearing about Patrick, I suppose,' she gasped, desperate for something to say, and finding that she had hit upon part of the reason why she was so unsettled. 'You have made me realize what I have missed.' She paused then went on more slowly, 'When I hear you and Mrs Trimmer talking together, I wonder whether Patrick and I might have teased one another in the same way.'

'Almost certainly, I would have thought.' He looked at her for a few moments, as if trying to take her measure. Eventually he said to her, 'There is one other thing that I want to tell you about Patrick, but it's something that I could never, ever tell your father, for I think it would distress him even more than hearing about childish tricks.'

'What is it?' Emily asked him apprehensively.

'He didn't want to enter the church.'

Emily gave a tiny gasp. She was so used to hearing that Patrick was almost a candidate for canonization that this revelation came as something of a shock. So surprised was she that she almost missed the baronet's next few words. 'Oh, he knew how much his father planned for it, and he was dreading disappointing him, but he felt that that life was not for him at all.'

'What did he want to do?' Emily asked him curiously.

'He wanted to be a soldier. He was trying to nerve himself up to come and ask your father to purchase his colours. So the next time you look at his portrait, Miss Whittaker, imagine him not in clerical bands but in the red and gold mess dress that he so much desired. No doubt, had he been spared, he'd have been itching to fight the French! Now tell me about the Lincoln imp, and in particular how to find the elusive little fellow.'

Emily pointed him out at the top of his pillar, and recounted the tale of how two imps had come into the cathedral to wreak havoc. They had been reprimanded by an angel, and one of them had climbed to the top of the pillar to throw rocks at his heavenly accuser. As a consequence, he had been turned to stone. 'And there he stays, but I cannot feel sorry for him,' Emily concluded.

'After all, he doesn't look at all sorry for himself, and he can see everything from up there.'

She smiled up at the baronet, and saw that he was looking down at her. An arrested expression came over his face, and for some reason, her heart began to beat faster. She could not know how very winsome she looked at that moment; so much so that the baronet, already unsettled by their previous conversation, found his usual common sense flying away and emotions taking over.

'So he can,' he said. 'Better give him something to look at, then.' Leaning towards her, he tilted her chin with one finger and kissed her lightly and swiftly on her mouth.

'Oh!' she gasped, looking up at him. 'Oh, goodness me! I . . . I must be going! I am needed to . . . to . . . ' She turned and began to hurry past St Hugh's choir in the direction of the west door.

'Miss Whittaker, wait!' called the baronet, hurrying after her. He caught up with her easily, and grasped her elbow, firmly, but gently. 'Wait, please. I don't know why I did that. I didn't mean to insult you, especially when you have been so kind.'

'Kind?' she exclaimed in response, staring up at him with an expression that he found impossible to read. 'I had supposed that you, also, were kind, Sir Gareth.'

At that, he released her, his face flushed. He ran a hand through his hair, the gesture betraying his agitation. 'You do right to rebuke me,' he told her. 'No, pray do not run away,' he added hastily, for he could see that she was about to flee. 'At least give me a chance to explain myself.' At first, when he had caught hold of her, she had pulled away from him. Now, she paused, ready to listen to what he had to say. After a moment or two, he said ruefully, 'That's confounded me. Of course there is no excuse for me. All that talk about Patrick unsettled me a little, I think.'

Looking away from him, she said quietly, 'Perhaps the Lincoln imp was trying to wreak more havoc.'

'Perhaps he was,' Sir Gareth agreed, with a light laugh. 'I would be grateful if you would lay the whole matter at his door, and forgive me for my discourtesy.'

'Yes, of course,' Emily agreed, in subdued tones, but deep down inside her, something was singing, *He kissed me!*

By mutual unspoken consent, they did not look at the rest of the cathedral in any detail, but instead walked slowly back towards the west door, talking idly of the number of services that were conducted in the building, and about the terms of Canon Whittaker's

141

residency in the close. It must be confessed, however, that for varying reasons, neither of them would have been able to have given an account of what was said during the conversation.

Light though it was inside, the brightness of the summer day caused them to blink as they stepped out into the warmth of the sunshine. Sir Gareth turned to Emily to thank her for conducting him around the cathedral, but before he could say anything, a voice hailed him from just inside Exchequer gate.

'Blades, m'dear fellow! Houghton swore we'd find you here, but I never believed it.'

If Sir Gareth looked a little out of place in Lincoln in all his London elegance, that was nothing to how incongruous this newcomer appeared. Tall and willowy, he was clad in an elegant blue coat with gleaming brass buttons, red silk waistcoat, yellow breeches and glistening black boots with snowy tops, and his cravat was so high as to make it difficult for him to turn his head. He looked to be about the same age as Emily herself.

'I don't see why not,' Sir Gareth replied easily. 'I have never known Houghton to lie.'

'Devil take me, that wasn't what I meant,' said the other. 'It's good to see you, even in this benighted place.' The two men shook hands.

'How kind of you to say so,' the baronet answered ironically. 'You can now make your apologies to Miss Whittaker, who happens to live here.' He turned to Emily. 'Miss Whittaker, this graceless fellow, who deserves to be taken to the top of the tower and hurled off it immediately, is Lord Stuart Fenn, youngest son of the Duke of Barnwell.'

Lord Stuart's rather thin, mobile features took on an expression of comical dismay. 'The deuce! Resident here, you say! A thousand apologies, ma'am. I would not for anything cast any aspersions upon your . . . um . . . abode.' He made an elegant bow.

'You would not be the first to do so, my lord,' Emily told him with a smile. 'We do contrive to keep ourselves busy, however.'

'Busy! It's the aim of my life to try to avoid being busy as much as I can,' he answered frankly. 'But I'm not alone. Look, Blades, I've a pleasant surprise for you.'

Two ladies were now drawing closer to them from the Exchequer gate. One, dressed in a modest gown and bonnet, looked to be about Emily's own age. It was not possible to determine the age of the other. All that Emily knew was that this was the most ravishing creature that she had ever seen. She was dressed in a gown of celestial blue with palest golden piping around the hem and bodice, and a straw bonnet with gold and blue ribbons. Her hair was a riot of black curls, her blue eyes sparkled, and she came forward to Sir Gareth holding out her hand.

'Gareth, you wicked man!' said the vision in a teasing tone. 'You fled Houghton's estate as if all the devils in Hell were after you, but here I find you in this seat of virtue.'

'Forgive me, Annis,' the baronet replied, lifting her hand to his lips. But he did not offer any explanation for his disappearance.

'Have you just been looking over this dreadful old pile?' the newcomer asked, gesturing towards the cathedral with her left hand. 'It looks as if it ought to have been pulled down years ago.'

Sir Gareth could feel Emily stiffening beside him. 'Before you blot your copy-book any more, Annis, I must introduce Miss Whittaker to you, who resides in the close. Miss Whittaker, this is Mrs Annis Hughes. And this is her companion, Miss Wayne.'

The ladies acknowledged one another politely. Mrs Hughes looked at Emily in amazement. 'You actually live next to this place? Good heavens, it would give me the frights to have that great monstrosity looming over me every day and night.'

'It does not have that effect upon me,' Emily replied, wanting to defend her beloved cathedral, but feeling more drab than ever in face of all this feminine elegance.

'Well it would me,' replied Mrs Hughes frankly. Now that she had taken a proper look at the newcomer, Emily could see that the lady was not as young as she had appeared at first. Tiny lines at the corners of her eyes suggested that she was in fact probably about Emily's own age or even slightly older.

'Now, now, Cousin,' said Lord Stuart, thus revealing his connection to the society beauty, 'you can't say that. I mean to say, get used to anything given time, y'know.'

'Miss Whittaker has just been escorting me around the cathedral,' Gareth remarked.

'Indeed,' murmured Mrs Hughes. 'Did he flirt with you dreadfully, my dear?' she asked Emily. 'He is a shocking flirt, you know; he has quite a reputation for it.'

'Flirt? In the cathedral?' exclaimed Sir Gareth in outraged tones, taking Mrs Hughes's attention away from Emily.

'No indeed, certainly not,' Lord Stuart declared. 'It would be like . . . like . . . well, like flirting in church. I mean to say, it *would* be flirting in church.'

'No one's conversation elevates the soul quite like yours, Stuart,' remarked the baronet. 'Tell me, are you staying in Lincoln, or just passing through?'

Stuart opened his mouth to speak, but before he could say anything, Mrs Hughes said, 'We are staying for a few days. Our plans are not fixed. We have taken rooms at the White Hart. It seems quite tolerable. Would you care to join us for luncheon?' Then, after a moment's thought she turned to Emily. 'And you too, of course, Miss Whittaker: would you care to join us?'

'Thank you, but I am expected at home,' Emily replied.

'Then I shall join you after I have escorted Miss Whittaker to her door,' said Sir Gareth.

'No, there is no need,' said Emily hastily. 'I am accustomed to walking alone here. Please join your friends, sir.'

'Very well,' the baronet replied with a bow. 'Then I will thank you for your informative tour, and bid you good day.'

'Good day, sir,' Emily replied, 'And thank you for . . . for . . . ' She was thinking of all that he had told her about Patrick.

He made a gently dismissive gesture with his hand. 'It was nothing, ma'am,' he replied, smiling down at her in an understanding way.

Emily bade them all a polite farewell, and turned to go home. As she left, she heard Mrs

Hughes saying, 'A sweet, mousy old thing. Who is she?'

Who was she? Once upon a time, about a week or so ago, she had thought that she knew. She would have said then that she was simply Canon Whittaker's spinster daughter, dedicated to good works. Then Sir Gareth had appeared, and suddenly she had begun to see things differently.

Emily hurried away from the three fashionables, but instead of going back home, as she had told Sir Gareth she would, she walked around the cathedral and entering it again by the door that she usually used, she made her way to the seat that she had so recently occupied with Sir Gareth.

For as long as she could remember, the cathedral had been the place to which she had gone when she wanted to express how she really felt. Not since her brother's death had she been able to do such a thing safely at home. Now, she recalled how she and Gareth had spoken about Patrick; how he had been so moved at the memory of her brother's death, and she blushed as she thought of how she had caught hold of his hand to comfort him. After that, they had walked round to look at the Lincoln imp, and there, under the little creature's mischievous gaze, he had kissed her. I will never look at the imp again without remembering that moment, she told herself.

In her mind, she went over the scene again, recalling Sir Gareth's deep tones, the strong feel of him as she had cannoned into him, the touch of his lips. Suddenly she recalled how on the day when they had first met he had suggested that perhaps she might not have liked the look of him. Not like the look of him? She would be mad not to do so. In her mind, she had come to think of him as the hero of some kind of story. Well, now another character had appeared: a character called Mrs Hughes, who might, she feared, turn out to be the heroine. One thing was certain: however much she might like the look of Sir Gareth Blades, she was quite sure that Mrs Hughes liked the look of him as well.

11

'That lady is Miss Emily Whittaker, as I have already told you, Annis. I cannot think your description of her very kind or even very accurate,' said Sir Gareth as he strolled back to the White Hart with Lord Stuart, Mrs Hughes and Miss Wayne. He strove to keep his tone pleasant, but truth to tell, he was rather surprised at how annoyed he felt at this criticism of the canon's daughter.

'Hoity toity! I had not realized that she was a favourite of yours,' Mrs Hughes exclaimed, prompting him to realize that he had not been entirely successful in disguising his feelings. 'Well, I did say she was sweet. Anyway, she's certainly dowdy; you can't deny that.'

'I should say not,' said Lord Stuart quickly, then glanced sideways at the baronet and cleared his throat in a rather embarrassed way.

'She's not fashionably dressed, I agree,' the baronet admitted. 'But then, my dear Annis, you will find that fashions are somewhat behind London here in the provinces.'

'You do not need to tell me so,' the lady

agreed fervently. 'Why, as we were travelling through the town, I saw a richly dressed woman in a gown that was quite ten years behind the times. Can you imagine?'

'Ten years? You shock me,' declared the baronet in amused tones.

Inside the White Hart, they were shown into a private parlour and there served with a light lunch of cold ham, bread, cheese and a ginger cake. 'You seem to be well catered for here,' Sir Gareth remarked as he carved a slice of ham for Miss Wayne, then cut another for himself.

'It is tolerable,' Mrs Hughes drawled; then recollecting that she was choosing to remain there, and without a very good reason, save that which naturally she could not disclose to the baronet, she added, 'Very tolerable; surprisingly so, in fact. I assume that you are staying with your sister.'

Sir Gareth inclined his head. 'As you say. Aurelia will be pleased to receive all of you.' He smiled at Miss Wayne, in order to indicate that she was included in the invitation.

'Devilish good of her,' declared Lord Stuart, as he carefully inspected the cheese and cut himself a large piece. 'Her husband's a clergyman, ain't he?'

'That's right,' answered the other man.

'Well, no one's perfect,' declared his

lordship largely. Then realizing the infelicitous nature of what he had said, he added hastily, 'That is to say, someone has to do it. Take old Clumber, now; youngest son; no income; what else is the fellow to do?'

'Ah, but Alan, my brother-in-law, has a substantial private income, but is a clergyman by choice,' Sir Gareth pointed out.

'Oh,' said Lord Stuart blankly. 'No accounting for taste, I suppose. But tell us, old fellow, what the deuce is there to do here? Nothing much, I suppose.'

'Nonsense,' replied his cousin, as she selected a piece of ginger cake, and nodded to her cousin who was offering her another glass of wine. 'I'm sure it is a charming place.'

'I thought that you had judged it to be years behind the times, with accommodation that is merely tolerable, within sight of a gloomy old pile that needs pulling down,' remarked Sir Gareth pleasantly, but with a slight edge to his voice nevertheless.

'Gareth, my dear, surely you know by now when I am merely funning,' Mrs Hughes replied with a trill of laughter. 'Travel broadens the mind, you know, and I am sure that I will benefit from learning a little more about this place.'

'I am sure that you will, Annis,' replied the baronet, smiling. 'The only trouble is that I am not sure you are taking the matter seriously.'

'Oh, I am quite sure that I know when to take things seriously,' she answered, smiling back at him over the top of her glass. 'But tell us, Gareth, what *is* there to do here?'

'I am sure that Miss Whittaker could tell you better than I, but in her absence — '

'Miss Whittaker!' exclaimed the beauty scornfully. 'Why, anyone can see that she has never been anywhere or done anything. What would *she* know?'

'I should imagine she knows a good deal about the cathedral, ma'am,' Miss Wayne suggested.

'Unsurprisingly,' Mrs Hughes murmured.

'But, as I was saying,' Sir Gareth went on, 'in Miss Whittaker's absence, I can tell you that there are some Assembly rooms in which functions take place; there is, apparently, some good society here in the upper town, and at certain times, although not presently, there are race meetings. *And*, Annis my dear, just a few doors along from here is a fashionable milliner's.'

'*Really?*' answered the lady, with the first real sign of interest that she had shown in anything that Lincoln had to offer yet.

'Certainly. Would you like me to escort you there later?' Sir Gareth replied, reflecting inwardly that if travel broadened the mind, it did not seem to have that effect upon present company, despite what Mrs Hughes might have said.

*　*　*

That afternoon, Emily remembered that she had promised to purchase some soap for the housekeeper. She left the house, went back into Bailgate and made the necessary purchase. She was just walking past the milliner's shop, when the door opened, and Mrs Hughes came out, all smiles, accompanied by Sir Gareth. The baronet lifted his hat politely.

'Ah, Miss . . . Whittaker, isn't it?' smiled Mrs Hughes. 'Such a charming shop! Do you not find it so?' Her eyes lit on Emily's bonnet and her enthusiasm seemed to fade a little. Then she went on, 'Gareth has been giving me such good advice. He is a fount of wisdom with regard to fashions.'

'Wisdom?' murmured Emily in a quizzical tone, which caused the baronet to glance at her with a slightly narrowed gaze.

'Why yes,' replied Mrs Hughes. 'No one can advise upon female apparel as well as he. You must beg him to go with you, next time you shop.' She glanced at the package in

Emily's hand. 'But I see that you have been shopping today, in fact.'

'Yes,' replied Emily, colouring a little. 'It is soap; for the housekeeper.'

'How useful,' murmured Mrs Hughes in a mystified tone.

'Miss Whittaker, my nephews have been plaguing me to take them up the tower ever since you mentioned the matter, but I have told them that I will not go without your escort,' said Sir Gareth, abandoning the subject of shopping without hesitation. 'Do you have any idea when you might be able to give us some of your time?'

'The tower?' exclaimed Mrs Hughes, horrified. 'Not that huge one in the middle of the cathedral, surely!'

'Most certainly,' replied Sir Gareth, laughing. 'Would you care to join us, Annis?'

'Don't be so absurd,' Mrs Hughes answered. 'I should be worn out for the rest of the day.'

'Perhaps tomorrow, if it is fine?' Emily suggested.

'Thank you. I should be very much obliged to you,' said the baronet devoutly. 'Perhaps then I shall get some peace.'

'From my experience of small boys, they will soon find something else that they want you to do,' Emily told him.

'My God, you are right,' he exclaimed, striking his forehead. 'Perhaps I had better put off the tower expedition for a little longer. At least, then, I shall know where I stand.'

'Don't blaspheme in Miss Whittaker's presence, Gareth,' said Mrs Hughes. 'She will be very much shocked.' She smiled at him intimately, as if to say, but I am not. Emily opened her mouth in order to state that she was not so easily disturbed, but before she could say anything, Mrs Hughes spoke again. 'I am sure you will excuse us, but we are due to visit Aurelia for tea.'

'Naturally, you are welcome to join us,' put in the baronet.

'Gareth, do not be obtuse,' said Mrs Hughes patiently. 'Miss Whittaker must hurry home with her soap.'

'The housekeeper is expecting me,' Emily agreed, feeling a very strong desire to get out her soap and wash Mrs Hughes's silly pouting mouth.

'Then I shall see you tomorrow,' said Sir Gareth, as they parted.

★ ★ ★

The following day dawned bright and clear for the expedition up the tower and Emily, who had climbed it many times and never

155

with any thought as to what she looked like, now found herself torn by indecision as to what to put on. Strong shoes were essential, of course, but should she wear her lavender gown, the dark brown, or perhaps the navy? The navy was undoubtedly the most becoming, but the lavender would probably be a more sensible choice, in case she brushed against any stonework. After a moment's thought, she donned the navy.

Now, the question arose of what bonnet to wear. She did have one that went with the gown, but she seldom wore it, knowing that her father thought it rather frivolous. She had heard Canon Whittaker go out earlier, however, so she quickly put it on, and looked at her reflection with rather guilty pleasure. It was a very modest item of headgear by London standards, but the silk trimming to the crown and the bunch of daisies stitched to one side, near to where the ribbons were tied, made it look rather pretty, she decided.

Sir Gareth was due to meet her at the west front with the boys, but shortly before their time of meeting, as Emily was coming down the stairs, there was a knock at the door, and her heart gave a strange little skip as she heard his deep voice speaking to the maid.

'Good morning,' said Emily as she reached the bottom of the stairs.

'Good morning,' replied the baronet with a bow. 'Oliver and James could not wait like civilized people, so I have brought them round here.'

'So that they can be uncivilized in our house?' she asked him wryly. Then she turned to the boys. 'Good morning,' she said to them, smiling. 'Are you feeling strong today?'

'Yes, thank you, ma'am,' replied Oliver.

'If you'd seen what they ate for breakfast this morning, you wouldn't ask,' the baronet replied. 'I'm surprised my sister has any food left in the house.'

The boys laughed then Oliver said, 'How high is the tower, ma'am?'

'Two hundred and seventy-one feet,' Emily replied, as they left the house.

The boys' eyes grew very round. 'My stars!' James exclaimed.

'But it was taller once, wasn't it?' Oliver asked with interest.

'Yes, indeed it was,' Emily agreed. 'When there was a spire on top, the height was over five hundred feet.'

'How I should have liked to have climbed to the top of that,' declared Oliver with relish. 'Would not you, Uncle Gareth?'

'No I should not,' the baronet replied firmly. 'The present two hundred and seventy-one feet are quite enough for me, thank you.'

Clearly regarding his uncle's comments with deep contempt, Oliver turned back to Emily.

'Are people allowed to climb up the spires on the other two towers?' He asked.

'I suppose someone must, if they need to be repaired, but ordinary people are not allowed to do so.'

'But our uncle is not ordinary, he is a baronet,' declared James.

'Let me assure you, you objectionable brat, that this baronet is not even going to attempt climbing the spires, however extraordinary he may be,' declared Sir Gareth frankly. 'Didn't I hear somewhere that there had been a move to take them down?' he asked Emily.

'Yes, in about 1730, I think, but there was such a riot that they gave up the attempt.'

'A riot!' Oliver exclaimed. 'My stars! Miss Whittaker, were you there?'

'No, she was not,' interrupted Sir Gareth. 'That would make her well over seventy years old. Beg her pardon at once!'

Master Whittaker did so, although it must be said that he did not look noticeably abashed.

Emily smiled. 'Much though I would hate to see them go, something really must be done, for they are not very safe.'

'She tells me this, while I am still staying in a house just below the west front,' he mused. 'What a delightful prospect.'

'You mean, they might fall down?' asked Oliver with relish. 'How I would like to be there to see it!'

'Not if you were underneath it,' his uncle pointed out. 'I suggest that you confine your interest to the tower that we are about to climb today.'

To Emily's surprise the boy did so, saying to her eagerly, 'How many steps are there? Has anyone ever fallen off the top?'

'You can count them as you go,' the baronet told him firmly. 'And you might very well find yourself falling off the top if you don't give Miss Whittaker a chance to draw breath. Now run along ahead, both of you.'

'No, wait,' Emily said quickly. 'I will show you another way in.'

'Is it a secret door?' James asked.

'Not exactly secret, but not everybody uses it,' Emily replied. She ushered them in through the door which she customarily used, and which the choir boys also employed. She was impressed to see that both boys took off their caps without being told, and desisted from running about. Clearly Canon Trimmer's wife had given careful instructions to her children as to how they were to conduct themselves when in church.

Sir Gareth closed the door behind them and, smiling down at Emily, said, 'With having to take responsibility for these two boys, I have forgotten to mind my own manners. You are looking charming this morning, ma'am, and I quite forgot to say so.'

Such comments seldom came Emily's way, and she smiled and coloured, her pleasure out of proportion to the mild nature of his compliment. Not knowing how to respond to his words, she simply said, 'Well . . . well, come this way,' as she led them towards a very humble-looking door set in an easily overlooked corner in the south transept.

'We won't get locked in, will we?' Oliver asked, his voice rather hinting that he hoped that this might happen.

'No,' replied Emily. 'This door is not locked.'

'Never? Is that wise?' asked Sir Gareth, wrinkling his brow. The boys had already begun to climb after having been told by Emily where to wait part way up.

'Where would be the danger?' Emily asked. 'The choir boys have all been up these stairs, for the choir master takes them up himself, in order to satisfy their curiosity.'

'But what of those to whom Oliver

referred; those who might want to do themselves a mischief?'

'I don't *think* that anyone has flung themselves off the top,' Emily replied cautiously. 'It's rather a long way to climb for such a purpose, and I think that most people who set off with that idea in their minds would generally have thought better of it by the time they reached the top.'

Sir Gareth gave a short laugh. 'Very well, then, ma'am,' he said. 'Let us ascend. Do you want me to precede you, or would you like to go first?'

Emily opted to lead. 'There are one or two places where there is something to look at, and I will be in a better position to point things out if I go first.'

Ahead, they could hear the echoing of the boys' voices. 'Aurelia will be very grateful to you,' said the baronet from behind as they began the ascent. 'This should wear them out quite nicely.'

At the first stopping place, they passed along a narrow gallery which gave an unusual view down into the cathedral, and a look at the bishop's eye from a very different angle. 'Glorious,' murmured Sir Gareth. 'Quite glorious.'

'Are we nearly there yet?' James asked.

'No, I'm afraid not,' replied Emily. 'Have

161

you had enough? Do you wish to wait downstairs?'

'No,' replied James positively. 'I was just hoping that there was further to go.'

'Is is too much to expect you two brats to linger for a mere ten seconds in order to take in the beauty of this window?' their uncle asked, addressing their retreating backs as they headed for the next flight of stairs.

After this, the staircase became narrower and more difficult to negotiate, but the boys scrambled on ahead, as full of enthusiasm as ever. Emily smiled at the sound of their childish voices, and paused briefly to listen to them, trying to recall when she had first climbed the tower. For a moment she forgot that Sir Gareth was behind her, and was surprised when she felt him touch her lightly on the arm.

'Are you all right, ma'am?' he asked her. His voice sounded barely out of breath.

'What? Oh yes, yes! I beg your pardon. I was just listening to the boys. Shall we continue?'

'By all means.'

Now, as they resumed the climb, Emily found herself suddenly conscious of the baronet behind her; not so much the noise of his boots on the stairs, or the sound of his breathing, even and steady, but simply his solid presence. She found her heart beating faster in a disconcerting manner that had nothing whatsoever to do with the exercise.

For his part, Sir Gareth dropped back a step, anxious not to crowd her. As he did so, however, he realized that he now had an excellent view of the canon's daughter as she ascended. He noted with interest the sway of her shapely hips and realized that she had an excellent figure, a fact which the unfashionable nature of her clothes tended to conceal. He also noticed the suppleness of her trim ankles, and was torn between disapproval of his own voyeuristic behaviour, and a rather urgent desire to make sure that she conducted them up the other two towers another day, so that he might admire this appealing vista on another occasion!

After two more brief halts, at the second of which they were able to look up and admire the wooden beams that had supported the roof for over 400 years, they were able to complete the climb. Emily opened the door, and then they were out into the sunshine, the battlements all around them and the roof itself rising in a gentle slope from their feet.

'May we climb up them?' Oliver asked his uncle, pointing to the leads.

The baronet glanced at Emily and, when she nodded faintly, he said, 'Carefully, then;

no leaning over the sides.' He turned to Emily. 'This is a fine view; well worth the climb.'

'I always think so,' she answered. Her face was flushed from her exertion, and some tendrils of her carefully arranged hair had come loose, and Sir Gareth thought that she looked much younger and prettier. 'When my life seems confined, or limited, I always come up here, and I feel better straight away.' She turned and pointed into the distance. 'I'm told that the cathedral can be seen from those hills. They are in Derbyshire, forty miles away.'

'I must make a point of looking, next time I am in Derbyshire,' he replied, shading his eyes and looking in the direction to which she had pointed.

'Do you visit Derbyshire often?' There was a note of envy in her voice.

'Yes, quite frequently,' he told her. 'I have friends who live there, and I go to visit them whenever I can. I imagine that walking in the hills there, I experience much the same kind of freedom as you find from coming up here.' He paused briefly, then said, 'We must make a pact, Miss Whittaker. Next time I go to Derbyshire, I will arrange to climb to the top of a high hill on a certain day at a certain time, and if you climb to the top of this tower on the same day, then we could wave to each other.'

'That's absurd,' she replied, unsure whether or not he was being serious.

'Yes, it is. Has no one ever talked absurdities to you before?'

'No, never.'

'Not even Dr Pustule?'

She giggled guiltily, then stopped herself. 'Dr Boyle? No, certainly not.'

He opened his mouth to say something else, when Oliver exclaimed, 'Uncle Gareth, come and look at this!'

Emily looked after them. No, certainly no man had ever spoken nonsense to her, she reflected. She was a canon's daughter. She was supposed to be sensible and serious. Talking absurdities smacked of flirtation, and no man had ever wanted to flirt with her. All at once an extraordinary idea had come into her mind. Could Sir Gareth have been trying to get up a flirtation with her? The idea was at once so shocking and yet so exciting, that she had to press her hands against her hot cheeks. She was glad that no one was looking at her at that moment. She turned her back on the rest of the company until Oliver claimed her attention by saying, 'Miss Whittaker! Can we see our house from here?'

When they had had their fill of looking round, the boys said, 'Can we go first down the stairs again?'

'Yes, but be careful,' Emily answered. 'The steps are more tricky as you go down.'

'Careful, and small boys?' murmured the baronet wryly. 'I don't think the two go together. Shall I go first this time?'

'Very well,' Emily replied. In truth, she always liked to have someone else precede her when going down, especially near the top where the steps were more awkward.

Sir Gareth sighed. 'A pity,' he said playfully. 'I so much enjoyed the view on the way up.'

'The view?' Emily asked, confusion mixed with indignation.

'I could not take my eyes off your boots, ma'am,' he replied, his eyes twinkling. 'Why, what else did you think I meant?'

More absurdities! She thought to herself, as they descended; this time she was almost sure that he was trying to flirt with her. Might he try to do so again when they were back downstairs, she wondered? She was not to find out, however, for as they emerged from the door to the tower, they caught sight of Mrs Hughes and her companion, escorted by Lord Stuart.

'Gracious, wherever have you been?' asked Mrs Hughes, her eyebrows soaring.

'Good morning, ma'am,' replied Oliver with a bow, proving that he remembered his manners. 'We have been climbing the tower.'

'Well that would certainly explain how dusty and dishevelled you are,' replied the beauty gently, with a brief glance at Emily so that she knew she was included in the description. 'Miss Whittaker, what remarkable footwear.' Mrs Hughes was becomingly, if frivolously clad in palest pink, and she made Emily feel clumsy and drab.

'Stout shoes are a necessity when negotiating such difficult stairs,' replied Sir Gareth, recalling with pleasure the sight of Miss Whittaker's very feminine ankles. 'Your slippers, now, would never stand the strain.'

'No, I am sure you are right,' replied Mrs Hughes in satisfied tones, delicately pointing her foot so that one cream kid slipper could be seen. She clearly regarded this as a cause for satisfaction. 'In fact, I have walked halfway round this cathedral and I am not sure that I have not done enough walking already.'

'I think you must have done, Annis,' replied the baronet in amused tones. He had noted that Mrs Hughes's ankles were on the thick side. 'Shall we repair to my sister's house and take some refreshment?' He looked round at the whole company.

'I think that perhaps I — ' Emily began; but the baronet interrupted her.

'Miss Whittaker, I insist that you accompany us,' he said. 'Aurelia will never believe that I have been right to the top if you do not corroborate my story.'

'No indeed, for he is a terrible fabricator,' put in Mrs Hughes. 'You really cannot believe a word he says.'

'I protest, Annis,' replied the baronet. 'I am the soul of truthfulness.'

'With gentlemen perhaps,' agreed Mrs Hughes. 'But with ladies, you will tell any story in order to gain an advantage.' She tucked her hand into Sir Gareth's arm. 'The tragedy of it is, that we are too easily convinced.'

So that is how flirting is done, Emily thought to herself, as she followed behind, and turned to engage Miss Wayne in conversation. The two boys walked with Lord Stuart, telling him all that they had seen, to which account he listened with commendable attention.

'This is such a splendid cathedral,' Miss Wayne remarked. She was a little younger than her employer, with light brown hair, modestly dressed, and brown eyes.

'Is it your first visit to Lincoln?' Emily asked her.

'No, I came once as a child. My father, like yours, was a clergyman.'

'Are either of your parents still living?'

Miss Wayne shook her head. 'I am alone in the world,' she admitted.

'For how long have you been working for Mrs Hughes?'

'For a few months only,' Miss Wayne admitted. 'I would really prefer to be a governess. That is the work that I was doing before. But I needed employment, and there were no posts for governesses available, so I came to work for Mrs Hughes.'

She did not say that she hoped that the position would only be a temporary one, but her tone only confirmed what Emily had already suspected, namely, that Miss Wayne was not entirely comfortable in her present situation. Seeing the boys talking with Lord Stuart, and remembering a previous conversation with Mrs Trimmer, Emily began to think that here there might be a solution to a problem.

They were soon out in the sunlight, and then, only moments later, they were being welcomed into Mrs Trimmer's drawing-room with offers of wine or lemonade.

'You didn't wave from the top,' said Mrs Trimmer reproachfully to her sons. 'And I watched for you especially.'

'We were at the wrong angle,' Oliver told his mother. 'Miss Whittaker said so.'

'Miss Whittaker would be quite correct in that observation,' agreed Miss Wayne. 'Is it possible to see the top of the great tower from your house, Master Trimmer?'

'No, it is not, ma'am,' Oliver replied.

'Then you would not be able to wave to your mama, would you?' she suggested.

'It is possible to see the tower from Derbyshire, however,' put in the baronet, as the boys were taken upstairs by a maid after thanking Emily very politely for the morning's outing.

'The day would have to be very clear, I would imagine,' answered Mrs Trimmer thoughtfully. Sir Gareth and Emily exchanged a smile as they remembered their conversation on top of the tower. Mrs Hughes, noticing this exchange, narrowed her eyes a little, and deftly turned the conversation towards London, knowing that Emily would then be unable to play any part in it.

Mr Trimmer, however, who had far better manners, soon introduced the subject of the local countryside. 'Lincolnshire is supposed to be flat, but this area seems to be anything but,' he observed. 'Tell me, Miss Whittaker, are there any places to which I ought to escort my wife? This part of the world is very new to both of us.'

'Gainsborough is an interesting town, and very old,' replied Emily. 'I believe many people think it worthy of a visit.'

'I rode through Gainsborough on my way here,' said Sir Gareth. 'Would I have come through the Lincolnshire Wolds, ma'am?'

'Only if you had come from the coast,' Emily replied.

'The Wolds?' echoed Mrs Hughes, not entirely pleased that the canon's prim daughter had become the centre of attention.

'It is a name given to the rolling countryside to the east of here,' Emily replied.

'We must get up an excursion to visit some of these places, my dear Mrs Trimmer,' declared Mrs Hughes. 'For I am as unfamiliar with this part of the world as any of you.'

'What about tomorrow?' suggested Lord Stuart. 'We might as well make the most of this fine weather. Are you free, Trimmer?'

The clergyman agreed that he was. 'We can take the barouche,' he suggested.

Aurelia frowned. 'The barouche might be a little crowded with Mrs Hughes, Miss Whittaker, Miss Wayne, myself and the two boys.'

'Oliver would probably like to ride,' suggested Mr Trimmer.

Emily, surprised and pleased at being included, noted Mrs Hughes's expression of chagrin, but she felt bound to say regretfully, 'I fear that I cannot join you tomorrow. I am committed to going to the prison.'

The baronet clicked his tongue and shook his head, saying in mock disapproval, 'Oh Miss Whittaker, Miss Whittaker! When will you learn from the penalties of law-breaking?'

Mrs Hughes simply looked mystified at this, but Mrs Trimmer laughed. 'Gareth, don't be so absurd,' she said. 'Emily, if you cannot come tomorrow, then we will arrange the expedition for another day — perhaps the day after tomorrow.'

But Mr Trimmer had an objection to this. 'I fear that I shall not be able to join you that day,' he said regretfully. 'I am engaged to speak with the bishop.'

'And we do not know what the weather may do later in the week,' Mrs Hughes pointed out. 'Naturally, I should be very sorry to leave Miss Whittaker behind, but she has already seen something of the countryside around here, whereas Mr Trimmer has not. She can always come with us another day.'

'But we should then be without her local knowledge,' Sir Gareth objected. 'As for the weather, we do not know what it may do tomorrow, either. Alan, are you engaged three days hence?'

'No, I am not,' Mr Trimmer replied.

'Then let it be for Friday,' the baronet suggested, in such a positive tone that everyone else agreed at once, although Mrs Hughes looked a little grudging.

It was agreed that Oliver should ride with his father and the gentlemen, thus making more space in the barouche. 'James will make a fuss, no doubt, but he must learn that seniority carries certain privileges,' said Mrs Trimmer.

A short time after this, Emily begged leave to be excused. 'I am expected at home,' she said. 'Thank you for the lemonade.'

Sir Gareth and Mr Trimmer both stood as she made her farewells, but to her surprise, the baronet accompanied her to the front door. 'Thank you for this morning,' he said, taking her hand. 'The climb was invigorating, and the views were magnificent.'

'It was no trouble,' she replied, nervously conscious of the feeling of his large, capable hand enveloping her small one. 'I am always looking for excuses to climb the tower.'

'I shall send word to let you know on Thursday, what time we shall be setting out,' he responded, lifting her hand and kissing it lightly.

As she walked back to her own house, she cradled the hand as if it were something precious. His touch had sent tingles all along her spine. She reminded herself that Mrs Hughes, who clearly knew him well, had said that he was a flirt whose word was not to be trusted. This description did not match with the man who had chatted so easily with his nephews, and admired the cathedral and the views with such genuine interest. Unfortunately, she could also recall his bland assertion that he had been admiring her boots when she was sure that he had been looking at her ankles! Of course that was very shocking, but ruefully, she had to confess that she was no better, for, as she had followed him down the stairs, she had spent a considerable amount of time admiring his splendid shoulders.

He was just flirting, she told herself sternly, and no doubt he would have done so even more, had he known the shocking nature of her thoughts. Well, she would have the chance to observe him in Gainsborough to discover if he displayed the same flirtatious tendencies. The only problem with this reasoning was that if he decided he was going to flirt with Mrs Hughes, she really didn't want to watch.

12

Two days before the outing to Gainsborough was due to take place, Mrs Trimmer came round to see Emily. Canon Whittaker was at home and he stayed to talk with his daughter's visitor for a little while before going to his study.

Once the ladies were alone, Mrs Trimmer said rather diffidently, 'I was wondering, Emily, what you were intending to wear for our outing to Gainsborough?'

'To wear?' Emily echoed, uncomprehendingly. This was a subject to which she never usually gave very much thought, partly because her father had always discouraged any vanity in dress, and partly because she did not have a great deal to choose from. She had never had a dress allowance; had never dreamed of having such a thing, and there were no female relatives in her family to suggest to her father that such provision should be made for her. She saved what she could from the housekeeping money, and then bought for her own needs. Almost inevitably, everything that she purchased tended to be hard-wearing and sensible, and although she never looked shabby, she never looked fashionable either.

No one amongst her acquaintance ever said very much about her clothes, not even Dr Boyle. To tell the truth, she had got out of the habit of thinking about them. It had seemed as if from the moment that she had been judged to be on the shelf, that as far as society was concerned she had more or less disappeared.

Aurelia had thought long and hard about coming to see Emily, for she did not want to say anything that would seem like unkind criticism. But there was no denying that Emily dressed 'old' for her years, and Aurelia had not liked the way that Annis Hughes had regarded her friend with such thinly veiled contempt.

Mrs Hughes was not exactly a young widow. In fact, Aurelia suspected that there was not such a large gap in age between her and Sir Gareth, at forty, as she would have liked others to believe. But she knew how to make the best of herself, and there was no denying that she was a very attractive woman. Had her reputation been good, Aurelia would, she told herself, have nobly allowed her brother to follow his inclinations if they lay in Mrs Hughes's direction.

Unfortunately, however, there were some

rather unsavoury tales going around concerning that lady; whilst some of them could be dismissed as mere gossip, others came from a more reliable source.

The only child of Theodore and Rosemary Bing, Annis Bing had begun her adult life by following a conventionally acceptable path and becoming engaged to the son of a local landowner. Her parents had been very satisfied with this match. Before the marriage could take place, however, the young lady had become infatuated with one Granville Hunter, a notorious libertine. She had permitted his attentions causing her fiancé to react with a baffled distress that he could not hide. Inevitably, the engagement was broken, and Miss Bing married Mr Hunter in the teeth of her parents' opposition.

The newly married couple went to live in London, where they proceeded to spend freely, gamble recklessly, and flirt outrageously. Eventually, Hunter succumbed to the rigours of his way of life, leaving his widow to lavish huge sums on mourning attire, and then to continue her career with undiminished enthusiasm.

For a time, widowhood and a number of loose connections suited her very well, but her inheritance was not bottomless, and soon she began to look around her for a wealthy husband.

The late Mr Hughes had been a wealthy man, with a father in trade and a mother from the ranks of the aristocracy. When she had met him, he was a grieving widower, with a son and daughter both still in the schoolroom.

Mrs Trimmer had been acquainted with the wife of the vicar of the parish in which Mr Hughes resided. This lady had written to her about the callously manipulative way in which Mrs Hunter had sought to entrap Mr Hughes, persuading him into marriage before he had even finished his period of mourning.

The new Mrs Hughes had insisted on continuing a life of unbridled gaiety in London, regardless of the fact that this was not her husband's preference at all. She spent money more freely than ever, attending every possible function and, it was rumoured, taking lovers. Again, Mrs Trimmer had more than gossip to rely upon, for the brother of a friend of hers had become entangled with the lady, and her friend had written, telling her of the affair.

The marriage had not lasted long. Mr Hughes's heart had had a weakness that no one had ever suspected, and within three years he was dead. No sooner had he passed away than his widow packed both of the children off to school, with the instruction that they were not to come home, even during the holidays, until they were grown up.

Now, rumours were going about that Mrs Hughes might like to change her name again, but that this time she was hoping for a title.

Decidedly this was not the kind of person that Mrs Trimmer wanted to see married to her adored elder brother. She was far too wise to say anything against the lady, however, knowing that such criticism might have the very wrong kind of effect. Nevertheless she did long to see him settled as happily as she was herself with her husband Alan, and she could not resist doing a little match-making.

She had thought at first that Jennifer Cummings might do nicely for him. But on subsequent occasions when she had met the girl, both at her own house when Mrs Cummings had called, and at the Cummingses' home when she had returned the courtesy, she had revised her opinion. Jennifer was a pretty girl who would no doubt blossom into a charming young woman. At present, however, she was exactly the kind of debutante with whom Gareth had recently become very bored, and his manner towards her was decidedly avuncular. Slowly and surely, Mrs Trimmer was coming to the conclusion that Emily might do very well.

For one thing, she was unquestionably a lady, and the baronet appeared to enjoy her company. She had also, through sheer innocence, Mrs Trimmer suspected, employed with him none of the tactics that many society ladies had tried. There were no veiled glances from Emily; no calculated stumbling; no grasping of his arm and holding on for longer than necessary. As a consequence, she had quite unintentionally succeeded in intriguing him. If Gareth decided that he wanted to pursue the canon's daughter, then he would have to do all the work, which would, his sister decided, be very good for him.

True, Emily was past the first blush of youth but what did that really matter? Of course, Gareth would need an heir, but then Aurelia herself was much the same age as Emily and was secretly hoping that she might very soon have more news of a delicate nature to impart to her husband.

Clearly, Emily was not used to mixing in polite society, although there was nothing to blush for in her company manners, but then Aurelia sometimes wondered how much her brother really enjoyed London. True, he was popular and played his part in the season each year, but he also seemed to be happy spending time on his estate in Nottingham-shire, where he was a conscientious landlord. Emily would certainly find much to fulfil her in the traditional role of the lady of the manor, visiting the tenants, supporting schools, and encouraging young people to learn trades.

Just as Aurelia was too wise to criticize Mrs Hughes, however, she was far too astute to promote Emily's cause openly. Instead, she had made it her business to invite Dr Boyle to go with them to Gainsborough, and he had accepted with alacrity. Now, it only remained to make sure that Emily would be attired in something more becoming than her usual sombre gowns. Boyle must be made to be more attentive; if he seemed more interested in her, then Gareth could not fail to notice it. It would do him no harm to be reminded that Emily already had a suitor.

'I am told that tomorrow will be a warm day,' said Mrs Trimmer in pursuit of her goal. 'I am concerned that you may be too hot if you do not have anything lighter to wear. May I come and see what you are thinking of putting on?'

Emily had never had a friend with whom to compare clothes or discuss outfits, and so it was with a feeling very like excitement that she escorted Mrs Trimmer upstairs to her bedroom and opened the cupboard so that she could see her gowns hanging up inside.

Aurelia Trimmer barely repressed a gasp of dismay. No wonder Emily always looked older than she really was. Everything hanging there was sensible, serviceable and drab; there was nothing frivolous or pretty.

For her part, Emily was very used to seeing this unexciting selection; now, with Aurelia by her side, it was as if she saw her clothes with new eyes. Suddenly, she pictured their party going to Gainsborough on the morrow, with everyone dressed attractively apart from herself, trailing in the rear, no doubt with Miss Wayne. They would almost make a matched pair. 'Oh dear,' she said involuntarily.

Mrs Trimmer took a deep breath. If Emily herself realized how unsuitable her clothes were, then her work would be made that much easier. 'Now listen, my dear, I have an idea and I think that it will work splendidly. I have a gown, in a charming shade of buttercup yellow, and I think that it would become you to perfection.'

'You want to lend me one of your gowns?' asked Emily, her eyes opening very wide.

'I would like to give it to you,' Aurelia answered. Seeing a stubborn look come over

Emily's face and anticipating a refusal, the canon's wife went on confidentially, 'It is becoming a little too tight for me,' she said frankly, then dropped her voice. 'To tell you the truth, my dear, and this is a very great secret indeed, so secret that not even Alan knows, I am almost sure that I am expecting an interesting event in the spring. If that is the case, then I shall need new gowns anyway, for the ones I am now wearing will not fit me.'

'An interesting event?' Emily echoed, her face glowing. 'Oh, how wonderful! When will you know for certain?'

'Very soon, now. And then, if I am right, you will be able to take some of my gowns without feeling guilty at all. In fact,' she added with what she felt was great cunning, 'you will be doing me a favour, for they are far too good to be thrown away, and I do hate waste. I think it is a sin.'

Emily eyed her friend suspiciously. She might be inexperienced in some senses, but she was not naïve. 'Are you trying to pull the wool over my eyes?' she asked.

'Not at all,' replied Aurelia Trimmer virtuously. 'But, perhaps, a gown over your head?'

Emily had to laugh at that. 'Very well, then,' she answered. 'I confess that my

wardrobe is chosen for practical consider-
ations for the most part, and I shall be glad to
wear something pretty. But for the time
being, let us say that it is lent, until you are
sure about your . . . your condition.'

Realizing that she had won her point,
Mrs Trimmer said no more on the matter.
A short time after she had returned
home, a servant came round with a box for
Miss Whittaker. Trying not to show how
excited she felt, Emily hurried upstairs with
it, went into her room and closed the door.
She opened the box and could not hold
back a gasp of delight. The gown was
just the shade that Aurelia had described,
with short puff sleeves a high waist and a
deep frill. Inside the box with the gown
was a bonnet, with ribbons that matched
the gown, and a charming bunch of
buttercups fashioned from silk, and fastened
to one side. Inside the box was a note
which read:

I could hardly lend you the gown
without letting you borrow the bonnet
that goes with it, now could I?

Emily smiled and, impulsively, she went to
the mirror set on top of the chest of drawers
in her room and tried on the bonnet. She was

amazed at the transformation, and particularly at the way in which the colour of the ribbons and the buttercups added a glow to her face. All at once, she recalled the baronet's judgement concerning the white bonnet. He was right, she said to herself: I need colour.

She waited to try the gown on until she was sure that her father was out of the house and would be gone for some time. She was convinced that he would disapprove of her new appearance, thinking it frivolous. Once he was out of the way, she put on the gown, and stood staring at herself in the mirror for a long time. It was like looking at someone ten years younger. Where did my youth go? she asked herself. Then, before she could become maudlin, she made herself look more carefully at the gown to see whether it needed any alteration to make it fit properly.

In the end, she decided that although it was a little loose, this did not matter enough to signify. She was not as tall as Mrs Trimmer, so she would need to shorten the gown a little. She was not sure whether to simply take up the flounce, or remove it altogether and take up the body of the gown before putting the flounce back. After a little thought, she decided that since the gown was on loan and not yet given, the former course of action would be the easier to undo if she had to give it back. She was already coming to the conclusion that she did not want to do so.

Before she took the gown off again, she slipped out of her room and, being careful not to be seen by anyone, hurried along the passage to her grandfather's bedchamber.

'Look, Grandpapa,' she said, as soon as she was inside the room. 'Look at this pretty gown. Mrs Trimmer has lent it to me. I don't think I have ever worn anything so pretty before. Do you like the colour?' She twirled around in front of the motionless old gentleman. It was as she was just turning back towards the bed that she saw his eyelids flicker, and his eyes open fractionally. 'Grandpapa?' she said, hurrying to sit on the bed and take his hand. 'Grandpapa, can you hear me?'

The old man did not speak but slowly closed his eyes again. It was a tiny enough reaction, but it was more than anyone else had got from him in many weeks.

'I know that you heard me then,' she said, 'and I shall keep coming and talking to you every day. One day, I know, you will reply to me.'

She thought for a long time about whether to tell her father what had happened, but in the end decided against it. It had been such a very slight thing, and might mean nothing at all. If it happened again, she would inform him of it.

13

It was late that afternoon when Dr Boyle called round to see her. His face was serious and his manner grave and sensible so she knew that he had come to see her on a professional matter.

'Kennedy has been condemned to death,' he told her.

'Oh no,' she exclaimed, more in distress than in surprise. Rob Kennedy had always been an unreliable man, weak and easily influenced by others. Lately rumour had it that he had been spending too much time with a gang of men involved in all kinds of underhand activity. Several of them had broken into an empty house in order to steal property while the owner was away. The others had escaped, but Kennedy had been cornered by two grooms who had been sleeping above the stables. In his panic, he had killed one of them. Given his previous bad character, execution was inevitable.

'Although it was expected, I fear that Madge Kennedy will be much shocked,' the doctor said.

'Has she been told?' Emily asked.

The doctor nodded. 'The priest went straight round to see her from the prison. My fear is that such news will cause the baby to come too quickly. I am on my way to see her now, and would be grateful if you would come with me.'

'Yes, of course, I will do so,' replied Emily. 'Just give me ten minutes to collect my bonnet and find something for the family from the kitchens.'

They took the long, winding route down the hill, going through Pottergate and down New Road, for the more direct route, down Steep Hill, was far too precipitous to be attempted in a carriage. Of course, gentlemen had negotiated the hill from time to time as part of a wager, but the doctor would never do such a thing. She was conscious of a feeling almost of regret. She had often walked down Steep Hill, and made the challenging return journey as well and she had sometimes wondered what it would be like to make the descent at speed. Certainly they would never do such a thing in the doctor's modest gig!

The family that they were visiting lived in a mean dwelling in the lower town, not far from the Stonebow.

'When is the execution to be?' Emily asked the doctor as he helped her down from her seat.

'Tomorrow morning,' Boyle replied. 'Would you — '

'Yes, of course,' Emily replied, without a second thought. Then a moment later, she felt guilty for being relieved that her pastoral duties would not mean that she would have to miss the outing to Gainsborough.

Mrs Kennedy was pathetically glad to see them, and fell onto Emily's neck in gratitude. 'Oh, Miss Whittaker, I'm that glad to see you! Oh, my poor Rob! My poor fatherless children! Oh dear, oh dear!' Supported by Emily, she sat down in one of the only two chairs that the room contained and throwing her apron over her head, gave way to noisy grief.

Emily crouched down next to her, saying nothing for a time, but simply allowing the woman to feel that she was not alone. When her sobs had subsided a little the doctor, who had been talking quietly to the three children, (who looked confused and not a little frightened), said to Emily, 'Would you be so good as to make a cup of tea for Mrs Kennedy, whilst I take her into the next room and examine her?'

Emily had taken the precaution of bringing some tea with her, knowing that only thus would Mrs Kennedy be assured of a comforting brew. The Kennedys' own tea, as she knew from experience, tasted very much as if the leaves had been swept from the factory floor, and probably brewed once or twice already.

She had also put some bread, butter, and bacon in her basket, together with a few other items which she knew the family would not be able to afford. She now got these out, together with a bottle of claret, which she showed to the oldest girl, who was about eight years old. 'Jessie, you must give your mother a small glass of this every day. Put the cork back carefully each time, and do not have any yourself.'

'Why not, miss?' the little girl asked. The children were simply, even poorly dressed, but looked quite clean. Mrs Kennedy was evidently doing her best, although how long she would be able to do so, given this fresh blow, Emily did not like to guess.

'Because it tastes horrid,' Emily replied seriously. 'At least, you will think so.'

Dr Boyle soon came back into the room, and eyed Emily's preparations with approval. 'That tea will do her good,' he said. 'Why don't you take some in to Mrs Kennedy, and I'll cut some bread for the children.'

As she picked up two cups of tea, one for Mrs Kennedy and one for herself, she marvelled again at how much more attractive the doctor became when he was being professional. He ought to marry a nurse, she thought to herself, then his wife would see the best side of him all the time.

Mrs Kennedy was much calmer when Emily took her the tea, and she was soon willing to talk. 'I knew it would come to this, miss,' she said wretchedly. 'I knew it would; but would he listen? Hundreds of times I've tried to tell him, over and over, not to have anything to do with them scoundrels, but he always thought he was too cunning to be caught. Well, now, he's been proved wrong.' Emily was silent. After a few moments, Mrs Kennedy spoke again. 'No doubt you'll think me unfeeling, miss, but I'm not. I shall weep on the morrow, just as I've wept today, but it will be for the man he was, and not the man he is now. The lad I married disappeared long since.'

'Is there anyone you wish me to inform of this sad business?' Emily asked her. 'A friend or relative, perhaps?'

Mrs Kennedy opened a small box which stood on a rough chest next to the bed. 'This is where my sister lives,' she said, handing Emily a piece of paper with an address written on it. 'She married a man who works on the land out through Newport Gate and on a bit that way. She might help me.'

'Would you like me to write to her for you?' Emily asked, looking at the address.

'Yes, if you would, miss. I can write a bit, but I can't seem to get my head to it at the moment.'

A short time after this, one of Mrs Kennedy's neighbours came to sit with her, and Emily and the doctor departed. 'I am glad that the poor woman does not want to attend the execution,' said Boyle as they began the return journey. 'I do not think that that would have been at all wise. Would you like me to bring you down here in the gig?'

'No, thank you, there is no need,' Emily replied. 'I will walk. In any case, you will be needed at the execution, no doubt.'

He sighed. 'Yes, I fear that it is my turn,' he confirmed. 'It's not a duty that I relish at all, but someone has to be there.'

★   ★   ★

It had not been so hard after all, Emily reflected as she toiled up Steep Hill the following day. Unlike yesterday, Mrs Kennedy had been calm, and she had already told the children that their father had gone to Heaven. 'Not that I suppose he has really, miss,' she said confidentially when, after saying the Lord's Prayer with their mother and listening to a passage

193

from the Bible read by Emily, they had gone outside to play for a few minutes. 'Oh, my poor Rob! What would his mother have said, God rest her soul? Thank heaven she's not alive to see this day!' She did shed a few tears then, and gladly drank the cup of tea that Emily made for her.

Before leaving, Emily pressed a small purse of money into her hands. 'It's just a little from the church poor fund,' she said. 'It's not much, but perhaps you will hear from your sister soon. I sent the letter as soon as I got home.'

'God bless you, miss,' said Mrs Kennedy, waving her off at the door.

No, it could have been much worse; like the time when a woman whose son was being executed had insisted on going to the hanging. Emily had felt obliged to go with her and had had to restrain her from climbing onto the cart with him.

Thoughts of the morning's events, together with other sombre memories occupied her mind while she walked, so that she was surprised to discover that she was entering Castle Square already. She looked at the castle. It had been around the back of it, just to the right of the north gate, that Rob Kennedy had so recently been hanged. She could not repress a shudder.

'Why, Miss Whittaker!' exclaimed an affected society voice. 'How very energetic you are!' Emily looked around blankly to see Mrs Hughes, exquisitely dressed in powder blue with a white parasol trimmed with blue ribbons. One daintily gloved hand was resting on Sir Gareth's sleeve and a frivolous bonnet framed her face and contrasted charmingly with her dark curls.

'Good day, Miss Whittaker,' said the baronet, touching his hat politely. She looked weary, he thought, and not just because she had climbed the hill. She seemed inflicted with a weariness that had somehow seeped into her bones.

'Good day,' she replied, sounding as if her heart was not in it.

'Are you going to the prison again?' Mrs Hughes asked, eyeing Emily's dove-grey gown with barely veiled contempt. 'You certainly look dressed for it.'

At this, Emily's shoulders straightened and her eyes flashed fire. 'No, I am just returning from visiting a woman whose husband has been executed today. She was very distressed, as I am sure even you can imagine, Mrs Hughes. I need to go home and change, if you will excuse me.'

Without waiting for a response, she hurried away from them towards the Exchequer gate and the cathedral beyond, ignoring Sir Gareth calling after her.

'Well, really!' declared Mrs Hughes. 'Such provincial manners!'

At this point, Miss Wayne, who had been walking a little behind them, drew closer.

'Forgive me, my dear Annis,' said the baronet, his courteous tone at variance with the cold expression in his eyes. 'I have recalled an urgent errand that must be performed immediately.'

'Why, what upon earth can it be?'

'Do not concern yourself with it,' he replied smoothly, with a slight bow. 'It's just a provincial matter.'

★   ★   ★

After he had left Mrs Hughes, he went through the Exchequer gate and walked around the south side of the cathedral, heading for the Whittakers' residence in Priorygate. He was half expecting to discover that she had gone to the cathedral, but she had said that she was going home to change, and he did not think that Emily would deliberately tell lies.

'Yes, sir, she is in,' said Mary, dimpling up at him. 'I think she went into the drawing-room.'

Mary was opening the door, when they heard an enormous clatter from inside. They were just in time to see Emily picking up a cushion. She looked around at them, a guilty expression on her face. The fire irons were strewn at her feet.

'Thank you, my dear,' said Sir Gareth firmly, looking at the maid. 'Perhaps you could bring us some wine.'

'Yes, sir, at once,' replied Mary with a curtsy, before leaving the room, closing the door behind her.

'I suppose you have come to upbraid me because I was rude,' said Emily, still clutching the cushion. 'But I am afraid that I have no time for your silly society chit-chat.'

'Miss Whittaker — ' Sir Gareth began, but Emily would not allow him to finish.

'I am sure that you both looked very fine this morning, just as I know that I look exceedingly dowdy. I do not need Mrs Hughes's affected remarks or your admirable guidance on good taste to tell me so.'

'Ma'am — ' the baronet began again; but once more Emily interrupted him.

'But,' she said emphatically, 'I cannot see that a gown like Mrs Hughes's would have fared very well had she had to go where I have been. I am equally certain that Mrs

Kennedy did not care two straws what I was wearing.'

At this, she did pause to draw breath, and Sir Gareth took advantage of this by simply remarking, 'Quite right. I agree with you entirely.'

This was such a surprise to Emily that all she could do was stare at him open-mouthed. At that moment, the door opened and Mary came in with a tray bearing the wine that the baronet had asked for. 'Thank you, I will pour,' he told her. Then when Mary had gone, he said, 'A glass of this will do you good after your ordeal.'

At this, Emily put down the cushion and busied herself with setting the fire irons to rights, her face aflame. She had spoken hastily and emotionally; now she was remembering the infelicitous nature of some of the things that she had said and her criticisms of the baronet in particular. But, because he had startled her so much, she said, whilst still looking down at the fire irons, 'You agree with me?'

'Yes, of course,' he answered. 'I won't pretend that I've visited people in prison as often as you have, but I have made such visits at times, and would never wear my best clothes for those errands.'

'You have visited people in prison?' she

echoed in surprise.

'Certainly,' he responded, giving her a glass of wine, which she accepted. 'Sometimes members of tenant families or relatives of servants get themselves into trouble and I find myself obliged to try to sort things out. On one or two occasions I have been to see someone in the condemned cell. On both of those occasions it fell to my lot to break the news to some family members.' He paused briefly, allowing this information to penetrate her mind. Then he smiled and said, in a tone of gentle reproof, 'You really shouldn't tar all of us with the same brush, you know. May we sit down? I cannot unless you do so as well.'

Emily looked at him blankly for a moment or two then said breathlessly, 'Oh yes; yes, of course.' No sooner had she done so, however, than she sprang to her feet again. 'Sir Gareth, I must ask your pardon.'

'For what?' he asked teasingly. 'For making me bob up and down like a jack-in-the-box?' He, too, had risen.

She had to smile at his words. 'For that as well,' she agreed. 'But my apology is chiefly for the terse way in which I spoke to you in the street, and then my incivility to you when you came here just now.'

They sat down again. 'Your attitude was understandable,' said the baronet. 'You had just come from a scene of grief and hardship, and were confronted with two society people out enjoying themselves, who had no idea what your feelings might have been.' He paused briefly. 'You will have to excuse Annis. I fear she is not very sensitive.'

'No, but it was not fair of me,' Emily persisted. 'Had I given the matter but a small amount of thought, I should have realized that it was not for me to judge another person's actions. In any case, you are on holiday here, and I am not. I dare say that if I were staying on your estate, I should find that you would be very busy and I would feel idle.' It had seemed to be such a sensible comment when she had begun to make it. Now, she feared that he would think that she was angling for an invitation and she coloured.

He was sorely tempted to tease her, but his instinct told him that now would not be a good time. Instead, he said, 'I hope that you are feeling a little more yourself. I will take my leave, but I look forward to seeing you tomorrow on the outing to Gainsborough.' She looked at him, biting her lip, then glanced away. He narrowed his eyes. 'You are not thinking of forgoing that because of the tragedy you have witnessed today?' he questioned. 'You of all people need a little diversion, if only to refresh yourself so that you are ready to deal with the next crisis.'

They both stood up. He crossed to her side, took her hand and looked down at it for a moment or two. 'You know, if you *were* visiting my estate — and I trust that you will do so, before too long — I would set aside my tasks from time to time in order to show you around. Tomorrow, you will simply be doing the same.'

'Thank you,' she said, smiling as he lifted her hand to his lips.

He turned to leave, but before he did so, he looked back and said with a twinkle, 'By the way, I'm glad Aurelia taught you that thing with the fire irons. It always helps her, I know.'

★ ★ ★

She went up to her room early in the evening and sat by the window, taking up the hem of the yellow gown. While she was sewing, her mind was free to go over the incidents of the day. She was sorry that she had been so unguarded in her words to Mrs Hughes, and yet that scene had brought unexpected benefits. It had brought Sir Gareth round; had he not come, she would no doubt have spent all her time thinking about the Kennedy family. She recalled Sir Gareth's suggestion that she might visit his estate. Did he really mean it, she wondered?

Going to sleep proved to be difficult that night. It seemed a very long time since she had arranged to go out for the day on an expedition of pleasure, and she found herself feeling excited, almost like a little girl again.

Suddenly a memory came back to her from the recesses of her mind. She could not have been more than five years old, when she had wandered into the kitchen and had found cook very busy, working at the table and calling instructions to another servant. She must have asked what was happening, because cook had turned to her, red-faced and flustered, and had said, 'Why, Miss Emily, Master Patrick is coming home, and how I am to get all this done, I shall never know.'

Then Emily's memory did a little skip, and she now recalled being in the nursery, and hearing the sound of a door slamming, then footsteps coming up the stairs two at a time. The next moment, the door had opened, and suddenly she was flying through the air, screaming with laughter, and grasping at a head of wavy fair hair with her chubby hands.

That must have been Patrick, she thought to herself. Somehow, her father's constant emphasis upon the young man's virtues had fostered memories of which he would approve, and pushed others to the back of her mind. She thought of the recollections of her brother which came to her easily: of Patrick sitting decorously at the table; going to Father's study to read some Greek; sitting next to her in the cathedral.

Oh, but there was another memory! She had been sitting in the angel choir during the service, and getting very bored, when she had chanced to look up at where the Lincoln imp was perched. Then she had glanced at Patrick and in a flash, he had pulled a face at her of such unparalleled hideousness that she had started to giggle, and Patrick had hurriedly covered her face with a handkerchief, insisting later that she had been sneezing.

Lying beneath the covers, she laughed at the memory, then suddenly, driven by a sudden impulse, she got out of bed, lit a candle, wrapped a shawl about her and tiptoed downstairs to the drawing-room. Holding the candle so that it would throw light upon her brother's portrait, she stared up at the young man depicted there. *Imagine him in the red and gold mess dress that he so much desired*, Sir Gareth had said. As she contemplated the picture, she tried hard to do that very thing. Then, picking up the candle, she turned to go. Later, she decided that it must have been a trick of the light; but at that moment, she could have sworn that those hazel eyes sparkled with merriment.

14

When she woke up, the yellow gown was the first thing that she saw. The colour seemed to bring sunshine into her room, even with the curtains still closed, and after a few moments, she realized that she was lying in bed smiling.

A short time after this, there was a knock at the door and Mary, the maid, came in with a tray. Emily had told her father that she would be going out with the Trimmers and their party. Not wanting him to see her gown before it was time for them all to leave, she had taken the very unusual step of asking for breakfast to be brought to her in her room the next day. This meant that she would not have to go downstairs until she heard the door bell ring.

'It's a fine day, miss,' Mary said, putting the tray down on the bedside table, then adjusting Emily's pillows behind her when she sat up. 'I think you'll have a good run to Gainsborough today. Just enough rain in the night to lay the dust, I reckon.' Having spread a little cloth over Emily's knees, and given her the tray on which there was a slice of ham, a poached egg, some toast and a cup of tea, she turned to go. 'Oh, miss!' she exclaimed, halting in her tracks. 'What a lovely gown! Is that what you're planning to wear today?'

'Yes, it is,' Emily replied. Then, a little uncertainly, she added 'It is quite unlike anything I have worn before.'

'I should think it is, miss,' Mary replied approvingly. 'You'll look very becoming, too, if you don't mind my saying so. May I come up and dress your hair for you before you go out?'

'Thank you, Mary, I should be glad of your help,' Emily replied, almost shyly.

'I'll just be getting your hot water, then.'

Reminding herself sternly that it was only small, spoiled children who insisted that they were too excited to eat, Emily applied herself determinedly to her breakfast, and by dint of telling herself that she could not be sure when or where they might be eating next, she managed to get it all down shortly before Mary came back in with the hot water.

Once out of bed, she lifted the corner of one curtain and saw that, as Mary had said, it promised to be a fine day. Humming to herself, she washed and dressed, taking a little more time than usual, so as to put off the special moment of donning the buttercup-yellow gown. Then at last, when she could delay no longer, she pulled it on over her head and fastened it, trying not to look at her reflection until it was on properly. Then, quite deliberately, she crossed to the window, opened the curtains, then went to the mirror, and looked at herself.

The gown might have been made for her. The neckline was demure, much to her relief, but the way that it was cut seemed to give length to her neck, and the bodice made the most of her curves which were, in truth, a little more modest than those of Mrs Trimmer. The colour brought out golden lights in her hair and gave warmth to her eyes; and if she had had any doubts in her mind as to whether the gown became her, Mary's cry of 'Oh miss, you look beautiful!' immediately allayed them.

'Now come and sit down, miss, and I'll dress your hair,' said the little maid, taking up Emily's brush and comb. The girl worked quickly, and by the time she had finished, she had achieved a style that was both modest and becoming.

'Thank you, Mary,' Emily said gratefully. 'You have done very well.'

'I wouldn't mind doing more of this kind of work, miss,' the maid admitted. 'But you never seem to need me very much.' She sounded wistful, and Emily, who had always congratulated herself on not giving the servants extra burdens, wondered whether she had actually deprived them of some of the more interesting tasks thereby.

It was only as Emily picked up the bonnet that she gave a gasp of dismay.

'What is it, miss?' Mary asked.

'My feet!' Emily exclaimed, in a voice that was very like a wail. 'What shall I wear on my feet?' Her black boots were the newest and the most comfortable that she possessed, but she could not possibly wear a pair of black boots with a buttercup-yellow gown.

Mary thought for a moment. 'Wait a minute, miss,' she said. 'I've got an idea.' She left the room, and came back a short time later with a pair of light brown boots in her hand. They looked much daintier than Emily's black ones. 'Those would do, wouldn't they?'

'Why yes, if they fit me,' Emily answered, sitting down so that Mary could help her on with them. They did fit and felt as if they would be very comfortable. 'Where are these from?' Emily asked.

'They're my best ones, and nearly new, miss,' the maid answered proudly. 'I'd be honoured if you'd wear them.'

'Mary, this is very kind of you,' Emily declared. 'Are you sure?'

'Certain,' Mary replied. 'I've seen how well

you look after your own things, so they won't come to harm. Besides, I'll be right glad to think of them wandering around Gainsborough with that Sir Gareth! I wouldn't mind a stroll in the moonlight on *his* arm!'

'Mary!' exclaimed Emily in a shocked tone.

'Sorry, miss,' replied Mary, not noticeably dashed, 'but he is handsome, isn't he? And what a fine pair of shoulders!' Emily did not dignify this with a reply; but she noticed that Mary was grinning as she helped her on with her bonnet.

The door bell sounded promptly at half past nine, and Emily's heart suddenly started to beat rather quickly. Who would have come to collect her, she wondered. She glanced in the mirror one last time, and knew a moment's indecision. Briefly, she wished that she was wearing one of her own, uninteresting gowns so that she could blend into the background, but it was too late to change now, so with some trepidation she left her room and walked onto the landing. She could see her father talking with Sir Gareth in the hall. Gathering all her courage together, she began to make her descent. The two men glanced up and both fell silent, and Emily, looking down at the baronet, saw on his face an expression that could only mean admiration.

If those were his sentiments, they were undoubtedly hers as well. Today, he was dressed in a dark-green riding coat and buff breeches, and his clothes fitted him to perfection, his coat stretched without a single visible wrinkle across the shoulders that Mary admired so much. As for his boots, Emily could not remember ever seeing any so shiny before. Mary was right: he certainly was handsome. This very thought gave her cheeks a most becoming colour as she finished her descent.

Canon Whittaker was the first to speak, and to his daughter's great astonishment said, 'Emily, my dear, how lovely you look! Very pretty indeed! Would you not say so, Sir Gareth?'

'You have taken the very words out of my mouth,' the baronet replied, lifting Emily's hand and kissing it.

'Thank you, Papa,' Emily said. She had been preparing herself for all kinds of reactions from her father, ranging from a horrified insistence that she change immediately, to a sorrowful disapproval that she had squandered money on fripperies. So astonished was she at his unexpected praise that by the time she had remembered that Sir Gareth had also complimented her, it was too late to thank him without making it sound like an afterthought.

'I do not recall seeing that gown before,' remarked the clergyman, before she could make a decision one way or the other. 'You must wear it more often. It suits you.'

'I am glad that you think so,' Emily answered tentatively, replying to the second part of her father's speech and ignoring the first.

'Are you ready, ma'am?' Sir Gareth asked her.

'Oh yes, certainly. We must not keep the others waiting. Goodbye, Papa.'

'Goodbye, Emily,' answered her father, surprising her very much by leaning forward and kissing her warmly. 'Have a lovely outing.'

'You look puzzled,' said Sir Gareth, when they had got outside. He extended his arm to her and after a brief hesitation she took it, reflecting that when Dr Boyle had done so quite recently, she had quite deliberately put her hands behind her back.

His comment took her aback, and before she could think of another reply, she found herself saying, 'To be honest, I was preparing myself for Papa's disapproval.' Then she felt disloyal for voicing such a sentiment.

'Of your gown, or of your going on an

211

outing?' he asked her.

'Of both, I suppose, but chiefly of the gown, I confess.'

'Perhaps you have tried too hard to make up to him for the fact that he lost his son,' the baronet suggested.

'What do you mean?' she asked him.

'Of course you could not become a priest instead of Patrick, but you have in every other way sought to do the kinds of things that you believed that Patrick would have done, and of which your father would have approved. The consequence is that your father has readily accepted your self-effacing diligence, but has never until today seen you for the very attractive woman that you are.'

'Oh,' whispered Emily, blushing at this mild compliment. Glancing down at her rosy face and shy smile, the baronet suddenly felt his heart give a little lurch. If such a modest compliment gave such pleasure, he wished that he had said something more extravagant. Fortunately, since Emily could not think of a response, they soon turned the corner and saw Mrs Trimmer's elegant barouche standing outside. A little further away, two grooms were looking after a fine black horse, a chestnut with a lighter mane, and a piebald pony.

Mr Trimmer and his two sons were talking

to one of the grooms and, as Emily drew nearer, she could see Oliver shuffling impatiently, whilst James was saying 'Papa, why can I not go on my pony as well? I don't *want* to go in the barouche.' Involuntarily she smiled and glancing briefly up at the baronet, saw that he was smiling too.

At that moment, Mrs Trimmer came out of her front door looking very attractive in a gown of deep rose, with a shawl of a lighter shade of pink. 'Emily, how lovely you look, and what a pretty gown!' she exclaimed, without a blush.

'Thank you,' Emily answered, a little self-consciously. 'You are looking delightful too, Aurelia.' She could not help wondering whether it was entirely appropriate that the wife of a clergyman should be so unashamedly duplicitous!

'Would you like to step inside for a few minutes?' asked Mrs Trimmer. 'Annis and Stuart should have been here by now, but I must admit that I am not entirely surprised that they are late.'

'They will be here quite soon, I'm sure,' replied Sir Gareth reassuringly. As soon as they had arrived at the Trimmers' house, Emily had drawn her hand out of his arm. She was surprised, and a little annoyed with herself, at how much she missed that contact.

'You are very optimistic,' murmured his sister. 'Do you have any grounds for your belief?'

'Oh yes,' Gareth replied. 'Very good grounds. The time is now almost ten o'clock. I informed them that we wanted to set out by nine, and they are merely an hour late.'

Both ladies laughed at that. 'Gareth, for shame!' his sister exclaimed, as soon as she was ready. 'Such deceit!'

'My dear sister, you would be surprised how mendacious I can be, given the necessity,' answered the baronet blandly.

Sure enough, moments later, and before the members of the party already assembled could go inside, Lord Stuart and his cousin came through the Exchequer gate, with a groom leading the gentleman's horse. To Emily's surprise, however, they were accompanied by Dr Boyle.

Dressed in a riding coat of hair brown, he looked more rodent-like than ever; and this expression was accentuated when, on catching sight of Emily, he poked out his nose and, as soon as he was close enough, exclaimed, 'Miss Whittaker! Where upon earth did you get that gown?'

Emily flushed with mortification, a feeling which was only increased by the sound of Mrs Hughes's smothered laughter.

Before she could say anything, however, she heard Sir Gareth's deep voice, but speaking in the accents of a society drawl that she had not heard upon his lips before. 'Gad, Dr Wen — '

'Dr Boyle, sir,' interrupted the doctor, not sure whether to take offence or not.

'Boyle, then; where the deuce do you think she got it? Off a mulberry bush? It's from a modiste's of course.'

'Yes. I dare say,' the doctor agreed. 'But when did you get it, Miss Whittaker, and from where?'

'Upon my soul, Doctor, you are impertinently curious about where a lady gets her gowns,' declared Aurelia, her brows soaring.

The doctor flushed an unbecoming red. 'Just so; I beg your pardon, ma'am.'

'It is not my pardon you should be begging,' Aurelia told him roundly. 'Emily will be far more forgiving than I, if she permits you to give her your arm for so much as a step today.'

'Of course,' the doctor answered in mortified tones. 'My apologies, Miss Whittaker.'

Mrs Hughes was not so easily satisfied, however. Scenting a mystery, she said curiously, 'Miss Whittaker, I trust that I too, will not be condemned for unseemly curiosity, but I confess that I should be interested to know where you procured such a charming gown. If Lincoln boasts such fashionable modistes, I might be tempted to purchase something on my own account while I am here.'

Emily stood silently, unable to think of anything to say. For her own part, she would have been happy to say from the very beginning that she had borrowed the gown from Mrs Trimmer. Now that Aurelia herself had come so powerfully to her defence however, she could not help but realize that to reveal the truth at this juncture would not only make her look foolish, it would make her friend look foolish too.

Before the silence could become embarrassing, however, Sir Gareth spoke again. 'Annis, my dear, you have no need to question Miss Whittaker any further. I can tell you everything you wish to know about this gown.' To Emily's consternation, he walked slowly around her, quizzing glass in hand, whilst Aurelia tried not to look anxious. 'Firstly, I can tell you that it was not made in Lincoln. It is from a London modiste; Mme Claudine, I would say, if I had to hazard a guess. Secondly, it displays the unmistakable stamp of my sister's taste, and I would say that she probably gave advice on the colour and style. My guess, Annis, would be that Aurelia procured it from London on Miss Whittaker's behalf. Am I correct, Aurelia?'

Mrs Trimmer laughed and clapped her hands, as much from relief as amusement. 'You are quite correct, Brother,' she told him. 'I certainly ordered the gown myself from Mme Claudine. See how well it becomes Emily. Did I not make a good choice, Mrs Hughes?'

'Very good,' answered that lady briefly. She was by no means pleased to see how pretty Emily looked, or to hear how promptly Sir Gareth had defended her, or even to discover in what good standing Emily appeared to be with the Trimmers. 'Shall we set off now? We do not want to stand in the street talking about Miss Whittaker's gown all day, surely.'

There was general agreement with this sentiment, if not with the way in which it had been expressed, and Sir Gareth and Lord Stuart stepped forward to help the ladies into the barouche. James had been reconciled to travelling with the ladies, since he had been promised that he could sit next to Phillips, the driver, for both journeys.

'I suppose Wayne could have come after all,' Mrs Hughes remarked, noting that there was an empty seat. 'I told her that she must stay behind because there was no space.' Mrs Trimmer, naturally, had taken the front facing seat, so that she could keep half an eye on James. Mrs Hughes had arranged herself next to her hostess, leaving Emily with no alternative but to face the back.

She did not mind. This was such an unusual treat for her that she did not care which way she sat. As she observed the gentlemen mounting their horses, and her eyes chanced to take in how athletically Sir Gareth took to the saddle, she realized, colouring, that this position had unforeseen benefits!

'Poor Miss Wayne,' Mrs Trimmer was saying. 'Indeed there is plenty of room. We could send for her now, if you wished.'

'Good heavens no,' responded Mrs Hughes. 'I only keep her for form's sake; I take no pleasure in the woman's company, you know. Besides, she set off quite early this morning to go for a long walk. I think that she is planning to visit the cathedral later.' Her tone suggested that she could not understand why anybody could possibly want to do such a thing.

Emily glanced at Mrs Trimmer and then had to look away. She could tell that they were both wondering whether Miss Wayne disliked her employer's company as much as

Mrs Hughes disliked hers! All at once, Emily recalled her idea that Miss Wayne might make a suitable governess for James and Oliver. She resolved to try to speak to Aurelia about it that very day.

15

It was about seventeen miles to Gainsborough, and they reached the little country town shortly before midday. The gentlemen rode beside or just behind the carriage for the most part, a fact which soon became apparent to Mrs Hughes. Her attempts to keep them in her eye became quite ludicrous at times. Of course, she could not keep turning around, for that would have been openly rude, but she did turn as much sideways on the seat as she possibly could. This meant that at one point, when they went over an unexpectedly bumpy place on the road, she was very nearly thrown onto the floor of the carriage, and rapidly had to take up a more sensible posture in order to avoid being made to look even more ridiculous.

Lord Stuart rode his horse with the careless ease of one who has been taught to do so from the cradle. Out of all of the horse-riders, it was he who rode alongside the barouche most frequently, sharing his attentions equally between all the ladies. Dr Boyle attempted to do the same, but he did not have the same facility on horseback, and after nearly falling off on one occasion, he kept to riding behind the barouche.

Oliver trotted gamely along on his pony, and Emily noticed that either his father or his uncle always stayed close by, keeping a careful eye on him. Emily could see the gentlemen quite clearly most of the time, but she took care not to stare at any of them, although Sir Gareth certainly cut a very fine figure in the saddle. This determination of hers was made rather difficult, however, because for some of the time, there was an excellent view of Lincoln Cathedral that was different from the one to which she was accustomed. Strangely enough, this view often seemed to be just behind Sir Gareth.

After gazing at the building for a little while, Emily became conscious of being observed, and glancing away from the cathedral, her gaze met that of Sir Gareth, who guided his mount alongside the barouche.

'A magnificent spectacle, wouldn't you say?' he declared, a twinkle in his eye.

At once, there came into Emily's mind a memory of how they had stood on the threshold of her house, and she had breathed the word 'magnificent' whilst looking straight at him. 'What can you mean, sir?' Emily asked defensively, her cheeks suffused with colour. She looked across and saw to her relief that Mrs Hughes and Mrs Trimmer were engaged in conversation.

'Why, the cathedral, of course,' he answered. 'What other spectacle did you have in mind?'

Confused, she did not know how to answer him. She was relieved when Mrs Hughes claimed his attention, and she was able to calm herself by looking at the passing scenery.

On arriving in Gainsborough, they made their way immediately to the White Hart. 'How odd,' murmured Mrs Hughes. 'We are staying at the White Hart in Lincoln, too.'

'Dashed odd,' her cousin agreed. 'We'll have to take care we don't forget where we are, eh Blades?'

'You should be quite safe, Stuart,' the baronet responded. 'If you do not see the cathedral, then you will know you are in Gainsborough.'

'Ah, but that won't work,' the young lord pointed out triumphantly. 'Y'see, you can't see the cathedral from the White Hart in Lincoln. Too dashed close, don't you know?'

'You'll just have to ask someone if you're not sure,' the baronet told him.

'But no one would be so confused by the name of the inn that he would forget which town he was in,' the doctor protested.

'I wouldn't say that,' Lord Stuart returned.

'Take me for instance; went out for a night's gambling with a few fellows. Popped into Old White's; drank a bottle of as smooth a red as I've tasted in a long time — have you had any from there, Blades?'

'Not recently,' Sir Gareth answered, keeping his eye on his two nephews whilst their father was seeing to the disposal of the barouche.

'Well, make sure you do before it's all gone. Anyway, left White's, popped in to Boodle's — or was that another night? Never mind; thing is, I chanced to bump into Freddy Gorringe — you know him?'

'Slightly,' the baronet replied.

'Went to his lodging for a hand of cards. Had devilish bad cards, too. No luck all evening.' He stopped speaking, and beamed around at the other members of his party who were preparing to go into the inn. Aware that some of them at least were looking at him expectantly, he said, 'What? What is it?'

'We are all longing to hear the end of this enthralling tale,' prompted Mr Trimmer.

'Tale? Oh, of course! Brain like a sieve.'

'That retentive, eh?' Sir Gareth murmured.

Lord Stuart grinned good-humouredly. 'Well, we left Freddy's and went to Slaughters, then on to another place or two, and finally home. And it was then that I noticed I'd not got my cane. Went back in my mind. Did I have it at White's? Yes, because some fellow said 'Fine cane, Stuart' — or did he say Fenn? — and I said, yes it is, or something like that. Did I have it at Boodles? Yes, I put it on the floor by my chair. Did I have it at Freddy's — '

'Yes, we have grasped your thought processes,' the baronet interrupted. 'You went back in your mind through all the places that you had visited, and were convinced that you had had your cane on every occasion.'

'Marvellous!' exclaimed Lord Stuart. 'Now why didn't I think to put it like that? But that's just what I did. So the next day, I got up and went back to all the places I'd been, starting with the last which I think was Hamilton's. Went in; found a waiter: said 'Have you found a cane with a silver top — might have left it here last night?' 'No sir,' was the answer. Went to the next place . . . '

'Allow me to précis that for you,' Sir Gareth said kindly. 'You went back to all the places that you had visited and asked them if they had seen your cane.'

'I don't know how he does it,' remarked Lord Stuart, shaking his head. 'Did just that; and guess what?'

'You'd left it at White's all along?' the baronet suggested.

Lord Stuart stared at him in amazement. 'It's uncanny,' he breathed. 'How did you work that out?'

'Perhaps he was of your party,' suggested Mrs Trimmer, smiling at Emily, who had been listening to the dialogue in amazement. She could not remember hearing such a conversation in her life before.

'No, never,' Lord Stuart answered shaking his head. 'He runs with a much more dangerous set. Anyway, it just goes to show.'

'Goes to show what?' asked Mr Trimmer cautiously.

'I lost my cane; thought I'd had it all along; didn't have it at all. Fellow could easily think he was in Gainsborough and find he was in Lincoln. Easiest thing in the world.'

They all laughed as they went into the inn, but Dr Boyle, who brought up the rear, followed his polite laughter with a contemptuous snort.

None of the party was ready for food just yet, so they decided to have a cold drink — the day being decidedly warm — and stroll about the town a little before a light lunch which Mr Trimmer bespoke on their behalf as soon as they arrived. The gentlemen each had a glass of the landlord's home brew and pronounced it very good, whilst the ladies, together with Oliver and James, were very grateful for a drink of the landlady's own lemonade. Oliver had looked rather tired when they came into the inn, but the drink, together with a few cakes which the landlady brought in on a plate, soon revived him. Under cover of some other conversation, Mrs Trimmer told Emily that the ride was the longest that her son had attempted.

'He has done so well, but he was quite determined to ride with the men. He idolizes his uncle, as you have probably noticed.'

'At least he will have a good rest before the journey back,' Emily pointed out.

'Yes, and if he is too tired, Gareth will manage by some means to persuade him into the barouche.'

None of them wanted to be sitting about for long, so as soon as everyone's drink was finished, they left the inn and walked out into the sunshine. The boys were all for going to have a look at the river, and as the White Hart, situated in Lord Street, was not very far from there, the whole party agreed that such a stroll would occupy the time before luncheon very well. Needless to say, the boys were full of questions, and Dr Boyle, who had had relatives living in the town at one time, quickly found that he was being looked to as the authority on all matters pertaining to Gainsborough.

Noticing this, Sir Gareth informed Emily that he was sorry about her change in status.

'My change in status, sir?' she asked him, wrinkling her brow.

'Why certainly, ma'am,' he replied. 'We changed the day for this outing in order to take advantage of your local knowledge, if you recall. Now you find yourself outshone completely.' They were standing quite close to where the doctor was describing the dramatic effects of the spring tides to two fascinated young boys, whilst Mr and Mrs Trimmer looked on. Mrs Hughes and her cousin had wandered a few steps away and were talking quietly together.

'It is quite true,' Emily replied. 'What is to be done?'

The baronet looked down at her, pretending to consider the matter. 'Well, it's too late to take you back now,' he said eventually in tones of mock regret. 'I'll just have to make the best of your company, won't I?' His words, taken at face value, were ungracious, but his eyes told a different story.

What a contrast she was, the baronet thought to himself, looking at her as she turned her face away, her cheeks flushed becomingly. In some ways, she was far more experienced than other women of her age. Her visits to the prison, her work for the poor, her time spent with the sick and the dying had given her a breadth and depth of understanding that was rarely found in gently bred ladies. Her interest in the world about her, too, was, in his experience, unusual. Yet in anything concerning intimate relations between men and women, she shied away like the most innocent of very young debutantes. His sister had suggested that there might be an understanding between Miss Whittaker and Dr Boyle. If there was, then it could not be a very passionate one.

Conscious that he had been staring down at her for a little too long without saying anything, he murmured in a low tone, 'By the way, you do look delightful in Aurelia's gown. It was an excellent choice.'

She looked up at him again, a startled expression on her face. 'You know, then,' she exclaimed, her tone matching her expression.

'My dear Miss Whittaker, I was with her when she chose it,' he returned. 'I thought it charming then, and I still do.'

'Then you don't mind?'

He laughed. 'Why should I mind?' he asked her. 'My sister has a perfect right to do what she wishes with her gowns, especially when the results are as pleasing as they are now.'

At that point, Mrs Hughes and her cousin joined them, with some question about the new bridge over the river, and they all strolled on a little, looking at the water. This time, Emily found herself walking with Mr Trimmer, whilst the boys ran ahead under the watchful eye of their uncle, and Lord Stuart chatted with Mrs Trimmer on his right and his cousin on his left.

Emily was just trying to decide how to bring up the matter that was disturbing her, when Mr Trimmer made the whole business easy for her by saying, 'Have I told you how delightful you look, Miss Whittaker?'

By now, Emily's conscience was troubling her so much that instead of thanking him for his compliment, she simply said rather vaguely, 'Oh dear.'

'Pardon?' responded the clergyman, somewhat startled.

'You know of course that . . . that . . . '

'I know the *source* of your gown,' Mr Trimmer interrupted. 'Are you worried that I do not approve? I can assure you that I do. Aurelia was very apprehensive about moving to Lincoln, but came because she knew that I wanted this appointment. Thanks to you, she feels that she has found a friend. Any kindness that she can do you in return must be approved by me.'

'You are very good,' Emily answered, her brow still wrinkled in anxiety. 'I value your wife's friendship, and am grateful for her kindness.'

'But you cannot approve the deceit that has been practised?' he hazarded.

'That is exactly it,' she agreed. 'I would not have minded everyone knowing . . . ' Her voice tailed away, as she imagined the reaction of Mrs Hughes, and even of Lord Stuart, had they known that her dress was only borrowed.

'Miss Whittaker, I think you are not being entirely truthful,' Mr Trimmer observed acutely. 'Besides, from what I did hear of the conversation, and from what Aurelia has told me briefly, there was no real deceit. The maker of the gown was named, my wife was mentioned as being the one who ordered it and whose taste was consulted. If you never have any misdemeanour more serious than this with which to belabour your conscience, you will be a very happy woman. Now, forget all about it and enjoy the day.'

Taking this sensible advice to heart, Emily dismissed the matter from her mind, and while they completed their stroll, she told Mr Trimmer about her other friend, Mrs Fanshawe, and the new baby that surely must be born soon.

Lunch at the White Hart was well served and tasty, but not too heavy. Afterwards, Mrs

Trimmer said that she would like to lie down, and Mr Trimmer bespoke a bedroom so that she could do so. Emily, looking at the tender expression on his face as he told her that he would keep his eye on the boys, wondered whether she had told him about her condition.

Mr Trimmer then said that he would take the boys down to the river again and see if he could find a boat that would take them for a ride. Dr Boyle recommended a walk around Gainsborough Old Hall, and then a visit to All Saints church.

'It was built in the late 1400s,' he told them, 'and in its time, it was visited by royalty. It has now, I fear, become much neglected, but the outside is still worth examination.'

The party of five set out from the White Hart, but turned to the right before they reached the river, so as to visit the Old Hall. This time, Mrs Hughes managed to manipulate the situation so that she was holding on to Sir Gareth's arm, whilst the doctor offered his to Emily. It was the first time that she could remember his ever having done such a thing. Lord Stuart strolled along on his own, addressing an occasional remark to his cousin or to Sir Gareth.

'That is indeed a pretty gown you are

wearing,' remarked Dr Boyle rather shyly, remembering his *faux pas* earlier.

'Thank you,' Emily answered demurely. She had learned her lesson from Mr Trimmer and, since it seemed more likely than ever that the gown would be hers, decided to say no more on the matter.

'I . . . er . . . that is to say, I . . . '

'Yes, Dr Boyle?' Emily prompted.

'I can think of nothing wrong in the daughter of a clergyman wearing something pretty,' he went on in rather painstaking tones. 'Or a daughter of a doctor doing so.' He glanced at her quickly sideways and ploughed on. 'I am of the opinion that a wife of a clergyman or of a . . . a . . . doctor, could also wear such a gown with a clear conscience.'

'Then since I am a clergyman's daughter, that must be of great comfort to me,' Emily answered him.

'Yes indeed,' agreed Dr Boyle. He opened his mouth to make his meaning more plain, but before he could say anything, Emily spoke.

'There is something that I have been wanting to tell you, Doctor, but I did not want to say it within earshot of my father, for fear of building up his hopes. A couple of days ago, I saw my grandfather open his eyes.'

'You are certain?' Dr Boyle replied, turning towards her now with that confident assurance that characterized all his professional dealings. 'Many a person has thought that he has witnessed such a thing — in a mirror perhaps, or from a distance, but it has only been a trick of the light.'

'No, it was not an illusion,' Emily replied. 'I was looking at him at the time, and I saw him slowly open his eyes, then close them again. Does this mean that he will recover, do you think?'

'It is too early to say,' he replied cautiously. 'But I have known cases when a person has remained immobile as your grandfather has done for some time, then regained many of their faculties. It is as if the body decides that it needs a complete rest, and simply takes one. But although we must not be hasty here, I must say that it is a good sign.'

'Oh, thank you!' Emily cried, turning a glowing face towards him.

Sir Gareth and Mrs Hughes, following behind, were in an excellent position to see how the doctor beamed down at his companion in response. 'What a charming end for this expedition it would be for Dr Boyle and Miss Whittaker to announce their engagement,' mused Mrs Hughes. 'A doctor and a clergyman's daughter, neither of them in the first flush of youth. What match could possibly be more suitable?'

The baronet's response was merely a grunt.

Gainsborough Old Hall was indeed an impressive building at first glance, but on closer inspection, neglect could clearly be seen, from the untended garden, to the shabby paintwork and the occasional broken window.

'What a pity,' exclaimed Emily. 'I can remember visiting it when I was quite a young child, and I'm sure it was not as bad then.'

'Scenes from one's childhood are always rosy,' remarked the baronet.

'No they ain't,' replied Lord Stuart. 'I still remember the beating I got for climbing up onto the barn roof. That's not a rosy memory.'

'No, but I'll wager your backside was,' the baronet retorted.

'Sir Gareth! You are in the presence of ladies!' declared the doctor, shocked.

'I beg your pardon, ladies,' answered the baronet, bowing slightly, but there was still a twinkle in his eye.

When they had looked their fill at the Old Hall, they walked on to All Saints Church, which was only a short distance away. This time, Emily found herself walking with Sir

Gareth, whilst Mrs Hughes set out to charm both Lord Stuart and Dr Boyle at the same time.

'I suppose I should feel guilty that I have deprived the good doctor of his companion, especially when he was clearly enjoying your conversation so much,' the baronet remarked. Moments later he could have kicked himself for a comment that would have been picked up by such as Mrs Hughes as an example of jealousy.

Emily, however, simply took his words at their face value. 'He was telling me some good news about my grandfather,' she said, and proceeded to inform him of the doctor's opinion.

'That is indeed encouraging,' Sir Gareth answered. 'For how long has he been in his present condition?'

Emily told him, and as she did so, he reflected what a strange household it was for a young woman to grow up in. No wonder she was different from other women he knew.

While these thoughts were going through his head, Emily began to speak once more. 'Since we are talking about my family, sir, I must take the opportunity of thanking you for . . . for giving Patrick back to me.'

'I beg your pardon?' the baronet asked, mystified.

'You told me your memories of him, and by doing so, in some way enabled memories of my own to be released,' she explained. She began to recount the things that she had recalled as she lay in bed a short time before, together with one or two other cameos that had returned to her mind since then. He chuckled as she did so, and so did she, but suddenly, to her astonishment and mortification, she found that she was crying as well.

'My dear Em — Miss Whittaker,' he said concernedly. He glanced round. They were a little ahead of the rest of the party. 'Come, we'll walk round the outside of the church,' he said. 'It will give you a chance to compose yourself.'

Emily's tears did not last for long. 'I don't know why I did that,' she said apologetically. 'Please forgive me.'

'There is nothing to forgive,' he answered, putting his handkerchief back in his pocket when he saw that her own was quite adequate for her needs. 'I suspect that you were never really given a chance to mourn Patrick, and you are doing a little of that now.' He paused briefly, then seeing that she was still looking a little downcast, he said teasingly, 'You can have me for a brother, if you like.'

'I don't want you for a brother.' The words

were out of her mouth before she could recall them.

The teasing expression vanished from his face. 'Forgive me,' he said, inclining his head gravely. 'I didn't mean to presume.'

Emily stared at him in consternation. She wanted to explain to him that he was not presuming, but she could not think how to tell him so without revealing that the reason why she did not want him for a brother was because the feelings that he kindled in her breast were not sisterly. She did not know how to say this without sounding either brazen or immodest. All she could manage before they came within earshot of the rest of the party was, 'You were not presuming. You simply took me by surprise. It was a strange idea, that is all.' The smile returned to his face, but it was not quite as warm as it had been before.

Although All Saints had a fine medieval tower, the body of it had been remodelled about fifty years before, and the visitors were pleased to approve the light, modern interior. As they were leaving, they were very surprised to find Mr and Mrs Trimmer entering but without Oliver and James.

'The landlord came down to the quay and offered to take the boys back to the inn to play in the garden, since there were no boat rides available,' the clergyman told them. 'I knew that Aurelia would want to see the church so we came straight here.'

The others offered to wait, but Mr and Mrs Trimmer insisted that they would be quite happy to walk back alone, so the other five wandered towards the White Hart, taking a look at the market place by way of a small diversion.

'No, no, I am going to walk back with Miss Whittaker,' Mrs Hughes declared. 'You gentlemen can keep your distance. I am going to tell her what wicked fellows you all are.'

'I say, coz, I protest!' exclaimed Lord Stuart. 'Look at Boyle! He's a physician! What could be more respectable? As for me, there's no vice in me at all, I swear it. Ask anyone you like. Ask Blades here! Mind you, the things I could tell you about *him* . . . '

'Balderdash!' retorted Sir Gareth cheerfully, but there was a hint of worry behind his eyes.

'Now, my dear, we have got rid of the gentlemen so you can tell me everything,' said Mrs Hughes in a confiding tone.

'That would take rather a long time,' Emily responded. Then, because she knew she must and because this was such a perfect opportunity, she said, 'Mrs Hughes, you must allow me to beg your pardon for being so abrupt when I met you in the street, yesterday. The fact of the matter is — '

'Oh, think no more of it,' replied the other carelessly. 'I am sure I have not. But come, let us talk of more interesting topics. You know perfectly well that I am longing to know how matters stand between you and that charming doctor.'

Emily turned upon her an expression that was wholly baffled. She might have described the doctor as many things, but charming was not one of them.

For a moment, an impatient look crossed Mrs Hughes's lovely features. Then, trying another approach, she said, 'Has he proposed yet? I made sure that he would do so this afternoon. In fact, I was telling Gareth of my suspicions as we were walking behind you.'

'And did he entertain the same suspicions?' Emily asked.

'Oh yes,' responded Mrs Hughes, with a ruthless disregard for the truth. 'In fact, I believe that it was his idea to invite the doctor today, to give him that very opportunity.'

'That was very kind of Sir Gareth,' answered Emily, finding that this notion hurt, but not really understanding why.

'Oh, Gareth can be the kindest of men,' replied Mrs Hughes blithely. 'So much so, that many ladies have mistaken his kindness for something rather more . . . intimate, shall we say? And of course he cannot bring himself to repulse them; especially if they are past their last prayers.' She stopped abruptly as if she had suddenly realized the infelicitous nature of what she had just said. 'Of course, I do not mean you, dear Miss Whittaker,' she went on rather awkwardly. 'You are already spoken for. Though even there, I fear, dear Gareth can sometimes be rather naughty — testing just how faithful some ladies really are, you know. Of course, I am never jealous. I know where his affections really lie. And here we are, back at the White Hart Inn. What a lovely chat we have had, have we not? Such a pleasure to hear all your views.'

Emily was left reflecting that in fact, it had been Mrs Hughes who had been doing most of the talking, and half the time, she had been saying things that it had given Emily no pleasure to hear.

Mrs Hughes had not failed to notice that Emily had had a much better view of the gentlemen on the journey there, so on their return, she insisted on taking the backward facing seat. Mrs Trimmer was noticeably tired, and after Emily had assured her that she had no particular desire for conversation, the clergyman's wife closed her eyes and dozed. Mrs Hughes exchanged desultory conversation with her cousin whilst Mr Trimmer and Sir Gareth kept a careful eye on a rather tired Oliver. This left Emily free to think her own thoughts for much of the time. Almost inevitably, in view of what had taken place during the day, she found herself thinking about the baronet. She found that she only had to think about Sir Gareth Blades, the smile in his eyes and the touch of that strong hand, and the colour came to her face, her breathing became shallow and her heart began to beat twice as fast as usual.

How kind he had been that afternoon, and how sensitive to her needs! She did not need Mrs Hughes to inform her that Sir Gareth Blades was kind. She had seen that in evidence in his care for his nephews, his sensitivity to her father's feelings, even in his forbearance over Lord Stuart's silliness. Might not his attentions to her spring from that same well of kindness; a kindness which had also prompted him to include Dr Boyle in the outing, believing him to be the man of her choice?

The problem with this theory was that there had been things that Sir Gareth had done and said which, if proceeding from kindness, could only indicate kindness of a very odd nature. Flirting with her, for example; looking at her ankles; even kissing her beneath the imp. Of course there was always the possibility that a society man might think that by showing an ageing spinster such attentions, he *was* being kind.

This was a lowering reflection, but it made no difference to the way that she felt about him. She had been aware for some time that she was becoming fond of him; she had not really understood the nature of this fondness until that afternoon when he had offered to be her brother, and she had refused him. The affection that she had for him was of a very different nature.

I must be in love with him, she told herself in wonderment. It was such a powerful moment of self-awareness that she found herself looking at the other occupants of the barouche, certain that those around her must have picked up some signal from her. It was almost surprising that Mrs Trimmer should still be dozing, and that Mrs Hughes should be gazing idly at the passing scenery. For Emily, this new understanding meant that nothing could ever be the same again. The fact that Sir Gareth would never ever glance at a plain clergyman's daughter of thirty except to be kind to his old friend's sister made absolutely no difference to her feelings. Nor did the appearance of the elegant lady whom she had met so recently, and who was clearly intimate with the baronet; quite how intimate, she did not dare guess.

She had never before had any personal experience of love. She had learned something of its nature by observing the very real affection between Nathalie and her handsome husband, but naturally these observations were at second hand.

At one time, she had considered marrying Dr Boyle for all kinds of reasons of expediency. Now, she could hardly believe that she had even contemplated such a step. It almost seemed as if her love for the baronet had transformed her into a completely different person. All at once, to her astonishment, she realized that she could not marry the doctor, or, indeed, any man; for if she could not have the man whom she had met and fallen in love with so recently, then she did not want anyone at all.

16

The following day Emily woke up to the sound of heavy rain, and when she opened the curtains and looked up at the leaden sky, she could only be thankful that the expedition to Gainsborough had already taken place. It had, after all, been a very enjoyable occasion, despite Mrs Hughes's barbed comments.

She had a suspicion that she might have dreamed about Sir Gareth the previous night. I love him, she said to herself and, as she prepared to rise, she allowed her mind to savour the occasions when their eyes had met and she had almost felt as if they might be kindred spirits. She was still thinking about these times and staring into space when Mary arrived with hot water.

'Kindred spirits indeed,' she muttered to herself, as she pulled on her grey gown. 'Who am I trying to deceive?' But she could not stop smiling all the same.

As she reached the bottom of the stairs, she paused in some surprise, for she could hear voices proceeding from within the drawing-room. It was far too early for a social call.

As she approached the room, Canon

Whittaker, hearing her footsteps, opened the door and said, 'Come in, my dear.' Then turning to the other occupant of the room, he said, 'Here is Emily. I know that she will be prepared to do her Christian duty, whatever her personal feelings.'

On entering the room, Emily found that her father's visitor was Mr Fanshawe. She went forward to shake hands with the young clergyman. 'How is Nathalie?' she asked as she did so, trying to ignore her father's reproachful *Mrs Fanshawe, my dear!* 'I do hope your arrival means that she is feeling better.'

Fanshawe smiled, but it was a smile tinged with anxiety. 'She says she is better,' he replied, 'but I really did not want to leave her. You know how she falls prey to foolish imaginings. The dean has summoned me, and I have to tell you, Miss Whittaker, that I was very close to writing back and telling him that he must manage without me.' (Here, there was a tsk tsk sound from Mr Whittaker.) 'But Nathalie told me that she would be happy for me to leave her if she could be sure that you would come to her. And the dean himself suggested in his letter that you might perhaps come again.'

'Then of course I shall go,' Emily told him. 'When would you like me to leave? At once?'

Mr Fanshawe looked very guilty. 'I would not presume so far as to expect that,' he said respectfully.

'But you would be grateful if I did,' she surmised.

'You are forgetting your grandfather, Emily,' said her father reproachfully.

'I could sit with him now, Papa, whilst Mary packs my things,' she suggested. 'Are you to remain in Lincoln?' she asked Mr Fanshawe.

He shook his head. 'The dean wants me to attend to certain duties in his living in Louth,' he said. 'Nathalie has my direction.'

So it was that in a very short space of time, Emily found herself setting out for Mablethorpe again, but with different feelings from on the first occasion. For one thing, the first time she had travelled to Mablethorpe, she had had company, for she and Nathalie had travelled together. This time, however, she was alone and furthermore, the weather did not favour her, for the rain which had begun early in the morning continued relentlessly throughout the whole of the journey.

She had brought with her *The Mysteries of Udolpho*, which Nathalie had lent her, and which she had only managed to read very slowly, partly because she had to be secretive about it, and partly because she wanted to

savour it and make it last. After a short time, however, she set the book down on the seat beside her in Mr Fanshawe's comfortable carriage and thought about the young woman that she was to visit.

She had been very sorry to hear that yet again Nathalie was prey to imaginary fears. She did so hope that all would go well. She had visited far too many homes where either mother or baby had died in childbed for her to be foolishly optimistic on that score. But after all, Mrs Fanshawe did have youth and general good health on her side, and her husband was able to ensure that she had the very best treatment.

Nevertheless, Emily was conscious of an oppression of spirits as she travelled, and put it down to a combination of the depressing weather and fears for her friend. Even as she came to that conclusion, however, another picture came into her mind — that of a dark-haired, well-built man with a deep voice and a smiling mouth. Would he still be there when she returned? Could her every hope of happiness so quickly have become dependent upon the actions of another?

'Nonsense!' she exclaimed out loud, and picked up the novel again, but when at one point she leaned back and dozed, she woke up thinking of Sir Gareth's face.

Her welcome by Mrs Fanshawe made up for all the inconvenience of the unexpected journey. 'Emily! Dearest!' Nathalie exclaimed, laughing and crying at the same time as her visitor was shown into the sitting-room which had been put aside by the landlady for her use. 'How I have longed for you! Your letters have been cheering, but they are not the same thing as having you here in person.'

This effusive welcome, so unlike any kind of behaviour that Emily had been accustomed to in her own home, took her a little aback, but did her heart good nonetheless, and she returned her friend's embrace willingly. From this, as much as from the evidence of her own eyes, she could tell that Mrs Fanshawe's pregnancy was well advanced.

'I am so glad that I was able to come,' she replied. 'You are looking very well.'

'You mean I am looking like an elephant,' Nathalie answered teasingly. 'Do go up and put off your bonnet, and I will order some tea.'

Emily was pleased to find her friend in such good spirits, but she was not deceived. She had found during her previous visit that Mrs Fanshawe was capable of being in alt one day and then being very low the next, and she therefore prepared her mind for dealing with a bout of depression before too long.

Furthermore, although she had said that Nathalie was looking well, there was a waxiness about her complexion that Emily could not like.

The following day was bright and sunny, and Nathalie, responding to the sunshine like a summer flower, was all smiles; the next day though, the weather was wet again, and they had to stay inside, and the expectant mother was then inclined to indulge in morbid imaginings. In order to raise her spirits, Emily told her a little about the new arrivals in the cathedral close. She did mention Sir Gareth in passing, but she did not tell Nathalie his name. If asked she would have been hard put to it to say why she was so secretive.

After their luncheon, Nathalie went to lie down, but Emily, tired of being inside, put on her outdoor clothes, and went out to look at the sea. Mablethorpe was only a little place, hardly more than one street, so it did not take her long to get to the water's edge, and breathe in the sea air, whilst the waves came rolling gently in, and the rain fell in a fine mist.

As she walked along beside the breaking waves, her mind wandered to Lincoln and the people that she had left behind there. Would any of them enquire about her or miss her? Or would they simply be thankful not to have to include the drab little spinster in any of their entertainments? The very idea filled her with dismay.

Certainly Mrs Hughes would not be sorry at her absence. She would be spending her days ingratiating herself with the baronet, flirting with him in her practised London way. No doubt if she ever left him alone, Jennifer Cummings, prompted by her objectionable mother, would be ready to make cow's eyes at him on every possible occasion.

She paused in her walking, astonished at her own thoughts. Where had that bit of cattishness come from, she asked herself. She scarcely knew Mrs Hughes, and as for Jennifer, the girl had never done her any harm.

Determinedly abandoning this line of thought, she turned round and began to walk back. This time, she made herself think instead about the prison visiting that she had missed, and about the Kennedy family, and what assistance she might reasonably offer them over the coming weeks.

On arriving back at the house where they were lodging, she took off her bonnet and cloak in the hall and gave them to the landlady with a word of apology. 'I did not think it was raining so much as that,' she confessed.

'Ah, it's that fine rain,' replied Mrs Sealey, taking Emily's outdoor things. 'It gets into everything. I'll get these dried in the kitchen. Missus is upstairs. I did pop in to ask if she wanted anything, but she said no.'

Emily thanked her and went up to her room and as she passed the door into Nathalie's chamber, she heard the unmistakable sound of crying. At once, she tapped on the door and went in.

Nathalie turned to look at her. Even with her eyes drowned in tears, she still looked ravishing. 'Oh Emily!' she sobbed. 'Oh, I am so glad you have come back! I have wrestled and wrestled with my conscience, but it will not do! I must tell someone of what is such a burden to me.'

'Nathalie, my dear,' exclaimed Emily, her voice full of concern. 'What is it? What can have happened to distress you so? Is it bad news from home, perhaps?' She thought about her walk that afternoon and tried to remember whether she had seen anyone who might have been coming with tidings.

The other woman shook her head. 'No, no, there has been no news.'

'Then what can it be? When I left you, you were a little low in spirits, but not like this.' She got up from her place on the bed, and went to a drawer where she knew Mrs

251

Fanshawe kept her handkerchiefs.

'That was before Mrs Sealey spoke to me,' Nathalie answered, taking the handkerchief and wiping her eyes.

'Mrs Sealey told me that she had spoken to you, but she said that she had asked you if you wanted anything,' Emily replied.

'Yes, she did, but that was not what has upset me,' said the other. She paused, twisting the handkerchief in her hands. At last, she added in a low voice, 'She told me about a girl from a family of her acquaintance who had got herself into trouble.'

'Well, that is very distressing to be sure,' Emily remarked, after waiting for a few minutes to see if there would be anything further. 'But, my dear Nathalie, surely you must know that such things do happen?'

'Yes, I know,' Nathalie agreed in the same subdued tone. 'This girl met a . . . a man who led her into bad ways, and when he left her, she lied to her parents about who was responsible. Then the innocent man that she blamed denounced her.'

Again there was a long silence. 'That was very wrong of her, to blacken his reputation,' Emily agreed. 'She will have to live with the consequences of that falsehood.'

At this point Nathalie burst into tears again. 'But she will not do so for she died yesterday,' she declared, the words barely audible through her sobs.

Making a sudden decision, Emily rang the bell, and on hearing Mrs Sealey's footsteps in the corridor, went to the door and stepped outside. 'Mrs Fanshawe has been much overset by the sad tale you told her earlier,' she said. 'Would you be so good as to send up some claret to lift her spirits?'

Mrs Sealey looked very anxious. 'I wouldn't have upset the lady for anything, ma'am,' she assured Emily. 'To be sure I had forgotten how very sensitive she is.'

Emily smiled reassuringly. 'Of course you are in no way to blame,' she said. 'But the claret would certainly help.'

When Mrs Sealey had gone, Emily went back in and sat down next to Nathalie, taking her hand. 'I have sent for some claret for you,' she said. 'I know that Mr Fanshawe left several bottles here for the sole purpose of building you up.' She paused briefly then went on, 'I can well see how the sad tale of that young lady might be distressing to you, but pray recall that your own circumstances are so very different.'

'Yes, but they might not have been,' Nathalie replied. Gradually her crying subsided until she was calm again. When Mrs Sealey brought the wine, Emily took it from her whilst the other lady slid off the bed and went to stand looking out of the window.

'I'm very sorry if . . . That is, ma'am, I . . . I beg your pardon,' said Mrs Sealey, looking anxiously at Nathalie's back.

'It's all right, Mrs Sealey,' Emily said quietly. 'She'll be better presently. One of your excellent dinners will do her good.'

The woman brightened at once. 'I'll go and see about it straight away,' she said.

It was while Emily was pouring out the wine that Nathalie began to speak, and now her voice was calm. 'There is something that I must tell you,' she said, 'but you must promise by all that you hold sacred not to reveal what I am to say, for it would mean the ruin not just of myself but of Ernest as well.'

'Of course I will not reveal it,' Emily responded, taking her a glass of the rich red wine. 'But if it is so secret and possibly damaging, do you really want to tell me? Might you feel differently about this tomorrow and perhaps regret saying anything?'

Nathalie shook her head. 'No. I need to tell someone. If anything should go wrong' — and here she slid a hand over her stomach — 'someone else ought to know my story.'

'Very well then,' Emily agreed. 'But will you not sit down? You have exhausted yourself today and that cannot be good for you or the baby.'

Nathalie did as she was bid. Then she looked at Emily again and said, 'Now that I have made up my mind to tell you, I am very close to changing it again, for fear that you decide to hate me.'

Emily leaned across and caught hold of her hand. 'I could never do that,' she said. 'But if even now you decide to say nothing, I will be content.'

'No, I am resolved to tell you.' Nathalie paused, then began her story. 'You will find that no one knows very much about my background. If asked, I say that I am a squire's daughter and that my family live in Devon. That much is true; except that my family have long since disowned me, and the name by which everyone knows me is not mine. I began life as Emily Thorpe; yes, I was christened with the same name as yours,' she added, responding to her companion's start of surprise.

'I was the youngest of three girls, and was always fascinated with the theatre. When I was seventeen, a theatrical company came to a nearby town, and after a performance which we attended, I became enamoured of the leading man in the company. I found a way of meeting him, and he appeared to be as interested in me as I was in him.

'At the same time as this was happening, my parents were encouraging me to become engaged to a local man. He was nearly twice my age and not exactly a figure of romance, so I rebelled. When the theatrical company left the area, I went with them in company with the leading actor, and we . . . we became lovers.' Emily uttered a little gasp.

'I have shocked you,' Nathalie went on. 'There is worse to come, I fear. Once we had reached London, he soon tired of me, for there were plenty of actresses with far more worldly experience than I.'

'Never say that he abandoned you!' exclaimed Emily.

'Oh no, he did not do that,' Nathalie answered in a cynical tone. 'He introduced me to a gentleman who was an *habitué* of the Green Room — a man about town, noted for his good taste and fine looks. Having nowhere else to go and with my reputation ruined, I had very little choice. So I exchanged an actor for a gentleman. Unfortunately, the gentleman did not treat me as well as the actor had done, and I soon began to fear for my safety. Then, when I had been with this man for a few weeks, I realized that I was expecting his child.'

'Dear heaven,' Emily breathed.

'I could not think what to do. I knew that my parents would never receive me at home. I had no friends in London for my new lover, being very possessive and also protective of his own reputation among the ladies, did not allow me to meet people; for which I am now very thankful. The only time I was permitted to go out was on a Sunday morning, to attend church. Even then my lover insisted that I should go to a small, unfashionable place of worship so that I would not be noticed; I did not anticipate being noticed by the vicar.'

'Mr Fanshawe?' Emily asked.

Nathalie nodded. 'Yes, it was Ernest,' she agreed. 'I did little more than slip in and slip out each week, but he noticed me which helps to explain what happened next. My lover — you will notice I do not use names; I think it best not to do so — got into a quarrel with another man. Not over me, I am thankful to say. Anyway, there was a duel, my lover killed his man, but was himself seriously wounded. He was borne off to be nursed in hiding by friends, and the lodging which we had shared was reclaimed by his landlord, to whom he was heavily in debt.'

'What on earth did you do?' Emily asked. She had often wished that her life could be more exciting. She could at least be thankful that it was not as exciting as this.

'Every duellist has a second,' Nathalie replied. 'Once my lover's second had delivered him up to his friends, he came in search of me.'

'Oh no!' Emily exclaimed.

Nathalie shook her head. 'No, you misjudge him, for he was a true gentleman, who treated me with respect and did not seek to use me as well,' she said. 'Instead, he asked if there was anywhere he might take me. I was on the point of saying that there was nowhere, when I remembered the vicar of St Saviour's. He had seemed so kind, and I knew that he would find me a place if he could. So I asked my lover's second if he would take me to the church, which he did.'

Now, Nathalie paused for a long time, looking down at her clasped hands. Then when she looked up at Emily, her eyes were filled with tears again. 'Ernest was there and I told him everything; my childhood in Devon; the loss of my reputation at the hands of the actor; my liaison with the gentleman; my pregnancy; everything. Emily, he listened, and in his face there was no condemnation, no disgust. Then he told me that he had loved me from the first; that he had always suspected that I was troubled because of my manner; that he still loved me, despite all that I had disclosed; that he wanted to marry me.

'Emily, what would you have done?' she asked, her voice breaking. 'I was desperate. Ernest offered me a way out. The appointment to Lincoln had already been offered and refused. He told me that he would accept it after all, and that we could marry at once, then go on a holiday. After that, we would proceed straight to Lincoln where no one would know us. Because I had nowhere else to go, I accepted him, and as soon as the licence had been procured, we were married.'

'How deeply you must honour him,' Emily murmured.

'I do,' Nathalie agreed. 'And although I did not love him when I married him, I do love him now as much as any wife could love her husband. But you do see, do you not, that I had to tell someone my story? If all should not go well, and I pray that it will, I feel that there should be someone else in the world who knows that my baby is not Ernest's child. And should he have to bring up this child alone — which heaven forbid — he ought to have the comfort that someone else is privy to our secret.'

'Does he know that you are telling me?' Emily asked.

'He knows,' Nathalie replied.

★   ★   ★

Nathalie went into labour that night, and Emily knew at once that Mr Fanshawe would have to be sent for. She had already found out from Mrs Sealey the name of a man who would ride to Louth if necessary, and she was glad now of her foresight. The maid was despatched to fetch the doctor, and then to take Emily's note for delivery to Nathalie's husband.

That done, Emily remained in attendance on her friend, mopping her brow when necessary, holding her hand when the labour pains came, and speaking reassuringly to her.

'Will he come?' Nathalie asked. 'Have you sent for him?'

'The doctor is on his way,' Emily told her.

Nathalie shook her head. 'Not the doctor; Ernest.' She gasped again, as a fresh pain assailed her.

'The man has gone,' Emily promised her. 'Your husband will be here as soon as he can, I promise you.'

The doctor, who arrived very quickly, spoke calmly and confidently to his patient, but after he had examined her, he took Emily on one side and said, 'Has the husband been sent for?'

'Yes, a man left over an hour ago,' she replied.

He looked at her solemnly. 'It's just as

well,' he said quietly. 'I have anxieties about this one; grave anxieties. The baby is the wrong way round, and the mother is the kind who lives on her nerves, with no real strength. To be plain with you, ma'am, I do not think that both of them will live.'

Emily just managed to stop herself from gasping at this news. 'But she seemed so well,' she replied, in the same low tone. 'In fact, I remarked on how well she looked when I arrived, although I was concerned about her colouring.'

'Well, I may be wrong,' the doctor temporized. 'But I felt that I must prepare you for the worst. I am glad that the father has been sent for.'

'What are you saying?' asked a faint voice from the bed.

Emily turned back to the bed. 'I am telling the doctor what a splendid mama you will be,' she answered cheerfully.

'I certainly mean to be,' Nathalie replied. 'Emily, you must get out the baby clothes that I have made.' Then she gasped as another spasm of pain gripped her, and the doctor came to her side.

'That's right, ma'am,' he said. 'The babe is making its presence felt. But we've a long night ahead of us, I fear.'

By the time Mr Fanshawe arrived, looking

exhausted and anxious not long after dawn, it had become clear that the doctor's predictions had been all too accurate. The baby was now very near delivery, but Nathalie was not going to survive.

The young clergyman was desperate to remain at his wife's side, but the doctor would not permit it. The midwife was now in attendance, and so Emily sat downstairs with Mr Fanshawe in order to wait for some kind of resolution.

'If only I had been here,' he said over and over again. 'What kind of husband was I to leave her in this way?'

'Mr Fanshawe, you could not have done anything,' Emily told him earnestly. 'From the moment that she went into labour, it was all in the doctor's hands.'

'Yes, and what kind of doctor is he, plying his trade out here in the countryside?' he retorted, his voice rising. 'She should have been in the town, with the best physician that money could buy in attendance upon her.'

'I have seen him at work, and I believe that he is a very good doctor,' Emily said calmly. 'Mr Fanshawe, I wish you would sit down and have something to eat and drink. Mrs Sealey had made these sandwiches — '

'Damn the sandwiches!' he cried, thrusting at the plate with his hand so that they fell to the floor and the plate smashed. 'Damn Mrs Sealey, and damn you for not sending for me sooner. Do you realize that my wife is dying up there?' He stared at her as the enormity of his words sank into his brain. Then in a broken voice he said, 'My God, my God,' and sat down heavily, his face in his hands.

At once, Emily poured him a glass of claret and, stepping carefully over the sandwiches and pieces of smashed crockery, she touched him on the shoulder and handed the wine to him, half afraid that he might thrust this aside as well. He looked at her through moistened eyes, then took the glass and drank from it.

'Thank you,' he said in a subdued tone. 'I'm sorry, I . . . I . . . '

'It doesn't matter,' Emily answered.

'It does. I know you sent for me as soon as you knew yourself that the baby was to be born.' He paused again. 'Did she tell you about . . . ?'

Emily nodded. She did not ask to what he was referring.

'It will be a strange irony, will it not, if the baby lives and . . . ' Again he seemed on the point of being overcome.

They sat for what seemed like a very long time until, from upstairs, there came the sound of a baby crying. Fanshawe sprang to his feet, his eyes wild. 'Nathalie,' he breathed.

He flung open the door, but before he could leave the room, Emily caught hold of his arm.

'Mr Fanshawe, you must be composed,' she urged him. 'You must show her that you can manage.'

He swallowed hard. 'I'm not sure that I can,' he replied, looking at her.

'But you must make her think that you can — for her sake.'

He stared at her, and some of the wildness went out of his face. He ran a hand through his blond, dishevelled hair, and walked to the foot of the stairs, but as he reached them, Mrs Sealey appeared at the top, a bundle in her arms.

'You have a daughter, sir,' she said.

'My wife?'

Mrs Sealey bit her lip. 'She is alive, but you must be quick.'

He ran up the stairs two at a time, not even glancing at the tiny bundle that the woman held, before entering his wife's room and closing the door. Mrs Sealey glanced after him for a moment, then came down the stairs to where Emily was standing. 'Just look at the little mite,' she said, pulling back the covers to reveal the sleeping infant. 'Poor motherless child. You take her, miss. I've already alerted a local woman who's had a baby a little while back to come and wet nurse this one. I'll have her sent for, shall I?'

'Oh yes, do,' Emily answered. 'We cannot risk her going hungry.'

'Will you hold her then, miss, while I do that? Do you know how to hold a baby?'

'Yes, I know,' Emily replied, taking the child in her arms. It would not be the first time that she had held a child who was never to know its mother, but she had never felt anxiety about a baby before as she did about this one; for although hardly anyone else knew it, this baby was fatherless too.

17

The next few days went by in a haze as far as Emily was concerned. There seemed to be so much to do, and everyone was looking to her. Mr Fanshawe had remained at his wife's bedside until she had passed away peacefully, breathing his name, but after that, had seemed to withdraw from any decisions that needed to be made. The only thing he had been adamant about had been that Nathalie should be laid to rest here, in Mablethorpe.

'She loved the place, and never really settled in Lincoln,' he said.

The funeral he left for Emily to organize in consultation with the local clergyman, simply saying when asked about any matter: 'Whatever you think best.'

Hannah Grant, the wet nurse, arrived soon after Mrs Sealey had sent for her, and she proved to be a gentle, cheerful woman, and very well able to feed the new baby. After a little negotiation, Emily managed to persuade her to come back to Lincoln with them, leaving her own baby, who was just weaned, in the care of the child's grandmother. Mrs Grant agreed to stay in Lincoln until a local wet nurse could be found. Emily could think of one or two women who had recently had babies who, if asked, might easily be glad to help in that way.

Then there was Mrs Sealey who needed comforting. After the initial shock of Nathalie's death, the landlady had taken to blaming herself. 'It was I who upset her so with that awful tale I told her, miss,' the woman said to Emily, with tears in her eyes. 'Do you think that that brought her on into labour too soon? Oh, if I thought that by my careless words I had killed that poor young woman. I would never be able to forgive myself.'

Emily reassured Mrs Sealey that this was not the case. 'The doctor said that the baby was the wrong way round, and no words of yours could have caused that to happen,' Emily insisted.

Nevertheless, Mrs Sealey could not lay the matter to rest, and brought it up over and over again, until Emily thought that she would scream. So, what with one thing and another, including writing to her father, the bishop, the dean, and Mr Fanshawe's housekeeper, each letter needing care and tact, she had no time at all to think about her own feelings in the matter. She did wonder whether Nathalie's family in Devon ought to be informed, but she did not know their address, and Mr Fanshawe was in no condition to be consulted on the matter.

They all travelled back together in a hired chaise. The wet nurse and Emily took turns holding the baby. Mr Fanshawe still refused even to look at her. Mercifully, perhaps, for everyone's peace of mind, she was a remarkably good baby, taking to Mrs Grant's breast without difficulty, settling down to sleep between feeds, and lying placidly in someone's arms when she was awake. Emily hardly dared imagine how the haggard young clergyman might have reacted had the baby been fretful on the journey. She had not dared ask him by what name he wanted to call the child, but secretly, she called her Nathalie.

The weather was cool and overcast but fine when they set off from Mablethorpe, and it remained so throughout the journey. Last time she had travelled this road, she reflected, she had been reading a novel. The experiences she had undergone over the past days had surely been the stuff of novels, but not of any novel that she wanted to read.

On their arrival in Lincoln, the chaise drew into Minster Yard, Emily helped Mrs Grant inside with the baby, commiserated with the tearful housekeeper, delivered Mr Fanshawe into the hands of his valet, then left the house, promising to return very soon. After all, she had two women to speak to, in order to discover whether one of them could take over as wet nurse. Hannah Grant, quite understandably, wanted to get back to her family as soon as possible.

The door of the Fanshaws' house closed behind her, she walked down the path, took a few steps into the yard, then stopped and turned. It was here, she thought to herself. This was where I was standing when Nathalie came running out of the house. I was standing here with Dr Boyle. This was where our friendship really began; I never had a chance to say good-bye.

She had not yet cried, because she had had to be strong for all the others who were around her and who seemed to be falling apart. Suddenly, all the tears that she had had to hold back seemed to rush into her eyes at once. She looked around blindly. Where could she go?

There was only one place. Hurrying to the west door, she fumbled for the handle and made her way into the heart of the building that had always been her sanctuary.

★ ★ ★

Sir Gareth had called to see Emily during the afternoon following their outing to Gainsborough. The whole morning had been wet and miserable, but after midday, the clouds had cleared and the sunshine had made everything look sparkling and new. He had hoped to persuade her to take a walk with him, but when he had arrived at the Whittakers' house, he had been greeted with the news that Emily had gone into the country to visit friends. No, unfortunately the maid could not tell him when Miss Whittaker would be back. No, she did not have her direction. Yes, she would certainly inform Miss Whittaker when she returned that he had called.

Two days later, he called again, but as he arrived at the house, Dr Boyle came out. 'I'm afraid that Miss Whittaker has not returned,' the doctor said. Something about his tone seemed to indicate that he knew where Emily was, and for a moment, the baronet was sorely tempted to use his justly famous left fist and lay the doctor out on the front step.

Instead, he smiled blandly and said, 'Yes I was aware that she was away. In fact, I have come to call upon her grandfather.'

'Her grandfather?' exclaimed the doctor incredulously.

'Yes. She informed me that she had reason to hope for an improvement in his condition;

270

perhaps she did not tell you that?'

'Of course she told me,' the doctor snapped. Then, realizing how rude he had been, he straightened his shoulders and said in a calmer tone, 'I am his physician, so naturally she would tell me. I fear, though, that he will not provide you with any conversation, sir.'

'Nevertheless, I would like to pay him the courtesy of a visit,' Sir Gareth replied.

'If you should see any improvement, I trust that you will apprise me of the fact,' the doctor said.

The baronet did not answer, but merely smiled, bowed slightly, and allowed himself to be shown up the stairs by Mary who, quite unknown to Sir Gareth, was thinking most improperly how she would not mind showing him upstairs on another account!

She let him into the elderly clergyman's room, then said softly, 'Would you like a glass of wine, sir?'

Sir Gareth accepted, then sat down at the old man's bedside and thought to himself, now what? Well, of course, he ought to introduce himself. 'Good afternoon,' he said. 'My name is Sir Gareth Blades. I'm brother-in-law to one of the new clergy here.' There was a long silence. He got up from his place and wandered over to the window to look out at the cathedral. 'That's a fine cathedral you have there,' he remarked. Oh God, I'm going to start saying that the grass is green and the sky is blue, and there's a dog walking past next. Who the deuce wants to hear about that?

Mary came in with a glass of claret on a tray, and Sir Gareth took it with a smile. He took a sip. It was good; very good. 'But then, Patrick had a good palate,' he remarked out loud. 'Still undeveloped, but with great potential. Did he inherit it from you, I wonder?' In a moment of sudden impulse, he went to the bedside, dipped his little finger in the wine, and brushed it on to the old man's lips. At first, there seemed to be no reaction at all. Then slowly, almost imperceptibly, his lips parted the tiniest fraction, the tip of his tongue emerged, and he moistened his lips. 'Like that, do you?' murmured the baronet, before doing the same again. He went through the same procedure perhaps three or four times before saying, 'That's enough now. Don't want to get you drunk, do we?'

He wandered over to the window again, and took a sip of wine. 'What does she do when she comes to see you?' he said out loud. 'Does she read to you? Does she tell you about her day, about what she has been doing?' He paused. 'Has she told you about

272

me? No, I don't suppose she has. I expect she spends all her time enlarging on the virtues of Dr Pustule, damn his eyes. She could do better than that, you know.'

He took a sip of wine and sighed reminiscently. 'If only you could have seen her on the day when we went to Gainsborough. It wasn't just the gown — although it was good to see her dressed for once as a lovely woman should be dressed; it was that she actually imparted sunshine to the gown; she made *it* look better! What I wouldn't give to have the dressing of her; throw out those dingy gowns — someone should have thrown them out years ago — and see her in gold, and burnt orange, and a certain shade of green. But what's the good of thinking about that? She doesn't even want me for a brother, for goodness sake!'

Briefly, he thought back to that moment in Gainsborough when she had said those words to him. At the time he had been hurt by them. Since then, he had turned them over in his mind, looking at them from all angles. Eventually, to his rueful surprise, he had come to the conclusion that if she did not want him for a brother, then neither did he want her for a sister.

Noticing her unusual quality, he had originally planned simply to indulge her with a flirtation that would at one and the same time raise her self esteem, and cause Dr Boyle to look to his laurels. The game of flirtation he had soon abandoned. A man of the world, he was all too well aware that Canon Whittaker's spinster daughter was developing a *tendre* for him, and the last thing that he wanted to do was to raise false hopes. But the more he thought about the matter, the more he came to realize that she deserved better than Dr Boyle. She deserved a man who would not just esteem her, but love and cherish her. She deserved a man who looked upon her not just as a help-meet-cum-drudge, but as someone with whom to share projects, interests and concerns. She deserved a man who would not carp at the cost of a gown, but encourage her to dress in fabrics that brought out the beauty of her creamy skin. In short, she deserved a man like himself.

Looking down, he saw that he had almost finished his wine, so crossing to the bed, he gave the clergyman one last drop, which the old man licked at delicately as before. 'I'll come and see you again,' he said, putting down his glass. 'Good day to you, sir.' Then, as politely as if the man was conscious, he bowed with all his customary elegance and withdrew. As he left, Dr Whittaker's lips turned upwards into a faint smile.

Sir Gareth visited Emily's grandfather on two more occasions before her return. Both times, he gave the old man a little wine as before and then chatted easily about what the boys had been doing. Towards the end of his second visit, however, he said 'Where is she? Do you know where she is? Would you even tell me if you did know? I keep tormenting myself with the idea that amongst the company she's visiting is some fellow who's going to carry her off. I wonder how Dr Excrescence would like that?' He paused briefly, then went on in a sombre tone, 'I wonder how *I* would like it?'

It was as he was returning to the Trimmers' house after this visit that he saw what he thought was a familiar figure hurrying towards the west door of the cathedral. On impulse, he turned and went inside himself, removing his hat and then looking about him to see if he could see her. Where might she be? Suddenly having an idea, he retraced the steps that they had taken when she had shown him around.

He heard her before he saw her. The sound that he heard was enough to tear at his own heart strings. Rounding the corner, he saw Emily, sprawled across the seat on which they had sat on that previous occasion. Her face was resting on her arms, and she was sobbing bitterly.

Sir Gareth had heard women cry on other occasions; sometimes at an affecting play, sometimes because of a disagreement; sometimes because he would not buy a coveted string of pearls. He had also heard Emily crying before, when they had visited Gainsborough and she had wept briefly at the memory of her brother. But this crying was different. Like her laughter, it came out as a sound that was seldom made, and it came from deep within her soul.

He did not even think about what he should do: there was never any question of it. Lifting the upper part of her body gently off the stone seat, he sat down next to her and pulled her into his arms, so that she could cry on his shoulder.

He let her have her cry out, but then when her sobs began to subside, he got out a handkerchief, and handed it to her, keeping one arm around her. 'Would you like to tell me about it?' he asked her gently. 'I've no wish to force your confidence, but it might help to talk. Besides, there may be something I can do.' It must have been a very serious occurrence in the household of her friends to reduce her to this state, he decided.

She shook her head. 'There is nothing you

can do,' she told him. 'My friend . . . ' She paused and gulped. 'My friend is dead, you see.'

'Oh my dear,' he exclaimed involuntarily, gathering her close to him again. 'Was it very sudden?'

'It was in childbirth,' she answered. She explained to him how she had gone to stay with her friend because her husband was away, and about how they had had to send for him in the middle of the night. 'At least he was there in time to see her, but you see, I know it sounds selfish but' — she gulped — 'but I did not have the chance to . . . to say goodbye.' She shed a few more tears. 'Of course I know that it is far more important that her husband should have been there. Mr Fanshawe is a clergyman here. Did you know?'

He went suddenly still. 'No. No, I didn't know,' he replied.

'He has not been here for very long; just a little longer than Mr Trimmer. I do not have many friends and Nathalie and I had become quite close in a short space of time.'

'I understand,' he answered. Then, in a changed tone, he went on, 'My dear girl, you must try not to berate yourself over this. You were with your friend when she needed you. It is very sad that you could not say goodbye, but it is far better that her husband should have been there, surely.'

'Yes, yes, you are right of course,' she answered, sitting up straight. She had just realized that she had been in the baronet's embrace for rather a long time, and although there was nowhere else that she would rather be, she knew that it was quite improper. 'Of course it was right that he should be with her at the last. And although I will miss her very much, he will miss her more, and that sweet little baby will never know its mother.'

'There is a child!' he exclaimed. Looking up at him for the first time, it seemed to Emily that he looked a little paler than usual and she wondered whether he had been ill.

'Yes,' she answered, puzzled. 'I told you that Nathalie had died in childbirth.'

'Yes, yes of course,' he said quickly. 'But I thought that perhaps the child had died as well.'

'Oh no,' Emily assured him. 'The baby is thriving at present, but that reminds me, I must go and find a wet nurse for her. We brought one back with us from Mablethorpe, but she is anxious to return to her own family.'

'Should you not go home and rest?' asked the baronet.

'No, no, I am better if I have something to

do,' Emily replied. She stood up, fumbling at the strings of her bonnet with fingers that were still not quite steady. 'Do I look a perfect fright?' she asked him.

He had risen when she did. Now he smiled down at her gently. 'Allow me,' he said. He unfastened her bonnet and handed it to her, then carefully smoothed back the strands of her hair that had come adrift. She found herself holding her breath at the occasional touch of his fingers against her skin. Then, when he had done, he took her bonnet from her again, placed it on her head, and fastened the ribbons with a bow which he tied stylishly somewhere between her ear and her chin.

'Thank you,' she murmured.

'My only desire is to serve you,' he responded, taking hold of her hand, raising it to his lips and kissing it, keeping his eyes on her face the whole time. She knew a sudden impulse to raise her other hand to his cheek, but she sternly repressed it. After all, he was just being kind.

She turned and hurried out of the cathedral. He stood watching her for a moment, then took a deep breath and followed her, walking slowly.

18

To Emily's great relief, the first woman that she approached was very willing to act as wet nurse to Mrs Fanshawe's motherless baby. She was the daughter of the landlady of the White Hart, and so the work would be very convenient for her.

'I fear that Mr Fanshawe is very distraught at the moment, and I do not know how much help he will be,' Emily told her.

'Oh that's no problem, mum,' said Mrs Pearce cheerfully. 'I can have the baby here with me for a while if he prefers it.'

Emily was not quite sure how appropriate it would be for the baby's formative days to be spent in an inn, but when she looked at the handsome, respectable young woman sitting in front of her, she came to the conclusion that it would probably do the child no harm at all.

Mrs Pearce looked at her curiously. 'You look a bit peaky yourself, mum, if you don't mind my saying so. Were she a friend of yours?'

Emily could feel the tears welling up again. 'Yes. Yes, she was,' she replied, her voice breaking.

'Well then, just let me get you a glass of father's good claret,' said Mrs Pearce. 'That'll help.'

In fact, Mrs Pearce fetched not only a glass of wine, but also her own little boy, who clearly had a very sunny nature, and took to Emily immediately. The young woman very wisely chatted about her son's doings whilst her visitor played with him, and after spending half an hour in this simple and undemanding way, Emily began to feel able to face the world again.

'I will go round to Mr Fanshawe immediately and tell him that you will be able to help out,' she said, standing up. 'Mrs Grant will be so pleased to be able to get home again.'

'Just send me word and I'll come round,' answered Mrs Pearce. 'Soon as I've got this one settled.'

At least that's one thing sorted out, Emily thought to herself, as she walked back into the Minster Yard and approached the front door of Mr Fanshawe's house. Then, just as she reached the garden gate, she hesitated. Of course it was important that Mrs Grant should be able to return home as soon as possible, but they had only arrived that day. It would hardly be fair to expect her to turn around and go back to Mablethorpe immediately. Furthermore, the household needed a little time to settle down after all the turmoil that they had all experienced. She would go back the next day and tell Mr Fanshawe about what she had arranged. Perhaps by then he might even be willing to hear it.

With no further reason for delay, she turned her footsteps reluctantly towards home. It was not that her father would be unsympathetic: it was simply that there was so much of Nathalie's story that she could not share with anyone. What she would have liked to have done more than anything was to talk to Mrs Trimmer about the loss of her friend, but she did not want Sir Gareth to think that she was pursuing him into the house.

It was, therefore, a great relief to her when she opened the front door to have Mary come hurrying up to her and say, 'Oh, miss, such a time as you have had! I'm that sorry! Mrs Trimmer has called to see you and is waiting in the drawing-room.'

Emily surrendered her bonnet and shawl to the maid and went straight in. As soon as she entered the room, Mrs Trimmer got to her feet and came towards her, her arms outstretched. 'Oh my dear friend,' she said in sympathetic tones. 'What a dreadful experience for you.'

Emily had been quite determined that she

was not going to cry again, but in the face of Mrs Trimmer's kindness, she could not help shedding a tear or two. 'Yes, it was truly one of the worst experiences of my life,' Emily agreed. 'I have attended in homes where someone has died on many occasions since I was an adult, but never before when the person was close to me.'

'Had you known her for very long?' Mrs Trimmer asked.

'Not really,' Emily replied. 'The Fanshawes came to live in Lincoln a few months ago, but I only really got to know Nathalie after I was asked to go with her to Mablethorpe.' She paused. 'It must sound silly to you, but I don't have many friends. There were never many girls of my age growing up in the close, and those that did so, married and moved away years ago. I know it must sound very selfish but it seems so hard to make a friend only to lose her and in such a terrible way.'

'It doesn't sound selfish at all,' Mrs Trimmer replied. At that moment, Mary, acting on her own initiative, came in with a tea tray, and Emily, who suddenly realized that she was quite thirsty, poured out for them.

She handed Mrs Trimmer a cup, saying, 'I am so glad that you were here when I came in. It was such a comfort to me.'

'You can thank Gareth for that,' Aurelia replied. 'He told me how distressed you had been in the church and suggested that you might be glad to see me.'

'Oh how kind of him,' Emily exclaimed involuntarily. 'How truly sensitive!'

Mrs Trimmer merely smiled in response to this, and after a brief pause said, by way of change of subject, 'The boys will be glad that you have returned. They are for ever asking when you might be able to take them up the other towers.'

'I should be delighted to do so,' Emily answered. 'Pray tell them that we shall go on the next fine day.'

With all that had happened, Emily had quite forgotten to bring Miss Wayne to Aurelia's notice. She did so now, and her friend listened thoughtfully. 'I do not know her well, but my impression of her has been good,' she said. 'I am not sure how well she would cope with two lively boys, however.'

Refraining from commenting that a woman who could cope with Mrs Hughes could surely cope with anything, Emily simply said, 'Perhaps you could ask her to keep an eye on them one day; possibly while you are entertaining Mrs Hughes yourself.'

'I have only one fault to find with that idea, which is that it will involve my spending an afternoon in Mrs Hughes's company,' Aurelia replied mischievously. 'However, I will then be able to find out if the boys like Miss Wayne, which is vitally important, so perhaps it is a sacrifice worth making.' They talked easily about Oliver and James for a little while and by the time Aurelia rose to go, Emily realized that she was feeling much better.

'Do you think that I ought to call on Mr Fanshawe to offer him some help?' Aurelia asked. 'I do not want to be insensitive and, of course, Alan must be the first to call, but his circumstances are unusual. I do not want to deny him any assistance that I might be able to give.'

'Leave it a day or two,' Emily suggested. 'He was very distraught and not fit to deal with anyone.'

'I know that Gareth means to call upon him,' Aurelia told her as she was leaving. 'Apparently, he knew him slightly in London.'

'How strange,' Emily murmured. 'He didn't mention it earlier.'

★ ★ ★

Later that day, Emily went up to her grandfather's room. There, in the silence, feeling as if she were in the privacy of the confessional, she told the recumbent old man

Nathalie's whole story. This time, although she did shed a tear or two, she was not distraught as before, and afterwards she felt more at peace, as if the experience had been cathartic.

'Thank you, Grandpapa,' she said, bending to kiss him. As she did so, she took hold of his hand and, unmistakably, but quite faintly, he returned the pressure. 'Grandpapa?' she said again. 'Open your eyes, Grandpapa.' He did not do so, but there was the merest flickering of his eyelids.

The next day, Dr Boyle called to see Dr Whittaker, and after he had come back downstairs again, Emily told him what had happened. He listened attentively. 'Those are very good signs,' he told her. 'Your faithful attendance has, I feel, done him a great deal of good.'

'Papa has also visited him every day,' Emily pointed out.

'Yes indeed, but a granddaughter can sometimes have a closer relationship with a grandparent than that which exists between parent and child,' the doctor replied. He paused briefly then said, in a more urgent tone, 'Miss Whittaker!'

'How is Mr Fanshawe?' she asked hastily, fearing a proposal.

It was a successful diversion. The doctor

shook his head. 'It was a tragic business, was it not? I have attended him of course, but naturally I cannot disclose anything to you about his condition.'

'Naturally not,' Emily agreed. 'It is simply that I am wondering whether to go round yet and introduce the new wet nurse. I know that Mrs Grant wants to get back to Mablethorpe as soon as possible, but I did not want to intrude.'

'I think you might go,' the doctor answered. 'He is naturally still distressed and will be for some time, but the child must be settled. She is thriving, I am thankful to say. How I wish that Mr Fanshawe would take some notice of her! But it is early days yet.'

To Emily's relief, he left without proposing. His timing would have been most inappropriate even had she been inclined in his favour. Recent events, however, had shown her that she could never accept him. When he took her hand before his departure, she had felt nothing other than a mild distaste at the clamminess of his touch. The salute of Sir Gareth, however, had seemed to cause every nerve end to tingle. How could she ever marry anyone and accept less than that?

She went upstairs intending to visit her grandfather, but as she was going, Mary appeared in the hall and said, 'Shall I bring a glass of claret, miss?'

'Claret?' echoed Emily, mystified.

'Well, when Sir Gareth comes to see the old gentleman, he has a glass and he gives him a little bit.'

'Sir Gareth visits my grandfather?'

'He came two or three times while you were away, miss.'

Feeling absurdly pleased, Emily said, 'Just a small glass, then.'

'Grandpapa, I have decided that I cannot marry Dr Boyle,' she told her grandfather when she was in his room with the door closed. 'I am sorry if you are disappointed, but you see I . . . ' She paused. 'Grandpapa, I'm . . . I'm in love.' It seemed strange to say it out loud. 'I'm in love with Sir Gareth. You know, the gentleman who comes to see you sometimes. Oh I know that he would never look at me in that way. In fact, I am almost sure that he thinks of me as another sister, but because I feel that way about him, I cannot bear the thought of marrying anyone else, even if it means a lifetime of loneliness.'

At that point, Mary came into the room with the glass of wine on a tray, and in getting up to make sure that there was a clear surface for the glass to rest on, Emily managed to conceal the blush that had crept into her cheeks.

'Shall I show you how Sir Gareth gives him the wine, miss?' Mary asked.

'Please.'

The maid took the glass to the old man, dipped her finger in the wine, and touched his lips with it. Emily watched in wonder as her grandfather's tongue emerged to lick the droplets. 'Let me, Mary,' she said.

'Of course, miss.' Smiling, Mary handed the glass over before leaving the room.

Emily sat next to her grandfather on the bed, and went through the same process several times before saying, 'You are getting better and better every day. I know you are. That was good, wasn't it?'

While she was watching, Dr Whittaker's lips moved to frame the shape of the word 'good'.

Emily stayed with her grandfather for a little longer. He made no further response to her presence, but she was satisfied. The death of Nathalie had been a shock, and it would take time to recover from the blow caused by the loss of a friend, albeit quite a new one. But hope could be found in other situations; in the health of the new baby, for instance; in the slow recovery of Dr Whittaker.

Knowing that the news would please her father, Emily sought him out and told him about the small signs of improvement in her

grandfather's condition. To her great astonishment, Canon Whittaker then told her that
he had noticed similar incidents. 'I did not
say anything, because I did not want to raise
your hopes for nothing,' he told her. After a
brief silence, he said, 'I was sorry to hear of
the death of Mrs Fanshawe. You had become
very attached to her, I think.'

'Yes . . . yes, I had,' Emily admitted. She
was glad that he did not say more. She had
not yet reached a point where she wanted to
discuss the matter.

She now felt strong enough to go to the
Fanshawe household and break the news of
the wet nurse that she had found. In truth,
although she had suggested to Dr Boyle that
she might go, she had felt very reluctant to do
so. The circumstances in which she had last
spoken with Mr Fanshawe had oppressed her
spirits. Now, however, a new feeling of
optimism buoyed her up, and resolving to
make the most of it, she put on her bonnet
and walked along the southern side of the
cathedral.

As she passed the Trimmers' front door,
she found her footsteps slowing, as if to
increase her chances of encountering Sir
Gareth, and she remembered the conversation that she had once heard between a local
girl and her infatuated friend. Don't be

foolish, she told herself, deliberately quickening her step.

Mr Fanshawe's housekeeper greeted Emily with pleasure. She looked markedly more cheerful than on the last occasion when Emily had seen her, and the reason for this increased cheerfulness soon became apparent. 'Such a dear little mite,' she said smiling. 'She's never a bit of trouble, and as for that Mrs Grant that you brought, such a pleasant person! I do declare the house will be quite dull without her, when she goes.'

'It is about that matter that I have come to see Mr Fanshawe,' said Emily. 'Is he within, Mrs Dainty?'

'He's just stepped out, but only for a moment,' answered Mrs Dainty, her face becoming anxious. 'We all want to help him, so we do, Miss Whittaker, but how to do it?'

'It isn't easy,' replied Emily. 'Time is a great healer, of course. I'll come back later, then.'

But this Mrs Dainty would by no means allow. 'You must step upstairs and see the little one while you are here,' she pleaded. 'She is so much like her dear mama that it's no wonder the master finds it hard to look at her. No doubt that resemblance will be a comfort to him in time.'

'All right then,' Emily answered, easily

persuaded because in truth she did want to see the baby again. 'Perhaps Mr Fanshawe will have returned when I come downstairs, if he has only gone out briefly.'

The housekeeper conducted her upstairs to the nursery, where Emily could see that the baby was thriving just as much as the woman had said. 'I do believe she has grown, even since I saw her last,' Emily said, as she took the baby from Mrs Grant, who had just finished feeding her and changing her napkin.

Whilst she was holding the baby, she told the other two women about how she had found Mrs Pearce to be the new wet nurse. 'I know the family well,' said Mrs Dainty. 'They're a respectable lot.'

'Well, I shall be sorry to say goodbye to this one and that's a fact,' said Mrs Grant. 'Not but what I'm anxious to see my own little ones again, but she's one that is easy to be fond of, if you take my meaning.'

'Yes indeed,' Emily agreed. 'Mrs Dainty, would you like to hold her for a little while?'

'That I would, miss,' the housekeeper replied, putting her arms out to take the baby. 'It's some time now since my own little ones were this size.' She had just done so, when they heard the sound of the front door closing. 'That'll be the master,' Mrs Dainty said, looking regretfully down at the dozing infant.

'Don't worry,' Emily told her. 'I am sure that Mr Fanshawe will not mind if I knock on the door and tell him the news.'

'"Twouldn't really be proper,' the housekeeper responded. Then a look of regret crossed her features. 'Mind you, it won't be the first thing that's happened to this household that shouldn't have done.'

'No indeed,' Emily agreed. 'I will see you both soon. Pray do not leave without saying goodbye, Mrs Grant.'

'No, indeed I won't, miss.'

Emily went down the stairs and tapped lightly on the drawing-room door, and when no one answered she went in. The room was empty, but the door which led from the drawing-room into the study was not quite shut, and she became conscious of voices in conversation. It had never been her intention to listen, but as she drew closer to the door, she recognized the timbre of Sir Gareth's voice and paused, not to eavesdrop, but simply to savour the pleasure of hearing his voice.

'I haven't come to interfere; I wouldn't dream of it,' he was saying.

'Oh no?' replied Fanshawe in the kind of sneering, hopeless tone that Emily had heard him use before.

'No,' Sir Gareth answered. 'God knows, I don't want the responsibility.'

'Then rejoice,' Fanshawe exclaimed sarcastically. 'You don't have it, do you?' He paused. 'God forgive me, but I can hardly bear to look at her.'

Deciding that she had heard enough, Emily raised her hand to scratch on the door, but before she could do so, the baronet said, 'Then give her to me. At least we have the same blood in our veins.'

'But the world thinks that I am her father,' Fanshawe declared.

'You and I know differently though, don't we?'

Suddenly, Emily felt sick. Clamping her hand to her mouth, she hurried out into the hall, where mercifully there were no servants to detain her, and then into the street. She stared up at the cathedral and for the first time could not feel able to run here for comfort. In the recent past she had met with Sir Gareth there on too many occasions. Staring about her like a frightened animal, she finally hurried home, praying that neither her father nor Mary would meet her in the hall or on the stairs.

19

Fortune favoured her and after what seemed like hours, but which in reality could only have been a matter of minutes, she gained the sanctuary of her room. There she sat on her bed and finally forced herself to consider the vile disclosure that Sir Gareth was the baby's father.

What other explanation could there be? The whole business had been very secret as Nathalie had informed her. How would the baronet know about it if he were not one of the principals in the affair? Furthermore, he had said that he and the baby had the same blood in their veins.

Now that she thought about it, there were other, small incidents which could have given her a clue. When he had first arrived, his sister had referred to an injury that he had sustained. That would have been the injury in the duel that he had fought. Lord Stuart had spoken of Sir Gareth as running with a dangerous set. Such a man would think nothing of taking part in a duel. Nathalie had spoken of her lover as a handsome man of taste, and that certainly described Sir Gareth.

Had not his sister and Mrs Hughes both mentioned the way in which ladies liked to consult him? Yes, and Nathalie had said that the father of her child had a reputation among the ladies.

A man who could treat Nathalie in such a way could have very few scruples, and Emily had seen how easily he could tell an untruth if he thought that a situation called for it. If this needed confirmation, Mrs Hughes had said more than once that he was a fabricator of lies. Once, she had thought him a hero. What kind of hero behaved thus?

'Fool, fool, fool!' she said out loud. 'How could I be so deceived?' Thinking of Nathalie, she knew that she was not the first. At least she had not been so unfortunate as her friend. As she told herself this, however, she realized that she was committing the greatest deceit of all. Although naturally she did not want to die in childbirth, and although there was a part of her that even now wished that she were dead, another, treacherous, weak-willed part could not help thinking how wonderful it would be to bear Sir Gareth's child. Then she burst into a storm of weeping as she realized that despite the wicked things that he had done, she still had a picture in her mind of those engaging dimples, that warm smile, and her body still tingled at the memory of the touch of his hand. Was there ever such a fool as she?

She did not go down to dinner that night, pleading a headache, and fortunately, because her father was engaged to dine with some of the other clergy, she did not have to explain herself to anyone. She sent her tray back untouched, slept only fitfully that night, and woke up with the headache that she had feigned the previous evening.

Remembering her errand of the day before, she wrote a brief note to Mr Fanshawe, telling him about the new wet nurse, but she did not leave her room. Mary came upstairs with a message to say that Sir Gareth and his sister had called, but she denied herself, pleading her headache as a reason. Later that day, a bunch of roses arrived from the baronet with a message to say that he hoped that she would soon be better. She tore the note into pieces, then cried over the bits, as she retrieved them all. The roses, she decided, could go in her grandfather's room. It would be shameful to waste them, but she did not want to be seeing them every minute of every day.

She put them in a vase, therefore, and took them to the old man's room, where she put them down on the bedside table so that he could look at them. 'Aren't they beautiful?'

she said to him moving one slightly so that they looked better. 'Sir Gareth brought them. He . . . ' All of a sudden, the bright cheerful words died in her throat, and exclaiming 'Oh Grandpapa!' she put her arms down on the bed, next to him and buried her face in them.

'Grandpapa, I thought . . . ' she gulped. 'I never, never supposed that he would look at me; not really. When I was in my pretty yellow gown I indulged myself with some hopeless dreams, but I suppose I knew deep down that that was all that they were. Oh there were times, when I thought there might be a chance for me, but even though the chance was very small, I loved the fact that he was honourable and kind and good. But he isn't, Grandpapa; he isn't! He's vile and wicked and I don't think I can bear it.'

Suddenly, she became aware of a very light pressure upon her head, and, looking up in surprise, she found that her grandfather was stroking her hair, and that his eyes were open.

'Grandpapa?' she breathed.

His lips moved. She leaned down to hear what he was trying to say. 'Good man,' he murmured.

She smiled at him. 'Yes, you are a good man,' she told him.

His brow wrinkled; his mouth worked as if in agitation. 'No, no; good man,' he insisted.

'Good man. Wine.'

'Do you mean Sir Gareth?' Emily asked him tentatively.

'Good man,' he repeated.

Moments later, there was a knock on the door, and Dr Boyle came in.

'Miss Whittaker?' he questioned concernedly, for it was quite clear that she had been crying.

'Look, Doctor,' she said, gesturing towards the old man. In truth, had she been crying for no other reason, she might easily have been shedding tears of thankfulness.

Dr Boyle lifted Dr Whittaker's wrist to take his pulse, then glancing at his face was so surprised to see watery blue eyes looking at him that he almost dropped the limb that he was holding. 'Dr Whittaker,' he said slowly, 'can you hear me?'

The elderly clergyman continued to look at the doctor, but made no further reaction.

'He stroked my hair,' said Emily. 'I looked at him and found that he was looking at me.' For some reason, she found that she could not tell him about what her grandfather had said. Her feelings were too raw on that particular issue.

'This is indeed very promising,' said the doctor, 'very promising indeed.' After a short time, Dr Whittaker closed his eyes again, and soon after that, the doctor left the room, signalling to Emily to come with him.

When they were downstairs in the saloon, Dr Boyle said, 'This is excellent. I must tell you that I had not looked for this degree of progress. Your father will be delighted to hear the good news. Is it your wish that I should tell him, or would you like to give him the news yourself?'

'I will tell him,' Emily replied, thinking that this would provide the two of them with a topic of conversation that had nothing to do with her broken heart.

The doctor shuffled a little, and began to look self-conscious, and by these signals, Emily know that he was going to raise a topic of a personal nature. 'Miss Whittaker, I was hoping that with the anxiety over your grandfather lessening by the day, you might be persuaded to hear me on a matter that is very close to my heart.'

Emily was on the point of refusing point blank to listen to him, but something gave her pause. It was partly the knowledge that she would have to listen to him one day; it was also partly because now that her illusions about Sir Gareth had been torn away, marriage to the doctor seemed to be a possible way of escape. She sat down therefore, folded her hands in her lap, and said, 'Very well, Dr Boyle, what do you wish to say to me?' Then she was obliged to listen while the doctor spoke of his respect for her, his regard for her intelligence, his thoughts about how she would make an excellent helpmeet for a busy doctor; throughout his speech, not one word of love did he say.

That was what made Emily decide that she would probably accept him. A marriage in which she was struggling with the guilt of not being able to return her partner's affections would be intolerable. And yet she could not say yes; at least, not yet.

'Dr Boyle, you are very kind and I thank you for your very flattering sentiments,' she said. 'However, I need some time to think about your proposal. May I give you my answer in a few days?'

The doctor fairly beamed, for this was a more encouraging answer than he had expected. 'Of course, of course,' he replied. 'I leave here a hopeful man, Miss Whittaker.' He took her hand and kissed it in quite the grand manner. Emily, remembering a very different touch, barely repressed a shudder.

The doctor left the house with a smile on his face and a spring in his step. He looked in on baby Fanshawe — who had still not been given a name — and pronounced her to be in excellent health. Mr Fanshawe acted like the perfect gentleman, but Boyle suspected that he was holding down a good deal of grief by sheer will power. He came away rather concerned, but even this occurrence could not dampen his spirits completely. So cheerful did he look that Sir Gareth, happening to meet him on his way back from an errand in Bailgate, asked him the cause of his good humour.

Well aware that Sir Gareth was something of a ladies' man, the doctor was very pleased to enlighten him. 'I have this morning been visiting Miss Whittaker, and so welcoming was she that I made so bold as to propose marriage to her.'

The smile on the baronet's face became rather fixed and he stiffened a little. 'From your demeanour, do I take it that congratulations are in order?' he asked.

The doctor looked a little crestfallen for a moment or two, but he soon cheered up again. 'Not precisely,' he replied. 'At least, she asked for time to think about the matter, so she has not exactly said no. How long do you think I ought to leave it before I go back to her?'

Repressing the urge to say at least forty years, Sir Gareth answered 'I would wait for a couple of days. Ladies do not like to be rushed.'

'A couple of days,' echoed the doctor. 'Yes, I shall do as you say, sir. I should not want her to make an unconsidered decision.' With that he walked on, completely unaware of the turmoil that he had stirred up in the other man's breast.

For his part, the baronet felt as if he had been punched in the stomach. Emily's attraction for him had been growing with every passing day, but when he had embraced her in the cathedral and she had poured out her grief onto his chest it had been as if he had reached a point from which there was no turning back.

Unlike Emily, he had loved before. He had also enjoyed casual connections with ladies of like mind. No other woman, however, had touched his feelings at such a deep level. He had always thought her pretty, although her attractiveness was often concealed by ill-chosen clothes. More significantly, however, he admired her courage in the face of situations whose sordidness would cause most society women to cringe in horror. He also admired her energy, seen for example in her climbing of the great tower. He liked the way that she talked to his nephews, and the way in which she had extended a hand of friendship to his sister. That little choking sound that she made when she thought she ought not to laugh captivated him completely.

Yet for all her courage and energy, at times she seemed very much alone. At those times he was conscious of a longing to draw her close and protect her. In short, almost without his knowing it, she had come to fill his mind and his heart. Almost as soon as he had arrived in Lincoln, Aurelia had told him that he ought to marry. How strange to think that he was now contemplating marriage in good and earnest.

But now, although he had been so sure that she had a preference for him, it seemed that she was considering a proposal from Dr Boyle. Why? Did she believe that his attentions were only flirting, and that they would never come to anything? If so, then he must go round and persuade her that she was mistaken in this belief.

He went immediately to the Whittakers' house, but was told that Miss Whittaker was not receiving. This was according to Emily's instructions.

'But miss . . . ' Mary had protested.

'Those are my express wishes,' Emily had replied, more imperiously than was her wont. 'Kindly understand that I am not at home to Sir Gareth either today, or at any other time.'

'Miss . . . ' Mary ventured.

'He is a rake and a libertine, Mary,' Emily

answered, trying to conceal the shake in her voice. 'Such men are not welcome here.'

Mary had rather expected to find that the elegant baronet had grown horns the next time she opened the door, but to her surprise he looked much as usual.

'Are you able to tell me when she will be receiving?' he asked Mary, with his attractive smile.

Unable to bring herself to repeat her mistress's exact words, Mary said, 'I couldn't say, sir.'

'Then I will come back later.'

He began to walk away from the house, but as he did so, something made him turn and look up. For an instant, he saw Emily standing at one of the upstairs windows, before she stepped back out of his line of vision. He frowned, paused, and nearly turned back. Then, reflecting that he could hardly burst into someone's house uninvited, he walked back slowly to his sister's house. After all, the room in which she had been standing was probably her grandfather's. Perhaps she had been busy attending to him. But then, if she had been doing that, why had she been standing at the window?

★ ★ ★

'Aurelia, I have decided to ask Emily Whittaker to marry me,' the baronet announced the following morning.

'Gareth, how wonderful!' his sister exclaimed, hurrying to embrace him. 'I thought that you were looking particularly well turned-out today.'

The baronet had indeed almost surpassed his usual elegance. His coat fitted his broad shoulders superbly, his breeches were without a crease and his top boots were polished until they shone like glass.

'Do you think she'll have me?' he asked her, his diffident tone quite at variance with his usual assured manner.

'Have you?' his sister echoed. 'Of course she will. What woman would not?'

'But then, you are not entirely unbiased, dear Sister.'

'No, maybe not,' Mrs Trimmer agreed. 'But I have observed her and I would say that she had a fondness for you.'

'And so would I have said so, coxcomb that I am,' he replied. 'But yesterday, she would not receive me. Furthermore, she had only just heard a proposal of marriage from Dr Stye.'

'You are not going to tell me that she accepted him!'

'No, but she did not refuse him. She wanted to think about the matter.'

306

'There you are then,' his sister answered. 'Probably she could not face anyone else after such a momentous occasion. She needed a time of quiet reflection.'

'Yes, but . . . ' He paused. 'Aurelia, why would a woman say that she needed to think about it, unless there was in her mind the very real possibility that she might accept?'

'Gareth, my dear, she knows you are rich and titled. You have come here for a time, and flirted with her, along with Mrs Hughes and other women. Why should she think that you are serious? She may simply be trying not to burn all her boats. Go and call on her again; and Gareth?'

'Yes, Aurelia?'

'Make your feelings clear. If you love her, tell her so.'

A short time later, Sir Gareth called again at the Whittakers' house, and was again told by an embarrassed Mary that Miss Whittaker would not receive him. This time, Gareth was prepared to question the girl further.

'Do you mean that she is not in, or that she is not receiving anyone, or that she will not receive me in particular?' he asked. Mary flushed, and shuffled her feet. 'I see,' he said, colouring as well. 'I suppose it would be too much trouble for her to come and tell me why?'

'You have been told that you are not welcome here,' Emily said, from a step halfway up the flight. She stood very still, her hands clasped tightly together to prevent them from trembling. 'I do not understand why I should be importuned in my own house.'

'And I do not understand what I have done to merit such treatment,' he answered her, his face set. 'If I have done anything to offend you, I wish you would tell me what it is, then I would be able to beg your pardon.'

'*My* pardon?' Emily exclaimed, descending the rest of the stairs. Mary bobbed a curtsy and disappeared into the back of the house. 'I am not the one that you have offended against.'

'I can assure you that when I visited your grandfather, I behaved with the greatest respect,' he told her, pushing the front door to behind him.

'Nor have you hurt my grandfather,' Emily said. Then, straightening her spine, she said, 'I am speaking of Nathalie. I know her story.'

He lost a little colour. 'I see,' he said, and the tiny hope that she had been keeping in her heart shrivelled and died. 'I suppose that you would not be prepared to allow me to explain the part I played?'

'What explanation could there possibly be that could excuse what you did?' Emily demanded.

'I only did what any other man in my position would have done,' he told her.

'Oh, disgusting!' she exclaimed, almost shuddering with revulsion.

'Disgusting?' he repeated, mystified.

'Dr Boyle would not have done it,' she said swiftly. He gave a short contemptuous laugh. 'Yes, I know that you choose to laugh at his name,' she retorted, 'but he has proved himself to be a greater gentleman than you, for at least I can trust him.'

'And when have I proved myself unworthy of your trust?' he demanded.

'When I discovered that you had played a part in that disgraceful affair and presumably never intended to tell me about it.'

He paused for a moment. 'You are right,' he conceded. 'I probably would not have told you. But that was because — '

'Say no more, sir,' she interrupted. 'You have proved yourself to be a scoundrel, a libertine and a liar. To think that I . . . ' She drew a ragged breath. 'Kindly be gone, sir,' she said. 'We have nothing more to say to each other.'

'I see that you have constituted yourself as

309

judge and jury and have already pronounced me guilty,' declared the baronet bitterly. 'I came here today to tell you that I love you and to ask you to marry me, but clearly such a proposal from a man so depraved as myself would only be disgusting to you. Have no fear that I will importune you again. It only remains before I leave for me to give you a taste of the libertine that you think I am.'

Before she could realize what he was about he had pulled her into his arms, lowered his head and kissed her full on her mouth. The kisses that he had bestowed upon her before had been gentle and respectful, and they had stirred her blood. This embrace was powerful and insulting, and it had her shaking from head to toe. When at last he released her, she fell back against the banisters, her hair disarranged, her lips swollen from his kisses.

'God keep you, madam,' he said savagely, 'and give you joy of Dr Pimple.'

He threw the door open and strode away and Emily, tears filling her eyes stared after him and thought to herself, God help me, I love him still.

A voice interrupted her reverie. 'Emily, my dear, I am surprised and disappointed. How can you fill a gentleman's house with uproar in this unseemly way? My sainted Patrick, had he been alive, would never have done such a thing.'

Emily turned to face her father and for the first time he saw her with her hair all anyhow, her face flushed, her eyes filled with tears. 'What do you know?' she demanded. 'Patrick wanted to be a soldier.'

'No; he was to enter the church,' her father replied, frowning slightly.

'He never wanted to enter the church,' Emily replied, her voice breaking. 'He only said that he would in order to please you. You have twisted and turned his memory until it bears no resemblance to the boy that he really was. And you have been letting me twist and turn my life ever since as I vainly tried to make up to you for the fact that your darling son had gone. But you don't know the real me any more than you knew the real him. Now my heart is breaking and all that you can say is, don't make a noise!'

She turned from him and ran up the stairs, oblivious to the sound of his voice repeatedly calling after her.

20

'Tomorrow? But you cannot possibly leave tomorrow!' exclaimed Mrs Trimmer, looking at her brother in consternation. She had known that something had gone terribly wrong, of course, when she had seen him returning from Emily Whittaker's house with a face like thunder. She had gone downstairs to find out what had happened, only to find that he had walked out of the Minster Yard to work off his anger elsewhere. Mrs Hughes and her cousin had popped in a short time later, and had lingered for far longer than was socially acceptable, but still he had not returned. It was only after Aurelia and her husband had retired for the night that she heard her brother coming in, using the key that she had given him for his use whilst he was staying with them. Now this morning, he had suddenly announced his intention of leaving.

'Why not?' Sir Gareth asked her. 'There is nothing to keep me here.' His tone was light, but his expression was bleak.

'I take it that . . . ' She allowed her voice to tail away.

'Then you take it correctly,' he told her. 'My morals are disgusting to Miss Whittaker and she wants nothing more to do with me.'

'But how could she say such a thing?' demanded Aurelia, indignant on behalf of her adored elder brother. 'You have always acted the gentleman towards her, have you not?'

'Of course,' he replied, then flushed a little as he recalled his behaviour just before he had left her house.

'Then what possible reason could she have?'

'She has misunderstood some of my actions, and has judged me on the basis of them,' he answered.

'But surely — '

He interrupted her. 'Oh have done, Aurelia,' he said wearily. 'There's nothing more to be said.'

But his sister thought that perhaps there was, and later that morning, when her brother had gone out for a last walk with her husband, she put on her bonnet and went round to see Emily.

It was with a certain amount of embarrassment that Emily welcomed her in. When she had dismissed the baronet so summarily, she had forgotten that she would have to continue to live in close proximity to his sister and her family. Now she realized to her great dismay that she was in danger of losing Mrs Trimmer's friendship. The problem was that she could not explain her reasons for refusing him, because the secret of the fathering of Nathalie's baby was not hers to share.

For her part, Aurelia had come fully prepared to do battle on her brother's behalf. He might be a suave man of the world, but Emily had hurt him, and she should be made to answer for it. As soon as she saw Emily, however, she could see that Gareth was not the only sufferer. She looked pale; there was no sparkle in her, and there were dark circles under her eyes as if she had not slept.

As soon as they were inside the drawing-room, therefore, Aurelia said, 'What a pair you are! I do not know who looks the more dreadful, you or Gareth.'

At once, from merely looking defeated, Emily looked stricken. 'Does he?' she whispered.

'He looks shocking. The awful thing is that he set out so hopefully yesterday, and, forgive me, Emily, but from my observations of your conduct towards him, it seemed to me that he had reason to feel that way.' Seeing Emily looking a little shocked, she held up her hand. 'Not, of course, that you behaved in any way improperly towards him, but there was, I think, a tenderness there.' Emily bit her lip and turned away, but not before Aurelia had seen tears sparkling in her eyes. 'There still is, I think,' she ventured.

Emily took a deep breath. 'Yes, there may be,' she acknowledged bravely. 'But that does not make any difference I'm afraid. It must not. Please do not try to persuade me. There are things that I cannot disclose.'

Aurelia sighed deeply. 'Very well,' she said. 'Perhaps you may be glad to hear that he is leaving tomorrow, so you will then avoid bumping into one another accidentally.'

'I *must* be glad of it,' Emily replied, in subdued tones.

'I will send you word when he is leaving, and I will pray that you will change your mind in the interim.' She went to the door, then turned around impulsively. 'You have not told me what the problem is, and neither has he, but he has dropped a hint that it may be to do with his reputation.

'I want you to know that these things are often very exaggerated, especially by the likes of Mrs Hughes. She has wanted him for a long time but he has never responded to her, so she can sometimes try to put other females off by hinting that he is involved with her, which is not the case. I cannot pretend that he has not enjoyed female companionship in the past, but he is one of the most honourable men that I know, and the woman who could call him husband would never have cause to regret it.'

It was only after Aurelia had gone, and Emily had stood for a long time staring at the closed door that she realized that there was something different about the room. The portrait of Patrick had been replaced by one of her mother. She thought about what she had said to her father after the baronet had left. Never before had she lashed out at him in such a way. Until now she had been too wrapped up in her own pain to think about his. Feeling suddenly guilty, she went to his study and knocked on the door. Hearing no reply, she went in and found her father by the window, examining the picture of Patrick, which had been placed on the desk.

He looked up at her, and she could see that there were unshed tears in his eyes. A sudden insight made her wonder whether the picture that he had created of Patrick had been a way of avoiding grieving for him as he should have done.

'Emily, have I been mistaken all these years?'

'Oh Papa,' she said, 'I am so very sorry,' and she ran across the room to him. In the manner of one to whom such a gesture is very unfamiliar, he opened his arms, and she went into his embrace weeping, though whether her tears were for her father, for Patrick, or for her lost love, she would have been hard put to it to say.

They stood like that for a long time, not speaking. Eventually, Canon Whittaker said, 'He never sat for this picture, you know. It was taken from a miniature.'

'No, I did not know,' Emily replied. 'He . . . Sir Gareth said that it was a good likeness.'

'Was it also he who told you that Patrick wanted to be a soldier?' her father asked. Emily nodded. 'Perhaps I should ask him to tell me more,' he said thoughtfully.

'He is leaving tomorrow,' Emily replied, in such a desolate tone that her father looked at her curiously. Before he could say anything, however, there was a knock at the door and the housekeeper came in.

'Beg pardon, Miss Emily,' said Mrs Ashby, 'but you haven't given me any instructions for today. Is there anything special?'

'No, nothing, thank you,' Emily answered.

The housekeeper was about to withdraw when Mr Whittaker said, 'There is one thing that I would like to ask you, Mrs Ashby. You knew my son Patrick well, did you not?'

The woman's gaze softened. 'That I did, sir,' she replied.

'Then would you mind telling me if you think that this is a good likeness?'

Mrs Ashby came round the desk so that she could look at the picture the right way up. 'Now there's a question that will be difficult to answer, sir,' she said frankly. 'I'm so used to seeing it hanging above the fireplace, you see.' She looked at the picture thoughtfully, and eventually she said slowly, 'In some ways it's a very good likeness.' Seeing that they were waiting for more, she added reluctantly, 'I've always thought that the painter's missed the twinkle, though.'

'The twinkle?' asked the canon.

'Yes, sir. Always had a twinkle in his eye, did Master Patrick.' She glanced at the clergyman, half afraid that she would be reprimanded, but in his expression she saw only genuine interest. Emboldened by this, she went on, 'Full of mischief he was; never cruel, mind you, but funny. Do you remember Doris, the kitchen maid, who married one of Dr Mitchell's servants? The young master caught one of the lads in town laughing at her and calling her fat. He blacked the other boy's eye for him, even though the lad was a year older and half a head taller than young Master Patrick.'

'That was . . . brave of him,' said Mr Whittaker slowly.

318

'Yes, he was that,' agreed Mrs Ashby. 'We — the staff — always thought he'd end up a soldier.' Suddenly aware that she might have said too much, the woman coloured a little. 'Well, I must be about my duties if you'll excuse me sir.'

Mr Whittaker looked at his daughter for a long time after the door had closed. 'It appears that I really did not know Patrick at all,' he said slowly, as he tucked a loose strand of Emily's hair behind her ear. 'I don't seem to know you very well, either, my dear. You must teach me.'

★ ★ ★

'I had to call in before I left in order to say goodbye,' said Sir Gareth. Dressed for riding, he had his hat and his crop in his hand. 'You know where to find me if there is any way in which I may serve you.'

Ernest Fanshawe smiled, an expression of sadness behind his eyes. 'You are very good,' he said. 'I'll admit that when the child was first born, I didn't want to look at her, and if you'd asked me then, I would willingly have given her to you. I still find it hard to look at her now. But she is all that I have left of Nathalie.' He paused, then forced himself to go on in a more cheerful vein. 'But you will be returning to Lincoln, no doubt, to visit your sister. You may see how the child progresses then.'

'I doubt if I will be returning soon,' the baronet answered, his face set.

'But I thought . . . ' Fanshawe's voice tailed away.

'So did I,' sighed Sir Gareth. 'So did I. But she will have none of me, I fear. She judges me on my reputation, you see.'

'And you are too proud to explain.'

'If she cannot trust me — '

'Blades, happiness can be all too fleeting,' Fanshawe interrupted in an urgent tone. '*I* know that. You have to seize it with both hands.'

'But what if you try to seize it and find that it slips through your fingers like sand?' Sir Gareth asked him.

Soon after this, the men parted. 'I will keep you informed of the child's progress,' Fanshawe promised.

'Thank you,' replied the baronet. 'And if there is anything I can do, please let me know.'

★ ★ ★

After Sir Gareth had left, it occurred to Ernest Fanshawe that he ought to enquire about the child's progress. Looking at her was still something that he had to steel himself to do, but it was getting easier. He therefore went upstairs to the nursery, where his housekeeper was talking to Mrs Pearce. He was a little surprised, for he had forgotten all about the new arrangements for the wet nurse, but he greeted Mrs Pearce politely, and thanked her for her good offices.

'It's a pleasure, sir,' the young woman answered, smiling pleasantly. 'She's no trouble at all.'

'It was very good of Miss Whittaker to find Mrs Pearce for the little girl, sir,' Mrs Dainty remarked. 'But then of course you know that, for she came to find you to tell you so.'

Fanshawe looked puzzled. 'No, Mrs Dainty, she did not,' he replied. 'I know that I have forgotten some things, but I do not recall that at all.'

'But she came round here just a day or so ago, sir. It was the day when Sir Gareth first came to call on you.'

'Are you sure?' he asked her. There was something very important here that he felt he ought to be able to grasp, but could not quite do so.

Mrs Dainty nodded vigorously. 'Oh yes, sir,' she assured him. 'I remember thinking that you had had two callers that day. It seemed to me, sir, if you'll forgive my boldness, that it would do you some good.' She coloured a little at her presumption.

'Yes, no doubt it would have done had I seen her,' he responded ruefully. 'Perhaps she heard us talking and realized that I had a visitor.' He frowned, looking thoughtful. 'Excuse me,' he murmured. Then, before he left the room, he turned, conscious that he was being impolite. 'Forgive me, I . . . I . . . have something that I must think about. Thank you for all your good offices — both of you.'

Since Nathalie's death, Ernest Fanshawe had spent half his time conjuring up her image and the other half trying to banish it. Now, however, he began to think about what his wife had said in one of the last conversations that had taken place between them.

'I am going to tell Emily about the baby,' she had said. When he had objected, she had remained obdurate, surprisingly so for such a gentle person. 'Someone else ought to know our story, just in case.' When he had objected a second time, she had agreed for discretion's sake not to tell Emily the name of any of the parties involved.

She knows the story but not the names, Fanshawe thought to himself. She did not know the name of the baby's father. She came here while Blades and I were talking. She refused Blades's offer because of his reputation . . .

He had been walking slowly down the stairs, and paused at about the middle of the flight. Suddenly filled with an energy that had deserted him since Nathalie's death, he was galloping down the rest, and running to fling open the front door.

★　★　★

One day, Emily thought to herself, I shall go to bed and sleep all night, without being kept awake by my own thoughts. She had only slept fitfully that night, dozing off to be woken by nightmares, none of which she could remember. Over and over again, she thought about Nathalie's disclosures and measured them against what she knew of Sir Gareth. Everything seemed to match up until she recalled his kindness to his nephews; his courtesy towards her father, together with his tact and discretion; his sheer humanity towards her grandfather; his chivalry towards herself.

The morning brought no respite; her mind still seemed to be struggling with itself, and although she knew that it would make no difference, she dreaded the moment when the messenger that Mrs Trimmer had promised would come to tell her that he was going.

The message arrived as she and her father were getting up from the breakfast table. They had still not decided what to do about Patrick's portrait.

'What was that about, my dear?' her father asked her.

'Mrs Trimmer promised to tell me when Sir Gareth was going, that is all,' she answered calmly. 'I will go and sit with Grandpapa now. He seems to be improving every day. Did I tell you that he spoke a word or two the other day?'

She went upstairs, not realizing that after a few moments, her father had followed shortly behind her.

'Why am I still so confused?' she asked her grandfather. 'I know about his wrong-doing. I could never ally myself to so base a man. Why, then, can I not feel peace of mind?'

'Good man,' her grandfather said, in as clear a tone as she had heard from him since his attack.

'Grandfather?' she exclaimed.

'Good man,' he said again.

'Grandfather, you don't know,' she replied in frustrated tones.

'Yes I do,' he stated haltingly. 'So do you.'

He paused. 'Loves you. Good man.'

As Emily stared at the old man, it was if all the confusion suddenly dropped away from her, and at that moment she was filled with the peace of mind that she craved. Whatever she had heard that day at Ernest Fanshawe's house, whatever Nathalie might have said, whatever Mrs Hughes might have intimated, she knew that Sir Gareth was noble and true, and she had let him go without allowing him to speak in his own defence, or telling him that his feelings were returned.

'Oh Grandpapa!' she exclaimed. 'He's gone, thinking I despise him. What shall I do? It's too late.'

'Not too late,' he breathed. 'Steep Hill.'

'Steep Hill?' she echoed, too dazed to think clearly.

'He used to run down it as a boy,' said her father. He had come in through the dressing-room and had heard a large part of the conversation. 'So did I. Sir Gareth will ride the long way, by New Road.'

For a brief moment, Emily stared at her father, before swiftly kissing him, then bending to salute her grandfather on his withered cheek. Then she fairly flew down the stairs and across the Minster Yard, not even stopping to put on her bonnet. She would not be too late. She must not be!

As she was nearing the West Front, Mr Fanshawe came rushing towards her at almost the same breakneck speed. 'Miss Whittaker!' he exclaimed. 'Matters are not as you think — about the baby, I mean.'

She only checked for an instant. 'Mr Fanshawe, I cannot stop!' she exclaimed. 'I must not miss him!' And she hurried on through the Exchequer Gate, and turning left, gathered up her skirts and prepared to run down one of the steepest city streets in England.

21

After visiting Fanshawe, Sir Gareth had only returned briefly to his sister's house before making his farewells. Mrs Trimmer had been hoping against hope that Emily would send some word, or even come herself, and she only managed to conceal her disappointment with extreme difficulty. Telling herself that it was her duty to send her brother off with a cheerful countenance, however, she waved him goodbye, smiling, before going indoors to weep on her husband's chest. 'Oh Alan,' she sobbed, 'I did so hope that they would be happy!'

'They might be yet, my love,' her husband replied. 'Do not give up hope. Who can tell what may occur?'

★ ★ ★

Although his quickest route would have been through the Minster Yard, Sir Gareth rode up Bailgate and through Newport Arch, then round to the right, in order to join the road that would take him gently to the bottom of the hill. So Emily would have none of him;

327

well, in that case, he did not want to risk laying eyes on her. Who knew what he would end up saying or doing? Better to begin to put her out of his mind altogether. He could go back to London and take up with someone like Annis Hughes, who would not expect him to be anything other than what he was.

My God, no! He exclaimed to himself. Better to hide away on his estate and look after his acres and his tenants. It was what he had intended to do anyway; it was just that he had not intended to do it alone.

By the time he had allowed these various cogitations to go round and round in his mind, he had reached the bottom of the hill and he paused at the point where the descending lane emerged onto New Road. He looked up towards the cathedral, remembering all that had taken place in and around it. Contrary to all logic, the soaring towers, the majesty of the place seemed to infect him with a most unexpected feeling of optimism.

'Damn it!' he exclaimed. 'I won't give up! She *must* listen to me!'

He was on the point of retracing his steps, when he became aware of a commotion going on in the lane above him, and looking up the street more carefully, he saw a female figure flying in his direction, her skirts gathered up almost to her knees. Those taking the route at a more decorous pace were obliged to get out of the way as she ran. Those standing about at the side of the road shouted encouragement.

As he recognized her, his heart seemed to miss a beat, and he dismounted hastily, for he could see that given the momentum that she had built up, she was only going to stop with extreme difficulty.

Hastily giving the reins of his horse to a passing lad, with the promise of a coin or two when he had leisure, he threw himself into Emily's path and braced himself for the impact.

She hurtled into his arms, he staggered, held her, swung around in an effort to keep them both upright, then lost his footing and fell, landing on his back with Emily on top of him.

Emily, thoroughly out of breath, but determined to explain herself before she lost courage, gasped, 'You mustn't go! I don't want you to go! I was wrong to believe it, even for a minute. You are good and honourable and . . . and I love you, Gareth.' The crowd, some of whom had followed Emily's progress from part way down the hill, although not as rapidly as she, broke into a ragged cheer, with some of them making various suggestions as to what this strange couple might do now.

'Give 'er a kiss, mister!' was both the most repeatable and the most audible.

Sir Gareth, grinned, answered 'I intend to,' in tones that only Emily could hear, and pulling her head gently but firmly towards him, suited his action to his words, whilst the crowd cheered again. 'My dearest,' he said, when he had broken off this brief embrace, 'I think perhaps we might get up now. We are attracting rather a lot of attention.'

Emily looked around, colouring as she heard comments such as, 'It's Canon Whittaker's daughter!' 'Well I never!' 'Who would've thought she had it in her?' The tone was admiring, rather than otherwise.

'Who indeed?' murmured Sir Gareth. 'Emily, my dear . . . '

Hastily she got up, whereupon the baronet did the same, brushing himself down as well as he could, given that most of the dirt was on his back.

He turned around, and finding the boy who was holding his horse, tossed him a coin, the size and colour of which made the lad blink. Then he turned to Emily, smiling. 'Come, my love,' he said. 'Let me take you home.'

They returned to the Minster Yard, retracing the route that Sir Gareth had taken just a short time previously, but with very different feelings. There was much to talk about, but this was neither the time nor the place. The baronet offered to put Emily up onto his horse, but she refused. She wanted to walk beside him, her hand tucked into his. For the most part, they walked in silence, exchanging smiles, and savouring this new joy of being together, knowing that the feelings of each were fully returned by the other.

'The cathedral?' Sir Gareth asked her, when at last their climb was finished, and he had entrusted his horse to a passing choirboy with the instruction to return it to Mr Trimmer's stable.

She nodded. 'You haven't been up either of the western towers yet, have you?' she said playfully.

'No I haven't, you baggage, but something tells me I'm going to climb one very soon,' he replied. In truth, he was glad that she had made this suggestion for there were things that they had to say to one another that ought not to be heard by anyone else.

The western towers were not so high as the central tower, and it was an easier climb. As on a previous occasion, Emily went in front. 'You will have gathered by now, my darling, that my real purpose in taking this position is to leer at your ankles and your shapely . . . ah

. . . outline,' remarked Sir Gareth provocatively as they neared the end of their climb.

'Gareth!' Emily exclaimed; then found herself smiling at how lovely it felt to be calling him by his Christian name.

At last they stepped out into the air, and Emily turned to Sir Gareth saying, 'There you are.'

'Yes; and there *you* are,' he answered, pulling her into his arms.

She gasped. They were both a little out of breath, and they stood, gazing into each other's eyes while the sun shone down on them and the noises of the city seemed very distant. Then, at last, he lowered his head and kissed her, pulling her close against him and holding her as if he would never let her go. He had kissed her before; once fleetingly beneath the Lincoln imp, and once with an intention of punishing her. This time his kiss was firm but tender, and with a hint of passion, and Emily responded fervently.

'Now tell me,' he said at last. 'The last time I saw you, you never wanted to see me again. Why did you believe so ill of me? Was it something that that she-devil Annis Hughes said to you?'

She shook her head. 'No, not really; although later her words about your unreliability came back to haunt me. It was more to do with Nathalie Fanshawe. I believe . . . I assume . . . ' She hesitated.

'Yes, I know her story. You may speak freely.'

Emily blushed. 'She told me that the father of her baby was a fashionable man about town, with good taste.'

'Well that cuts it down to several hundred,' the baronet observed.

'I know, but listen. She also said that he had been injured in a duel, and you arrived with a recent injury to your shoulder.'

'Again, not a strong argument for my guilt. In fact, my injury was sustained in a riding accident. Go on.'

'Lord Stuart said that you ran with a dangerous set.'

He laughed. 'Anyone who indulges in any activity more strenuous than rising swiftly from a chair is accounted dangerous by Stuart,' he answered. 'He considers my way of life, which includes regular boxing, fencing and swimming to be positively ruinous. Go on.'

'When I came to see Mr Fanshawe to tell him that I had found a wet nurse for the baby, I overheard you telling him that you and the baby have the same blood.'

'And you immediately leaped to the conclusion that I must be the baby's father.'

Emily hung her head. 'I'm so sorry,' she whispered.

'Well, it was an understandable assumption, given what you knew. What happened to make you think that you might be mistaken?'

'Nothing happened really,' she answered, 'Apart from Grandpapa actually saying some words. One of the things that he said over and over again was that you were a good man. I couldn't think how he could be so sure. Then I realized that he was trusting his own judgement, and I knew that I must do the same. I knew that I had to trust in your honour, and I do, Gareth.'

'My darling,' he murmured, feathering kisses across her brow and her cheek before covering her mouth with his own once more. 'And supposing I said that I could never tell you what the connection was between Nathalie and myself; would you still trust me then?' he asked her curiously, a hint of tension in his voice.

'Grandpapa said 'I know him; so do you', I know you Gareth; that's enough.'

'A jewel amongst women,' he remarked, his tone light, but an unmistakable look of sincerity on his face. 'But I *will* tell you, because since you know so much, there is no reason why you should not know the rest.

'Nathalie's lover was my cousin. Sadly, he had been thoroughly spoiled by his mother, his father having died, and he expected everything that he wanted to fall into his lap and belong to him exclusively. I never really knew Nathalie, because he was possessive over her. I did keep in touch with him, however, because our mothers were sisters, and my mother felt very anxious about the ruinous path that his life was taking. By the way, I want you to meet my mother as soon as possible. I have a suspicion that she will adore you.'

'Oh, why?' Emily asked, momentarily diverted.

'Because *I* adore you,' he answered, kissing her. After a brief interval, which proved to be agreeable to both parties, he continued his story. 'To resume, I was on hand when he issued a challenge to a duel, and much against my will, found myself involved as his second.'

'Then I know the part that you played,' Emily put in. 'After the duel, you took Nathalie to Mr Fanshawe.'

'I have never been sure that I did right on that occasion,' he told her.

'Oh, but you did,' she assured him, 'for they were most sincerely attached to one another. Is the baby's real father still living?'

Sir Gareth shook his head. 'After he had recovered from his injuries, he fled to Paris and perished there in a street brawl.'

'Mr Fanshawe must have wanted to tell me about the baby,' Emily exclaimed. 'He tried to stop me in Minster Yard, only I could not wait to listen to him. I was in too much of a hurry to catch you.'

'And so you ran all the way down Steep Hill.'

Emily nodded. 'That was Grandpapa's idea,' she told him. 'He used to run down it as a boy, Father said.'

'Your father knew that you had come in pursuit of me?' the baronet asked curiously.

'We have reached a new understanding,' Emily replied. 'After you had gone, I blurted out about Patrick wanting to be a soldier, and that my heart was broken.'

'So was mine, sweetheart,' he told her. 'Go on.'

'I think that you had already guessed that I have unintentionally been playing something of a part, to try to make up to Father for the loss of Patrick. After I had let rip at him, he began to ask questions about Patrick and about me too. I think that he might want to hear what you have to say about my brother; I think that maybe this time he will be ready to hear the truth.'

After a moment's silence, he said, 'You were telling me about how you came to run down Steep Hill.'

'I knew that that was the only chance I had of stopping you,' she explained, 'but when I started to run down, I suddenly realized that I did not know how I was going to stop. I have never been so frightened in all my life.'

'As well that I was there to catch you, then,' replied Sir Gareth, taking her hand and kissing it. After a moment or two, he went on, 'I am glad that Nathalie and her husband were happy together. I shall continue to take an interest in the child. That will be much easier now, of course.'

'Why is that?' she asked him.

'You will naturally want to keep in touch with your friend's child. I, as your husband, will support you in this.'

'As my husband,' pondered Emily, her finger on her lips, a tiny frown crossing her brow, even though her heart was beating very fast. 'It is strange, sir, but I do not remember a proposal of marriage.'

He pulled her into his arms, none too gently this time. 'You baggage, are you flirting with me?' he asked her.

'Trying to,' she replied demurely.

'Well, you are getting better at it,' he told her, before he kissed her again. 'My sister has been parading a series of females in front of me for years; but never have I felt the remotest desire to link my life with any of them. Now, having met you, I know that my life will not be truly complete without you. I love you, Emily Whittaker. Will you marry me?'

'Yes, Gareth, I will. I love you too.' More kisses. She looked around. 'I suppose that some people might say that it was improper to behave in this way up here.'

'I cannot agree,' her betrothed replied. 'What better place to plight one's troth? I assume that you will want to be married here?'

'It is what I have always dreamed of, but I never ever thought that it would happen to me,' she replied smiling. He was her hero after all.

★ ★ ★

They were married in Lincoln Cathedral just a few weeks later. Emily's father played a part in the service, which was conducted by the dean. Her grandfather, although not well enough to attend, was able to sit by his bedroom window and watch as she walked to church with her father and then returned on her new husband's arm.

It was generally agreed that never had there been a happier looking couple. Emily looked radiant in cream satin with tiny seed pearls stitched into flowers on the bodice of her gown. Sir Gareth, in white knee breeches and waistcoat and a dark-blue coat looked pleased and happy.

'Oh Alan, he looks ten years younger than when he came to Lincoln,' Aurelia said to her husband, smiling through her tears. 'I could not have wished for anything better.'

'Not even Jennifer Cummings?' murmured Mr Trimmer provocatively.

'Certainly not,' his wife answered positively. 'And definitely not Annis Hughes!' Mrs Hughes had congratulated the engaged pair in rather a forced manner, and had left Lincoln well before the wedding, pleading engagements elsewhere. Mrs Cummings had taken Emily's triumph in good part, probably reflecting that the new Lady Blades would be a good friend for Jennifer to have when she came out the following year.

Dr Boyle had accepted his disappointment as a gentleman should, even going out of his way to congratulate Sir Gareth, which kindness the baronet had acknowledged by thanking the doctor warmly and remembering at the same time to address him by his correct name.

'You were very badly behaved towards poor Dr Boyle,' Emily told her husband severely when they were on their wedding tour. They had travelled to Derbyshire and, climbing one of the hills there, had tried, but failed, to see Lincoln Cathedral on the horizon.

'Yes, I know,' Sir Gareth replied, pulling her close against him for the wind was rather strong. 'He made me want to behave badly. Every time I thought he might lay claim to you, it made me want to think up another stupid name for him.'

'Did it?' Emily asked, her severity disappearing in an instant.

'Yes it did. In fact, I was thinking up stupid names for him almost from the very beginning; so I must have known instinctively from the very first, that you belonged to me.'

Emily turned in the crook of his arm and lifted her face to his, so that he could kiss her. 'The sky is clouding over a little,' she said, as soon as she was able. 'Do you think that we ought to return to the inn?'

'An excellent idea,' replied the baronet, looking up at the sky, then looking down into her face with a wicked gleam in his eye. 'The effort of climbing this hill has quite worn me out. I fear that I may need to lie down in a darkened room.'

'That's funny,' Emily replied demurely with only the tiniest blush as she took his arm and prepared to make the descent. 'I was just thinking exactly the same thing.'

We do hope that you have enjoyed reading this large print book.

Did you know that all of our titles are available for purchase?

We publish a wide range of high quality large print books including:
Romances, Mysteries, Classics
General Fiction
Non Fiction and Westerns

Special interest titles available in large print are:
The Little Oxford Dictionary
Music Book
Song Book
Hymn Book
Service Book

Also available from us courtesy of Oxford University Press:
Young Readers' Dictionary
(large print edition)
Young Readers' Thesaurus
(large print edition)

For further information or a free brochure, please contact us at:
Ulverscroft Large Print Books Ltd.,
The Green, Bradgate Road, Anstey,
Leicester, LE7 7FU, England.
Tel: (00 44) 0116 236 4325
Fax: (00 44) 0116 234 0205